THE RISE OF TITANIUM

~A Kingdom Of Diamond Antlers Novel~

to Emily,
Thank you for your
support and kindness! I
hope your writing goes
well! ♥   - Zachary

Zachary James

D1515614

~*Praise for*~
THE RISE OF TITANIUM

"A compelling fantasy novel that will keep you clutching the back of your seat! Similar to Sarah J. Maas' *Throne of Glass* series, it's a world full of wonder with beautifully written details that James sweeps you into. Not to mention the harrowing fight scenes, plot twists, grim deaths, and a steamy romance that will have you hooked until the very end!"-**Nicole DiRienzo,** *avid reader and trusted novel enthusiast.*

"Zachary James lifts his literary paintbrush to create a majestic world of fantasy and adventure, creating the perfect recipe for romance. The unpredictable plot keeps readers grasping for breath while his dynamic characters bring life to the pages. With the turn of each page so turns the tables of good and evil, faith and vulnerability, as the characters test their physical inner strength in a struggle to find themselves and the truth about the past."-**Heather Falotico,** *English teacher and talented editor.*

Edited by: Heather Falotico
Cover Art by: Justin Shi
Cover Design by: Eight Little Pages
Ages: 14 and up

Second Edition
13 12 11 10 9 8 7 6 5 4

I made a promise, so this goes to you,
Heather Falotico

Pronunciation Guide

People

Ariadae Vox- *Are-e-ah-day Vox*

Zube Mindelow- *Zoo-be Min-dee-low*

Evaflora- *Eva-flooruh*

Sapientiae- *Sap-e-en-tay*

Pacem- *Pace-em*

Odi- *Oh-die*

Viate- *Vee-ah-tee*

Fae

Fae- *Fay*

Succumbus- *Suck-um-bis*

Mindinae- *Min-dah-nay*

Tempestatis- *Tem-pest-tah-tis*

Telekinae- *Tell-e-kah-nay*

Forsaken

Nymph- *Nim-fah*

Dreag- *Dray-guh*

Troglodyte- *Trog-low-dite*

Wendigo- *When-dee-go*

The Rise of Titanium

Part One
ELKWOOD FOREST

CHAPTER ONE

It's been two days since my father attempted to murder me. He had come home earlier than expected from traveling through Elkwood Forest. He was meant to be meeting a southern kingdom, which I am unsure of who, but all I know is that I was excited to have him back, happy to learn he had come home early, joyful with the thought of hugging my father upon his return. So with the thought of his smile and kind eyes, I practically ran to his chamber, tripping over my skirts. The door was ajar and there were guards posted out front, I should've noticed their shaken faces or the dark aura that had sucked the air from my father's room. But I wasn't observant, I didn't care enough to think about those things, or take in those details because I was blinded by happiness. My father was blinded by rage.

I called his name in the silent chamber that did not smell like him, but the scent wasn't an issue. I should've seen it coming, or hear his pounding steps, but I didn't scream until my body was slammed against the stone of his floor and he had a silver blade poised to dig into my throat. The scream ripped past my lips as I stared up into his green eyes, no longer clear like spring grass, but shadowed like darkened pine. The guards were at my aid in an instant and they saved me, they protected me and stopped my father from trying to kill me. I hadn't thanked them for saving my life, and although they stopped the attack, they couldn't stop the haunting nightmares that night and the internal damage that has seared my brain. I can't forget the look in his eyes; hatred, evil, bloodlust.

A chill pulls me from the recent memory and I look around my personal library. The hearth promptly lit and enveloping the room in an orange glow. The sentinels have been keeping my father and I separated from one another for safety. They fear he may try to kill me again, and in all honesty, I don't blame them. I just don't know why my father would do such a thing? He was always kind to me growing up; it was always just us around. My mother had gotten murdered after entering Elkwood Forest, the ominous wood that surrounds my kingdom. Growing up, I was never allowed to enter the tree line because of what happened to my mother, and now that my father had traveled into the forest and returned with darkness in his heart, I can't help, but wonder what is going on, what has changed my father and killed my mother.

The energy-draining questions that rattle my brain make me rise from the plush chair, placing the tome I wasn't focusing on atop the Elkwood coffee table near my knees. The book thudding against the surface with an echo that follows. I had learned everything I know from the books that fill these walls. I learned about philosophy, courtship, English, and proper manners. Mathematics was taught to me by my father who has written several tomes on astral theory and projection. I used to believe him to be an amazing author, and I'd sit on his lush bed reading the brick-sized books with glee, but I soon discovered other scholars and poets. They wrote of romantic encounters and terrifying beasts that lived in nightmares. No longer was I naïve.

I depart from the library and my chambers, the whispering blue silk of my dress in my fisted hands. The gown is alluring to the eye, but in all truth is just unbearable to move in. I try to ignore my attire and focus on the mission ahead. The guards will not escort me to my father because they will not want to risk another attack, so if I want my questions to be answered than I'll have to find another way to the throne room.

In a crouching approach, I shuffle my way down the hallways using alcoves, statues, and the occasional bustling maid to hide my form from the sentinels posted every few feet. I almost laugh at the blindness of some of the guards, but I keep the giggle rising in my stomach within my throat, as to not bring attention to myself. And although there seems to be many guards standing in the corridor I take in the lack there of. Typically there is double the amount, but suddenly I recall how every week a legion of warriors gets sent south to Solaria, the kingdom warring against my father, the king of Equadoria. Now that I am thinking of Solaria I also remember hearing that a guard has returned home from the south. He had undergone five years of unyielding torture, but is now with his family who must be beyond happy. I wish my father and me had a happier homecoming.

The towering doors that lead into the throne room rise up before me and my excitement is short lived. Two sentinels are posted out front and they lock eyes with me almost immediately and I realize that this was never going to be an easy task. The only heir to the Equadorian throne is trying to be in a room with the man who failed at an assassination attempt. I have to get into the throne room somehow and besides the doors, there is no way into the chamber except for the windows. It isn't an option to rule out, but I'm not in the proper attire for climbing.

Before I can open my mouth to speak, one of the sentinels shatters the silence. "You are not permitted entry, Milady," He says and I take in his words with consideration. I then shove his words away like they are a fly, buzzing too close to my meal.

"And why is that?" I question the obstacle standing in front of me.

"It is for your safety, your majesty," the other guard steps into the conversation and reaches for me like he can push me away. I recoil and look to the both of them.

"I am the princess of Equadoria and I demand to be allowed entry into *my* throne room," I order. Never have I used my title as leverage or to acquire something, but in this instance I have no other choice. They started to shut me down before I could even request to go inside, so I did it. I made the command.

The two guards look to one another and nod, reluctantly opening the doors revealing the familiar, yet opulent chamber. The sentinels escort me down the blue velvet carpet and I stare straight ahead at the man I love, the father who's always been around, the man I thought could never hurt a fly. He leans his head forward in a slight bow, allowing the maid to place a cobalt coronet of twisting thorns onto his head. I don't understand it's meaning because his old crown was silver with blue sapphires, the colors of Equadoria. My father's eyes are bloodshot and his yellowed teeth gleam as he grimaces from his dais.

"I thought I had ordered her to be executed?" he asks, the room carrying his voice. I shudder at the way his words are so void of emotion. What happened to him? What has caused him to have a violent change of heart, a cursed mind, an evil will?

One of the guards that escorted me says, "We can't execute the only heir to the throne, sir." I couldn't agree more.

"Then what is your business here, girl?" the king spits with what seems like every drop of venom he can muster.

"Why are you acting this way?" I erupt with a boiling anger from within me. He no longer is the man I love, the person I grew up with, and I want nothing more than to help him. "What happened to you?

His cackle floods my eardrums and I cringe. I never said anything funny, but he continues laughing as if I did. "What foolish questions, remove yourself from my throne room!"

One of the guards touches my forearm and I pull away from his fingers, stepping closer to my father. "No," I shout trying to ignore the tears flooding in my eyes. "What did Elkwood Forest do to you? Are you under some sort of spell-,"

"SHUT YOUR MOUTH YOU PRENTENTIOUS BITCH," My father screams cutting me off and a gasp escapes my lips, followed by a sob as the water falls down my cheeks. My hands tremble with confusion as my beating heart thunders against my ribcage. This isn't like him; this isn't the man I know so well. I have to learn what happened, but how can I do such a thing? I'm not even sure if he is under a spell or has had a change of heart.

"Please…," my voice quivers as I begin to taste the salt water and my runny nose.

"Don't beg for pity," My father seethes as he rolls his eyes at me and I crumple to the floor. My legs no longer working, no longer being able to carry the weight of my crushed heart and branded spirit.

"Milady," the sentinels whisper at the same time in my ear. They try to not stare at my laughing father and I barely hear their voices, my father's cackle. My body is shaking too hard and my senses are blinded by my tears and sobs.

I feel hands lift me from the floor and begin to carry me out of the chamber. My wicked father waving at me as the doors close him in, lock me out, and keep us separated from each other. I feel like I have nobody, like my heart has been ripped from my chest by the one person I know loves me.

I don't remember arriving in my bedroom or crawling beneath the blankets of my bed. Snow, my pet tiger, isn't with me, but I feel as if I can't move, can't breathe, can't focus on anything, but the sounds of my father's laugh. His words were so vile and yet they came from his lips. Where do I even begin to help my father from himself? What would a king like him, willing to kill his own daughter, do to a kingdom like Equadoria? The damage that he could cause because of his title is insurmountable.

CHAPTER TWO

After supper alone in the dining hall, my maids draw me a bath. I sit in the clawfoot tub and stare out the open balcony doors, into the balmy night. Candles flicker around the bathing chambers giving a warm glow to the stone room. I can't help but think of what my father called me. It makes me almost sick that those words came from his mouth. He is a King, not some foul mouthed fool. He used to love me. Treated me like the world revolved around me. He taught me not to be rude, arrogant, or demanding. *You pretentious bitch,* again and again, I can't stop hearing his words in my head. Where has my father gone?

Sometimes people leave and don't come back, but sometimes people do come back even though they may not be who they used to be. I try to drop my thoughts about my father and direct them towards Elkwood. The forest is right across the courtyard, behind the fence, enclosing me in. It holds secrets that need to be told, even though it doesn't want to share. I don't know where to go other than into the forest for my answers. It's my best chance at finding out what's wrong with my father.

Elkwood seems to call to me, almost beckoning me towards its cluster of dark tall trees. If I listen closely I can hear it. *Ariadae, Ariadae, Ariadae.* I snap back to reality and realize someone is actually calling me. I rise from the tub wrapping a robe around myself and approach the terrace. The wind rustles the dark leaves and makes the branches clatter together. Whoever is in that forest keeps calling my name;

Ariadae,

Ariadae,

Ariadae,

Ariadae! The voice is almost a scream.

Then it all stops; the wind, the voice calling my name, and even the insects' hum. My heart starts to beat and my dinner rises in my throat trying to come up. All of a sudden I feel as if I'm being watched. The forest is watching me, or whatever is *in* the forest.

"Hello," my voice breaks through the silence like a wind chime on the passing breeze.

"ARIADAE," the ear splitting scream sends me into a fit of tumbling and crashing back into the bathing chambers. I slam the balcony doors and lock them as I slowly back away from the terrace. Refusing to look away I begin to cry as fear destroys my curiosity. Whatever is in Elkwood is dangerous. That voice was rigid, evil, and sounded like nothing a human could make. What am I getting myself into? I sink to the floor when I bump into the corner of the room.

My sobs carry throughout the room with a deep echo as I try to control my breathing. My heart is drumming into my ears and I can't hear anything else. That scream seemed to have almost blown out my eardrums.

A maiden comes charging in and runs to me instantly. A worried look is on her face and I see her lips moving, her hand caresses under my ear lobe and when she pulls away I see blood on her fingers. I faint.

"You have to believe me," I told my maid what happened and she doesn't believe me. She thinks I fell while getting out of the tub and got concussed. She doesn't understand what I heard was real. It gives me chills as I think of everything. The evil king with the dark crown, (also known as my father), Elkwood forest talking to me, these aren't normal occurrences.

Snow the white tiger that has been my pet since before I can remember woke me up this morning. His heavy large body lay across my bed making me lose circulation in my legs after a while. The maid and doctor leave my chambers and I begin to stroke Snow's pelt. I whisper to him after I'm sure they're gone, "You believe me don't you?"

He chuffs and snuggles into my side. A smile spreads across my face as I think about the adventure we will begin tomorrow. I lost a day due to the unnecessary concussion tonic I was forced to drink.

The adventure will be the start of my answers, and hopefully will reverse this wicked evil that is controlling my father. I roll over and close my eyes ready to take on whatever Elkwood throws at me.

I woke before the sun rose. I had a quick breakfast and the sun only just started rising, so I decided to head to the weaponry to train a bit. I typically train almost every day but lately it's been hard. The royal guards have been so busy with keeping me safe from my father that I haven't been able to train with Jeremiah.

I enter the large golden room laced in large floor to ceiling windows. The vaulted ceiling carries the sounds of soldiers sparing and practicing. Jeremiah is outside in the middle of a sparring match. His swings are hard and fast and he moves like a shadow dancing through the night. Before heading outside to the patio area, I retrieve a bow and quiver to use when I go into Elkwood.

"What time are we heading out today," Jeremiah asks almost bored with his fight. I barely hide the shock on my face at his remark. How could he have known I was going into the forest? I look to him, but he doesn't lose focus even as I drop my stuff and take a seat on one of the iron chairs.

"What are you talking about," I play dumb, but my own voice sounded high and weak making me sound unconvincing.

"I know there is some plan churning in that head of yours… and the dumb founded look on your face doesn't help your cause either," he laughs. He still doesn't look away from his opponent and he still somehow noticed my shock. He always said to never take your eyes away from your enemy. "So what time are we leaving?"

He thinks that even though we grew up together that he can come. He is supposed to stay here to watch over the kingdom and hopefully not let my father kill innocent people. "I'm going alone with Snow."

His rapier pokes the chest of his opponent naming him the winner of the dual. He chuckles and approaches me; his large towering stature overpowers my small frame. The muscles of his shoulders shift underneath the airy white shirt he wears. His voice drops to a whisper not wanting the rest of the soldiers to hear, "You can't travel into Elkwood forest without some form of protection."

There he goes again. Ever since we met in the village twelve years ago he has always been protective of me. I was only four at the time, and he was six, but he pulled me out of the way of a carriage rolling down the dirt path. Now, I being sixteen and he eighteen, he still acts as if everything is that carriage rolling down the street, wanting to pull me away from danger and into his protection.

"I'm not that girl you met in the village anymore. I've grown and I learned to watch my back. Some adventures need to be taken alone," I sternly answer with a failed attempt at intimidation. I need to understand what happened to my mother and my father. I can't stop thinking about how my life keeps getting ruined by the forest and I want to know why.

"But others need to be taken carefully," Jeremiah tells me, "And knowing you, that won't happen, so we leave at noon." Before I can protest he marches off removing the shirt sticking to his back. The hard muscles in his tan skin shift and move down his back. I turn away trying not to stare.

"Just the two of us," I press knowing he isn't fond of the idea.

"Of course not, Dae." I shake my head and he grips my arms pulling my attention to his warm eyes as he whispers, "Don't worry, there are a few sentinels I trust here."

Heat rises to my cheeks as I blush. I then retrieve my bow and quiver and head into the weaponry. If Jeremiah wants to come I guess it will be better. I could use some help, I guess, but I don't think it is right. The forest talks to me, calls my name, and kills my family. Whatever is in there has a vendetta for the Vox family.

I grab three extra quivers and leave the weaponry. I travel down corridors passing Sentinels and other guards who only bow their heads quickly before moving on. I'm the heir to the throne they preside under; they don't have a right to question me. It sounds pretentious or rude but it's true. They wouldn't question why the princess is walking around the castle with four quivers and a bow. A few servants offer assistance and I accept their help and allow them to carry the quivers for me.

The people of Equadoria are so sweet and amazing, I couldn't ask for a different kingdom to rule. They don't think we are unfair, overpowering, or brutal. My father runs this kingdom with heart and mind, not force or power. I aspire to be like him, to control my kingdom the right way by protecting my people. The only way I can protect these people from something like Elkwood Forest, which surrounds our kingdom, I need to know what's in the forest. What lives and thrives there, what scares the young children, haunts my dreams, scares me, and talks to me.

"Are you alright, my lady," says one of the soft spoken maids. She hugs the quiver to her chest like the other three who stand in front of me. I stopped walking when I got lost in my thoughts. I plaster a smile on my face and say, "Oh my apologies. I am fine, just thinking that's all."

They bow and make the turn to the castle entryway where Snow waits with bags being holstered to him. Jeremiah is hoisting large baggage onto a lovely white mare. He wears the kingdom guard uniform. His shaggy brown hair falls into his warm chocolate eyes. In a few strides he is already next to me with a sly grin plastered on his face. "You aren't even dressed, Ariadae. What were you doing this whole time?"

"Getting here, you giant," I say laughing as I poke his hard stomach.

"Go change."

"Fine," I say as I start heading toward my chambers. Jeremiah has always had a way of making someone feel better. Just his smile can make anyone smile. I've always noticed the maids and other visiting noble ladies get weak in the knees when he passes. I have to admit he is handsome, but I've never thought of him in the way the other ladies do. He is my best friend, the ice to my fire, the hot to my cold, he is my only friend.

I quickly change into a dark scavenging outfit. A black tank top and black pants with a long viscose body wrap that crosses my chest with long strands that hang to my knees. Ankle high black boots made of cotton protect my feet and soft grey cotton strips wrapped around my arms will protect them from branches and sharp rocks; the perfect outfit for an adventure.

I get back to the castle entryway where Jeremiah, three other sentinels, and Snow wait, packed, armed, and ready to leave. Large swords are sheathed at their backs and Jeremiah holds a bow and dagger. He approaches me and whispers, his warm breath kisses my face as I look up at him, "This bow is a recurve, only the queens before your family have used it." He says this as he hands me the black bow with curvy limbs engraved with flames. "This," he says holding up a glittering dagger and a leather hip holster, "was your mothers." I take the dagger and holster from him and hug him.

I don't know what to say, and I certainly don't want this to seem inappropriate, so I release him shortly and begin to head over to Snow. He chuffs as I stroke his soft pelt and mount his muscular feline body. The sentinels and Jeremiah mount their own horses and I notice the mare's unnerving looks towards the tiger I sit on. Excitement fills me and I shout to nobody in particular, "Let's get on our way!"

The horse's hooves are *clack, clack, clacking* against the cobblestone as we bound through the streets of the kingdom. Snow's large paws don't make a sound as he flies past the mares and slows to wait for them to catch up. He seems to be playing a game with them. Copper strands of my hair flurry in my face, so while Snow plays his game with the mares I begin to braid the long waves.

Minutes pass and we are at the edge of Equadoria. The towering trees and thick brush making it almost impossible to see the path that goes into Elkwood Forest. These trees are Elkwood; it's where the forest got its name. The wind blows and I start to hear my name again. I try to ignore it but I can't. This is the moment where I discover everything, the secrets of my family; what is corrupting my father, what killed my mother, and what is whispering my name. *Sometimes people leave and don't come back, but sometimes people do come back even though they may not be who they used to be.* Hopefully I will come back who I am.

"Ariadae," Jeremiahs voice shatters the voice in the wind, "Are you ready?"

The word leaves my lips before I even think of the answer. Before I can protest or change my mind. My lips made the decision for me, "Yes."

CHAPTER THREE

The dirt beneath Snow's paws keeps his movements silent. Even though Elkwood is alive and rich of sound and color, I have this feeling something is watching my every move. Birds fly under the canopy of green leaves and afternoon sun beats down on our necks causing sweat to bead on our skin. We have been traveling for about four hours now and we might need to take a break soon. I don't want to stop but the horses are getting tired and the Sentinels are soaked.

Jeremiah rides up alongside Snow but doesn't look at me, keeping his ears alert and eyes searching he says, "What are we looking for?"

"Answers," is all I can say. I honestly don't even know where to look or go for these answers, but I need something, a clue, a person, a location, anything would be nice right now. I will take as long as I need to discover the clues and find answers to my father's behavior, but he is a king. Every passing minute can be the death or harm of an innocent person. My father wouldn't harm innocent people but that king, with the cobalt crown, is not my father.

"In about three hours nightfall will be upon us," says one of the young guards, to nobody in particular. "I don't think traveling at night would be safe, so I recommend we find a cave or some source of shelter to protect you, my lady," this time directed towards me.

"Let's find shelter then." The shadows grow as we don't take a break and push further into the forest. The sun is falling; calling it quits for the day but, still trying to help in any way possible. I notice the canvas of colors above me. My father has my mother's tapestries and paintings hanging around the castle and in galleries. She used to paint skies like this, above darkened forests. Maybe she was trying to paint Elkwood.

I would try to paint like my mother, but it never turned out so well. I gave up after a short period of time and seeing this makes me want to give it another try. My father would tell me that I reminded him of my mother, but I don't know how. In her portraits she has black hair and crystal blue eyes while my father and I have copper orange hair and green eyes. I can only assume he saw similarities in our manner or favor. What else would I have in common with her? I've never met her. How would I know?

The sun finally vanishes leaving Jeremiah, the three Sentinels, and I in the dark forest. Elkwood is different at night. The trees are towering giants giving everything alive cover from the sun. The insects' clicking is hushed and there is a pressure building in my chest. I feel eyes glaring through me. I even see the nocturnal animals' eyes blink in the brush all around. If I was out here alone, I would've gone crazy, more terrified than I am now. A throbbing stone pulses in my chest suffocating me.

The bushes rustle and I hear little whispers. The high pitch voices are barely audible but I catch a word or two, "Hungry…, Them…, Perfect…." The whole group stops and listens. My heart begins to thud in my chest as I wait for the owners of the voices to attack. One of the Sentinels cracks flint and steel sparking flames that light a torch illuminating the forest. The throbbing stone vanishes right when my eyes lock onto them. They hiss and scream, small little human like creatures with the skin color of marble. The tiny creatures are standing on either side of me and the sentinels, but Jeremiah doesn't notice anything. They begin to scurry towards him.

My bow is drawn and aimed at the creature closest to Jeremiah before the Sentinels can even unsheathe their swords. The squealing monster leaps for Jeremiah and I release my string, hitting the brittle creature in its middle as it flies and sticks into a nearby tree. Jeremiah thanks me by only a nod of his head as he starts swinging his large blade towards the small creatures.

I fire arrow after arrow into the leaping creatures that turned the quiet forest into a screaming skirmish. I am so focused on protecting the Sentinels' backs I don't even watch my own as a creature pounces onto Snow's neck. Its large black eyes glisten in the torchlight as its thick claws begin to rip at his pelt. I barely think as I strike the monster with the bow causing it to tear its claws across Snow. He howls in pain and bucks me into the air sprawling. My throat hurts as I scream into a speedy descent to the hard earth.

I land on my side and scream in pain as I hear the snap of a rib. The monster's corpses litter the illuminated area. The ground glistens from the blood of the small humans. I rise from the ground and clutch my side. The adrenaline coursing through my veins makes the pain from my rib unnoticeable as I pull out my mother's dagger. No more creatures emerge from the surrounding brush and Jeremiah pulls his sword from the last twitching corpse.

"What were those?" I question, running to him and looking for any wounds. He does the same to me and cringes when he sees me clutching my side.

"Wood Nymphs," a Sentinel answers wiping blood from his shining blade. "They eat the teeth of humans." A shiver races down my spine as I think about the little Nymphs hands in my mouth yanking my teeth from my gums.

"Gather the supplies, so we can get to shelter now," the order fires from Jeremiah. His voice goes low to a whisper, "Are you alright?"

"Probably a broken rib that's all." Fear crosses his face but disappears as quickly as it comes. "I'm fine. Just help me mount Snow." I look away from Jeremiah's sparkling eyes to go to Snow but something's wrong. I don't see him. The horses are calming down, but in the large illuminated spot of the forest, Snow is nowhere to be seen.

"Snow!" I call out into the darkness. I wait but he doesn't emerge from the brush. "Snow!" I yell. Again and again I scream out to him but he doesn't come, or move, or hear me. My childhood companion is missing. I start to scream for him and snatch the torch from a Sentinel and begin to dash between the trees running and screaming for Snow. Tears swell in my eyes. He doesn't know Elkwood. He is probably scared and injured somewhere in the dark.

I start to cry and sob loudly. I scream so loud that it rips my throat causing immediate pain. Snow is gone.

I sit on the ground ignoring the twigs and sticks stabbing into my shins. Jeremiah wraps himself around me. His warm body stifles the violent shaking from my heavy sobs. I can't help but lay into him. Jeremiah is the only anchor I've had, other than Snow. He strokes my hair and rocks me back and forth, attempting to comfort me like someone would comfort a wailing child. His heart thuds against my ear, his body shakes in what I assume is fear, and he says, "It's going to be okay. We will find Snow. He will find his way back."

Jeremiah's words don't help because Snow has never been in Elkwood. He doesn't know his way around, or what lives out here. I don't even know what lives out here. The thought brings me back to reality. I wipe away my tears and snatch the torch from the dirt rising with Jeremiah. I look up at him; his towering figure intimidates me but also makes me feel safe, especially in Elkwood.

"We found a cave," yells a Sentinel. I step towards where the voice came from but Jeremiah steps in my way and grabs my arm. His grip is gentle despite all the power he has in his arms. He looks into my eyes and pulls my chin to look at him. "Are you okay?" he asks.

"No," I whisper my voice hoarse. He's gone and could be dead by now. My companion is missing. I even named him Snow after the first snowfall in Equadoria. Jeremiah is here for me. The torch does justice on his stunning features. His tan jawline shaded with slight stubble and the high cheekbones on his symmetrical face glow caramel. My voice speaks louder this time, "I lost Snow and may never get him back, but I'm here for a reason, to find answers. Let's get back to the others before something else tries to maul us."

He sighs and steps out of the way. I walk back to the Nymph graveyard and soon see the clearing, which is still covered in the nymph corpses. Out of the corner of my eye, I see a bright light from a fire through some foliage. Pushing through the sharp sticks and plants, I see another clearing, but this one surrounds a rocky mountain wall with a cave. A fire is burning and roasting some kind of small finch a Sentinel caught while Jeremiah and I were gone. The Mares are roped to a tree and the three men are already unpacking and laying out sleeping packs around the fire.

They choose to sleep out in the open by the fire, but I don't think that is smart. Just because the wood nymphs hate the bright light doesn't mean other abominations will mind it. Some monsters could even be attracted to the fire and even the cooking meat. The worst thing about this adventure is that, other than Jeremiah, I don't know any of the three Sentinels' names. I notice my bow and quivers are leaned against the cave mouth along with many other weapons and supplies like clothes and herbal tonics.

I'm leading this exploration but I don't even know my own crew. I look over at Jeremiah as he takes a seat by the fire with the cave mouth to his back. I retrieve a threadbare blanket from the pile of supplies and take a seat next to him. I begin to notice each of my aches and bruises as I sit staring into the flickering flames. My rib is definitely broken because now, as the adrenaline leaves my veins, the pain is almost unbearable. It's not the physical pain I'm feeling though. I see him, Snow. My chest aches with the loss of my greatest companion. He protected me and helped me through so much more than any person has, but I couldn't return the favor. I couldn't protect him from the evil Wood Nymph that tore his flesh. He feels betrayed and I know it because I've been betrayed before. I was betrayed by my own father.

"He will come back, Princess," a young, blonde haired Sentinel says breaking the silence. He seemed to almost be reading my mind, but I know that would be a foolish thought. "You're not foolish," he adds. My heart skips a beat.

"How," my voice quivers in confusion. His features change under the flames and his hazel eyes grow dark and menacing.

"There is magic in this world. Your father has outlawed the use and practice, but many of his disciples have magic in their blood." He smirks and looks around, so do I, noticing the strange looks on the other guards' faces. Mine must look the most puzzled. Thinking back, I never understood why my father didn't let me read about Elkwood. Now I realize he didn't want me knowing about what he hid right beneath my nose, the truth about magic beneath the skin of our citizens in Equadoria. He hid the magic that he banished from our lands but he must have a reason. "Elkwood is holding all the magic on the continent. Hidden in this forest somewhere is the location of magic."

"Why would my father keep information like that from me?"

"I am not sure." What does this boy mean? I believed magic to be witchery thanks to him. An awkward silence begins to grow through the group as we stare at one another.

"What's your name?" Jeremiah asks breaking the looming silence in the air.

"Zube Mindelow," the blonde answers. He smirks at me and winks childishly and I can't help but be disgusted.

"You are childish and irrespective towards those above you. You use your title as Sentinel to make yourself seem better to others probably because your family has rejected you or you never even knew them!" My attack towards him was uncalled for, but also needed. His eyes are dark and deep showing his depression and the sleepless nights he stays up to acquire more hours being a Sentinel. His job is an escape to focus on instead of acknowledging what he needs and misses. His family. "I may not read minds, but I can see right through most people," my words are a feral purr in the night.

He dips his head in shame as pain rattles through his bones causing him to shake. "It was a late autumn night many years ago. My family sat around the table as a cauldron of soup boiled over a fire in the kitchen next to the table. We started talking, but my mother was silent. The baby started crying and screaming and my mother did not react. She grabbed the knife next to her plate and screamed at the child to stop but he didn't. My mother stabbed my baby brother in the heart with a knife," his voice is low, shaking and sad. "She then removed my father's eyes with the same blade and slashed his Achilles tendons so he couldn't run as she poured salt into all his wounds. As my father wailed in pain my older sister and I hid under the wooden table. We watched her gut my father and eat out his intestines. As I read her mind all I could hear was 'eat, eat, eat, eat, and eat.' She spun to face me and my sister, and when I saw her eyes, all light was gone. They were pure black like an urchin. My sister screamed and told me to run. I darted for the door and stepping into the cool night air and, as I looked back, I watched my mother drag my sister by the hair and hold her face into the burning embers of the fire. My mother became a Wendigo." I have no idea what a wendigo could be but the small goosebumps that have rattled my body make me never want to encounter one.

My body begins to shake for Zube. If I would've known, I wouldn't have said what I said. He is probably haunted every night by his mother, and I threw his past into his face. I want to apologize but I can't say the words. I don't want to do anything right now. He must sit with the pain and the thought of losing his whole family. I decide not to say anything for the rest of the night.

"I'm going to bed," Zube says rising and heading to the edge of the illuminated area of the forest. I can't shake the feeling of fear from my bones. My father did attempt to murder me and he most certainly isn't a Wendigo. Well I don't think he is.

Jeremiah wraps his arm over me and I lay into him. I ignore all of the inappropriate thoughts people may have if they saw us like this, but my main anchor is gone and Jeremiah is all I have. I want to keep him close for as long as I can.

Late into the night the other two sentinels tell their stories of their families and lives before becoming high guards of Equadoria. A gentleman named in his mid-forties, named Gaston, tells us about how he fought in the great wars of Equadoria. He was on the front lines battling the Solarians of the southern kingdom, Solaria. He even killed many of the Sun Guard of the Solarian army. The Sun Guard is the highest ranking warriors of Solaria. He tells us of the golden armor they use to glint the bright sun rays into the enemy's eyes to gain an advantage. I can't help but admire him. He is wise and much smarter than his age. Gaston is somebody I'm glad to have as a Sentinel because he is a strong fighter. He will go great lengths to protect my father and me from harm. I don't know if he has abilities, but supernatural or not, I think he could handle anything. I only hope he can handle whatever Elkwood throws at us.

The third Sentinel, Novid Wayland, is a twenty-five year old man who spent the last five years being tortured in a Solarian prison. Terror is behind those eyes and, after hearing what happened to Zube, I'm not ready for any in depth details about his stay at the prison. He has seen too much for his age and so has Zube. They both have deep troubling pasts, but how it affects them and the way they hide it amazes me. It may affect them in many ways but none I have witnessed, or noticed. We all notice Zube is asleep; Novid tells me Zube is only eighteen which is the same age as Jeremiah.

Zube's life was changed in mere minutes and it's scary to think that any minute my life could change, or be altered, forever. This whole experience has been changing me, and I can feel it. I may not be changing for the better, but I certainly am not changing for the worse.

"I'll take the first watch," Jeremiah mutters into the flames. "Go to bed guys." He smiles even though it doesn't reach his eyes and he keeps staring into the bright warm fire that is heating our cold faces. I don't think I will be doing much sleeping tonight but all I can do is try. Tomorrow we will travel further into the forest and I want to be well rested for the journey.

I wrap my arms around Jeremiah and hold him tightly. I'm so glad I didn't lose him in the attack. I wouldn't be able to move on with my life. I wouldn't be able to wake with a smile every morning, or have someone to talk too to maintain my sanity.

"Goodnight, Ariadae," he whispers into my hair. His hot breath wisps down my neck.

"Goodnight, Jeremiah." I release my grip on him and pull my threadbare blanket into the cave and curl into it. I watch Jeremiah as my heavy eyelids slowly close, sending me into the abyss of night.

Snapping of sticks startles me and I rocket into a sitting position. I look to the cave mouth and notice that Jeremiah still sits looking into the flames. The fresh sticks he fed into the burning fire were the snapping noises that woke me. The sky is becoming a light teal blue as the sun begins to peak over the far mountains. Jeremiah has been awake all night on watch. He wants to help and I know how determined he is to find answers with me, but he still needs to sleep and keep his head on straight.

I take a seat next to him startling him. My dry mouth and screaming from the night before make my voice hoarse, "I can take this watch."

"I know," is all he says as he does not focus on me but only the burning embers before him. He is thinking really deeply and I know this because he only gets this blank stare when something is on his mind. "Do you ever wonder what stops the human brain from wanting to share emotions?"

"No," I respond more coldly than I intended.

"The brain stops itself from letting the heart release its emotions because of fear but-,"

"I'm scared too."

"Ariadae, I wanted to always share my emotions with you, but I couldn't, and I'm trying not to be scared anymore." I'm really confused because he tells me everything, but now I can see he hasn't told me whatever is currently bothering him.

"What are you talking about? Are you-," His lips touching mine interrupt what I was going to say. An explosion of butterflies and fireworks erupt in my stomach as I flush. My cheeks are hot, but I don't stop the kiss. The emotion he was feeling was lust. Jeremiah, a warrior of Equadoria, felt lust towards the princess, towards *me*.

I pull away and look towards the forest behind me so he doesn't see me blushing but he pulls my chin forcing me to look into his warm chocolate eyes. His voice is a whisper, "don't let this change us." Then he rises and heads into the cave leaving me to think about his lips against mine.

CHAPTER FOUR

Jeremiahs lips are softer than they look. I can't stop my mind from drifting to our kiss several hours ago. The sun has reached above Archaic Mountain and now shines down on the open campsite.

Zube woke up first and immediately ignored me to go feed the horses. I watch him from across the clearing as he held the apple to the mare's mouth, his yellow teeth biting into the juicy fruit. Knowing Zube can read mind makes me worry about what I think. If I think about Jeremiah kissing me he might know and tell Gaston and Novid. If they learn they could tell my father and Jeremiah would potentially be hung. I let the thoughts leave my mind before Zube can raid it.

I rise from the blanket and wake up Gaston and Novid. As I approach him I notice his hair is tousled in a knotted mess atop his head. His sharp features are soft in the innocence of sleep. I don't want to wake him. I'm tempted to just stare at him even though that's very peculiar, I can't help myself. Jeremiah has always been a friend to me, basically a brother if I think about it, but how long will he be a friend? Part of me likes who we were but why not try and become something else.

After making sure that Zube and the other Sentinels' aren't nearby I place my lips to his and he wakes slowly and happily. A smile spreads across his face as he chuckles and says, "Good morning."

A giggle escapes my throat I whisper to him, "Good morning." His eyes light up as he realizes he is looking at me. The corners of my mouth pull, attempting to smile, but I try to keep my face straight. "We have to start traveling again." A groan escapes him as he stretches and rises leaving me in the dark cave to retrieve his threadbare blanket.

I have never experienced something like this. I've never wanted to push something more than friendship with anybody. Jeremiah might be the only person other than my father that I can't physically and emotionally be without. My father wouldn't approve of me being with

Jeremiah in a romantic manner, but he isn't around. He won't be until I find out what is wrong with him.

Zube, Novid, Gaston, Jeremiah, and I have finished our packing and unbound the mares for riding. There are only four horses, but five people. Pain stabs in my stomach as I'm again feeling the ache for the lack of Snow.

"Take my horse princess," Zube says holding the reins and brushing the white stead. I assume this is him finding a way to make up for his crude behavior last night, but I still can't help but feel sorry. What happened with his family is truly devastating and gruesome. I smile to the blonde boy and his green eyes twinkle.

I mount the horse and hold onto the saddle. "We head south," I say, sounding stern and brave even though I'm scared and nervous. We all head south into the brush of Elkwood's greenery and hold a steady pace. As we travel through the forest I can't stop my eyes from peering into the surrounding brush looking for Snow. I know he isn't going to surface but a part of me wants to believe he will. I'm staring into the forest, and the forest seems to be staring back. I can feel the watchful eyes glaring over my every bone. It keeps me focused and alert but shaking all the same.

Fear has a way of erecting a permanent camp inside my chest. It feels like a stone becoming bigger and colder with every passing hour. I try to remove it by looking to Jeremiah as he smiles and waves to me, but it only subdues the pain for mere seconds. I am feeling the same pain I felt when I learned something was wrong with my father. I knew when he held me against the stone floor with the blade against my throat, grimacing into my eyes, he was gone. He *is* gone.

An orange fox gallops ahead of us and prepares to pounce on something hidden in the leaves. It snarls heavily and turns instinctively primal. We all stop our pace and wait for the red haired animal to leave our path, but all it does is growl and stare into the brush.

"Why is the fox acting like that?" I question to nobody in particular. I look around to the others and they all stare at the fox just as confused as I am. The animal leans onto its haunches as its long neck hair rises in threat. A shudder crawls like a spider down my spine.

Gaston, knowing well about hunting and primal instincts, answers me. "The fox is either defending its territory or…" His voice slowly drifts as his face pales.

"What is it," Novid whispers beginning to panic. The stone is gone. The fear that has been so well placed in my chest has left but my head begins to pound.

"The fox is scared shitless." Right when the clipped words leave Gaston's mouth, we look to the animal. The sounds of the forest are gone and all I can hear is the pounding inside my head. Pain strikes like lightning across my vision leaving blurred circles in my sight.

A thin creature of skin and bones crawls around the trunk of the tree next to the fox. The animal howls at the abomination clinging to the tree. The creature screams back, and faster than I couldn't think possible, drops from the tree landing on slim tall legs. It grabs the fox in a spindly hand and darts into the foliage. The fox and creature are gone in an instant and a stream of curses escapes my team.

Jeremiah turns to me with his sword drawn and unmounts the horse. His words are stern and orderly, "Everyone protect the princess at all costs. We don't know what this thing is."

"Yes we do," says Zube. "It's a wendigo." That's what his mother became. He knows more about Elkwood's inhabitants than any of us do. We need to protect him too. I don't say anything about protecting Zube but I will make that my duty. I unstring my bow and nock an arrow as we make a kill circle.

Novid breaks the silence with his quivering voice, "Do you think it-." The wendigo sprints from the foliage wrapping its large hands around him and dragging him into the forest. We are left to his screams and cries from the brush. Several snaps of bone and Novid is gone. After surviving five years in a Solarian dungeon, being tortured for being by a wendigo is a horrible fate. I could've seen him walking out of Elkwood with us after we found out what was wrong with my father. I draw my bow and aim before me. Nerves begin to make me violently shake and the arrow falls from the bow and to the grass below me.

The white scalp peers around a trunk and something slams into my back pulling me towards the trunk. Hands hold my arms around the tree as I face the area where the horses wander in fear and my friends are all pinned against trees facing each other. A scream escapes me as my healing rib sends discomfort through my bones.

"There are five," yells Jeremiah. A wendigo strides from where the fox stood and the towering abomination turns on Zube instantly as he struggles to pull free from the hands of the monster his mother became. The Wendigo smiles and row after row of yellow grimacing teeth drip of saliva. Each tooth appears finely sharpened to tear and pull flesh from bone, specifically Zube's flesh from his bones.

The creature staring at Zube walks to him and raises a hand with long skinny fingers. It reaches towards his face as he closes his eyes and squirms away. The thudding in my ears pound harder and harder and I want to scream against the agony. I can't let Zube die the way his family did. It would be the worst déjà vu known to his mortal life.

I pull against the hands holding my forearms and they don't budge. I will my muscles into my forearms and the hands drop off and the thudding becomes subdued. My vision begins to clear and as I scream, "Don't touch him." The long fingers reaching for Zube's face contort and crack. Broken. The migraine in my mind clears instantly, giving amazing needed relief. The screaming wendigo runs into the foliage as does the other five.

We all have bruises lacing our forearms like tattoos but a few bruises are better than being torn to ribbons. Most of my pain comes from my rib. When the wendigo pinned me it must've stretched the muscles around the fracture. Jeremiah sprints to me in habit and we check over each other. And before he can ask *are you okay?* For the billionth time I smile and try to stand straighter.

"I'm okay. Just make sure Zube is still breathing."

"Gaston is with him now but after what happened to Novid I was scared that-," I interrupt him by gripping his waist and pulling him into a tight hug. He doesn't deny the affection and hugs me back. It feels good having his heavily muscled arms around me instead of the skin and bones of a wendigo.

Even knowing that the wendigo is probably long gone I can't shake the feeling of the surprisingly strong thin fingers gripping my forearm. I rub at the bruises and try to get rid of the shakes. Gaston and Zube wander back to me and I notice the pain in Gaston's eyes. He was a good friend of Novid's, and I wish I had seen that wendigo coming. I would've fired an arrow through the monster's bony scalp. It wouldn't have killed Novid. This is all tracing back to my fault because if my father wasn't the king of Equadoria he wouldn't have gone into Elkwood forest and came back as that monster with the cobalt crown. Novid's death is on my hands and I need to find out what is wrong with my father and avenge him. I need to find my answers before anyone else gets hurt.

We begin to gather the wandering horses and I mount a white stead. I grip her reins as it comes back. The abhorrent stone is back in my chest and with the weight of Novid's death, it's heavier than before. Something tells me it's only going to become heavier as this quest continues. With the bow on my back and the dagger on my hip I ride into Elkwood with my guardians on a search. The fate of my kingdom is left to us now and I can't fail. I *won't* fail.

The ground is becoming soft as we begin to head downhill through the dark glorious trees. We wander in silence as if breaking it will shatter some barrier that will keep us going. I feel so fragile in this broken forest. Abomination after abomination; we can't get a break from the attacks. These wood nymphs and wendigo may only be the beginning. This forest is dangerous, not only to me and my friends, but to the entire continent if they enter. All the otherworldly creatures that live in Elkwood remain in Elkwood.

Something evil lives in these woods. Every tree trunk provides cover for our next attack but something keeps me looking around each bark covered tree to look for a potential threat. The forest isn't only littered with mythical beasts it also has many animal inhabitants. A white stag seems to glitter under the broken rays of sun streaming through the canopy of leaves above and wanders near our group. The animal walks along almost as if it doesn't notice our presence. Not a single feral being is around. While the stone is back in my chest I can feel the weight lifting. The stag pulls away the pain of my rib, the ache for Snow, the fear of never fixing my father. It all just wisps away caught on the warm breeze of the summer air.

"Zube," My voice shatters the silence and the stag still wanders aimlessly. "What are you?" He holds the reins of his steed and is aware of exactly what I'm talking about. I'm only questioning his mortality because of the power he withholds. He holds one of the many abilities that are outlawed by my father. He kept his powers a secret even though it was a gift. It was probably given to him by the creators of our world. The Gods.

"I'm physically a mortal, but underneath my skin hides the immortal I truly am. I am an ethereal being, a myth, a legend, I am a Fae and like all of the others I can shift to my other form which happens to be mortal." His words take us all by surprise. I've only read novels of the Fae. They're immortal beings which carried magic within themselves. They were born to protect the lands from the harm of the mortals. "Centuries ago the Greek God Prometheus created the humans to inhabit the world, but once he noticed the damage the mortals were doing to each other and the lands, he needed something to stop them. He created the Tree of Light which holds all the magic in the world. He guided six individuals to the location of magic and gifted those human beings. These six individuals still wander the world and they have created the six royal Kingdoms in Elkwood; Spring, Summer, Autumn, Winter, Night, and Day Kingdoms."

"What Kingdom are you from," Gaston questions, his dark eyes confused and lost to what Zube is telling us. I'm almost as confused as he is, but I think I understand what Zube is trying to say. I look to Zube who pulls the cloak around him.

"I was part of the Spring Kingdom," his soft eyes turn sorrowful and lower to the ground. Something about his past at the Spring Kingdom pains him. I want to further question life as an immortal being but I look to the forest before me. "The High Fae who ruled over the grounds learned of my mother becoming the wendigo. She immediately banished me from the lands and warned every Kingdom of my Dreag history."

"What's a *Dreag*?" Jeremiah finally adds to the conversation.

"It's complicated to explain, but I'll try in the best way I can. You are a human and there are different ethnicities of you. I am a Fae and there are many different breeds of us as well. There are Succumbus, Tempestatis, Naga, Mindinae- which is what I am- and many others. There is also the Forsaken. They are beings of great terror and evil which were created by Prometheus to end war and protect Elkwood from non-ethereal guests. The Dreag, which are a clan in the Forsaken society, are the most wicked of all. Wendigo's are a breed of Dreag." His words were even and well-spoken the entire explanation but the way he shuddered when talking of the Forsaken. The stone only got harder now that I know of these creatures.

"They all inhabit Elkwood," Jeremiah says his voice shaking in fear. "Why did we do this?" He shakes his head and fear flashes across his face as he looks to me. Being frightened isn't the best look on him.

"Yes." Is all Zube says and we become silent, a bottle of nerves waiting to fracture any second. If these Dreag patrol through Elkwood how long do we have until they cross our path? The Wendigo were weak. A force from Zube fractured that Wendigo's hand and they all went running. If that is the strength of Zube's power, moving forces with his mind then what abilities do the High Fae control? Their powers must be unearthly and beyond powerful that nothing can stop them. A war between High Fae would most likely destroy the land around them instead of each other.

Throughout the conversation the white Stag sauntered off and is nowhere to be seen. Its calming presence was taken with it and I'm left to the balmy sun now beginning to lower. Night will be upon us soon and the Forsaken creatures will be wandering and looking for their next meal. I turn around and look to my followers and tell them that we need to cover as much ground as we can before nightfall. They listen as my white mare's hooves begin to pound.

She speeds along darting around tree after tree nearly missing many trunks as her hooves thud against the dirt. Her muscled body is tight between my legs as we bound through Elkwood moving as fast as our horses can. The thunderous hooves beating against the earth send reverberations through my bones, which make my teeth clatter together. We made our first push into Elkwood like this and we got a decent way in…I think. I want to be out of the Forest as quickly as I entered it. This place isn't made for mortal beings like me, Jeremiah, and Gaston. Zube, even though he is mortal, is truly immortal making Elkwood his domain. The Forsaken wouldn't kill him out of spite, but if they did I don't know what I'd do.

We must've traveled close to four miles today which is good. We have covered some decent amount of ground but we need to start searching around for maybe a village or town. If there really are Fae Kingdoms in these woods they need to appear at some point. I can't blindly wander through Elkwood waiting to see if someone will find me. I need to find someone else. The question is who though. I also need to find Snow. He is probably scared and injured from that stupid Wood Nymph. If I had just watched out for Snow as much as I watched out for everyone else he wouldn't have gotten scratched and wouldn't have…

I stop thinking about the gut wrenching loss of Snow. Novid died only hours ago and I don't think of him. For some odd reason every time I think of him dying I'm not even sad. I'm numb. These great companions of mine are dying and disappearing because of me. It's my fault that they are here and I can't stop seeing their blood on my hands. It's a matter of time before another one of us dies.

Our downhill decent into Elkwood drops us off at a small stream. The fast moving water sends trickling noises through the forest. I tie my mare to a trunk and remove my bow and quivers. I take off the dagger and strip off my clothing. I know I'm with three men, but this is the first source of water I've seen and I haven't bathed since three days ago. My ivory undergarments leave little to the imagination and I saunter into the frigid water. The biting cold water wakes up my nervous system. It makes me feel alive, awake, and alert. The clear water is now up to knees, so I take a seat and let the slow movement of the clear water rove over my skin.

The sky is blanketed in a dark sheet of blue violet and black making a beautiful abyss which would be impossible for even the most talented artist to replicate. I remove the braid from my hair and slowly pull my head under the water. I float, suspended in the river, almost as if I have nothing to worry about or care for. Zube, Jeremiah, and Gaston prepare the camp around a small fire and I just stay where I am. Waiting in time as everything moves by in slow motion. Wisps of my coppery hair flurry around my face and I lose a breath I didn't realize I was holding. The bubbles rise in a dance. A waltz. The dramatic chaotic world above the water is horrid compared to the serene silence of the river. The flowing water brushes against my skin sending goosebumps through my body.

A pain starts in my chest which isn't fear, but my lungs asking for air. Begging for air. I want to hold them and push them to their limits but I give them what they ask and rise to the surface. My serene silence is gone once my head rises from the flowing mirror.

"Jasmine or lavender," Jeremiah shouts from the shoreline. He holds my bathing tonics in his hands waiting for an answer. The moonlight shines down on his figure giving me some sight of his face more than just his silhouette from the flickering fire behind him.

"Lavender please," I answer and he tosses the small blue bottle through the air. I catch the little tonic and start to pull the liquid scent through my hair. Elkwood gave us a few challenges recently and I can't help but fear for the next one. I play with the slick stones beneath my feet which reminds me of the stone in my chest. Fear is always there waiting and growing and I don't know what it means. These strange occurrences like my migraines and this stone started once I entered Elkwood. There isn't any explanation for them other than fear. Fear that everyone might die. Fear that I won't find the answers I need to help my father. Fear that my entire kingdom will be destroyed by the tyrant with the cobalt crown in my father's body. I can't escape the terror that has become my life.

I use almost the entire bottle on my many wavy layers of hair and I use the last of the scented liquid over my body. I rise from the stream and head to shore where I snatch a towel from the satchel. Zube sits farther down river cleaning my clothes along with his. He sits shirtless in the frigid water scrubbing away at the many fabrics and his own skin. Zube and I never really got along but it's not too late to try and start over. He is a Fae and no matter how much we may not like each other he knows more about Elkwood than any of us, even if he doesn't know the layout of the forest. I decide to join him.

I take a seat next to him and grab the cloak he pinned underneath a rock. His pale skin shines from the water droplets reflecting the moonlight. His muscled, scarred back heaves heavy breathes. "Hello, I am Princess Ariadae Vox, Heir to the Equadorian throne."

He chuckles and looks to me. His green eyes seem to glow as he says, "Zube Mindelow, Sentinel to the Equadorian throne and warrior of Equadorian army," He runs his fingers through his wet hair and I see the cords of muscle beneath the skin in his arms. "Is this your way of starting over?"

"Yes." He can read my thoughts making me clear my mind giving him a blank slate. "I've noticed something about you." My voice is soft and clear. Jeremiah wouldn't like us talking let alone being next to each other in our undergarments. My face becomes hot as I obviously blush.

"What," he asks his brow furrowing. "You hate me more than I think?"

"I don't hate you and I noticed you're not... you're not that bad of a guy," He smiles. A crooked grin plasters across his face and a pink flush bites his cheeks. He must be blushing but if I call him out on it he might blame the cold water.

"I noticed something about you too," He looks to me and the air grows serious. The fun we were having is now gone and replaced by something harsh and dark. Zube must be using that powerful force ability he used on the wendigo. "You saved me from the Wendigo."

What is he talking about? He used his own ability to save himself from the Wendigo. He broke the Wendigo's fingers before it could mar his face. He read my thoughts again. He says, "I don't have a power other than the ability of reading minds. When the Wendigo's fingers broke it was because of you." No. It couldn't have been from me. My father and mother are mortals and my father banned magic from Equadoria. The Princess can't have powers. I'm not a Fae.

"You're crazy. That wasn't me and don't try and make me believe it was me. I don't want to be like you!" I rise from the water and run to the shoreline where I left my towel. I wouldn't want to be an immortal like him. I want to die of old age and grow old with someone. I don't want to watch my friends and family die around me. I don't have to worry about this cause that wasn't me. I'm not a Fae.

I put on a simple tunic and pants while my other outfit is still being scrubbed by Zube. I sit with Gaston and Jeremiah around the fire and we talk as I ring out my hair.

"He isn't that bad," Gaston says talking about Zube. He witnessed me marching away from him with an angered pout on my face earlier. "He is a decent boy."

"Whatever," It came out a lot angrier than I wanted. I shouldn't be taking out my anger on Gaston. He isn't the one who thinks I'm a Fae. "I'm sorry. I know he isn't a bad guy it's just I'm a little on edge recently and it's becoming hard to let people get close to me."

"Well always know that I am here to listen to you if you want to take the time and talk to me." Gaston has a way with words that makes me feel safe and calm. I love having a father figure around. He reminds me of the late nights me and my father would spend in the Library going through old manuscripts and discussing the latest scholars' works. My greatest memories are with my father and this whole situation with him saying *"You little pretentious bitch,"* is a smudge on my happy memories. I can't think of my father without thinking of the grimace in his eyes when he pressed the dagger against my throat.

It's gone again. The stone of fear in my chest is now gone just like it left before the Wendigo attacked. On cue with the disappearance of the stone, sticks began snapping in the foliage around us. I surge towards my bow and quiver as something black leaps from the brush. It pounces upon Gaston and he wails as he and a large black stick creature roll through the fire sending the camp into blackness. Our only light source is the moon above us and the embers still burning on the ground along with the ashes tossed into the air.

I nock an arrow and turn back to the fire pit where Gaston was attacked. Jeremiah is in the foliage grunting and swinging a blade at a charcoal colored creature. The Dreag is all I can think of. The creature Zube told us about is ironically attacking us now. I look to the streams edge where the creature is hunched over Gaston's still body. I draw back my bow and aim between its shoulder blades. The creature doesn't seem to know I'm standing behind it watching. A breeze blows strands of my hair into my face as I realize what the crouched creature is doing to Gaston.

Zube crashes through the water and up the bank to me where he screams "It's the Dreag." The Dreag turns to me and wails as Gaston's liver hangs from between its teeth. Small slits are its nose and it lacks eyes. There is just a flat surface of charcoal skin. "Shoot it," Zube yells and faster than I can comprehend the creature leaps over me onto Zube. They roll into the pile of supplies and begin to wail and fight. I fire an arrow into the charcoal black and the large Dreag slumps onto Zube. He grabs a sword and runs to aid Jeremiah.

Gaston is dead. The man I so knowingly liked was just murdered by Elkwood. Another friend was murdered by this place. I don't know how much more I can go on if people keep dying. I go to his body stand over him. The stream laps water onto my toes but the water is no longer clear. It is crimson, the color of Gaston's blood. My eyes begin to burn as I try to stop the tears. Everyone around me is dying and I can't stop it. The only way I know something is going to happen is when the stone vanishes mere seconds before an attack happens.

Jeremiah and Zube are still grunting in attack against the wailing Dreag, but I hear the crunch of sand behind me. I whirl fast enough to see the leaping Dreag pounce on me and pin me into the river. I'm back amongst the serene silence of beneath the surface of the water. I taste the metallic water of Gaston's blood. I didn't get a breath this time. My lungs begin to beg before thirty seconds pass. The strong Dreag has its dark long hands around my neck holding me against the slick stones of the streams' bed. Pain makes my body convulse and all I hear is the *thud, thud, thud* of my heart. My vision begins to blur and as the thudding continues my head begins to hurt as a headache begins. My chest is on fire as I scream into the silent water. My life begins to fade as my vision blackens. I close my eyes letting the pain and burn in my chest take me away. The Dreag's scream is ear splitting even from under the water. My back arches and my body forces my mouth open and I take a breath.

Air, balmy midnight air fills my lungs as my face is above the surface. I cough out a large amount of water as something grunts and yells deeper in the stream. Snow pins the Dreag beneath the surface of the water and shakes his head wildly. He rips out the throat of the Dreag. He saved me. My Snow is back and saved me from my imminent death!

"Are you alright?" Jeremiah asks gripping me in a tight hug. He notices what I'm staring at and he looks too. "Is that…," Snow flashes in a blinding light and I need to shield my eyes away. The spots leave my vision and Snow is gone, but the most attractive man I have ever seen is standing in the stream staring at me, Jeremiah, and Zube. What just happened? Where did Snow go?

"Who are you," I ask pulling out of Jeremiahs grip as the tall dark haired male walks towards me. He grabs my arm and pulls me into the forest.

"I'm Jax. I am a Fae, but you grew up calling me Snow. There can be a lot more of Dreag around so stay here." His eyes are as blue as the moon. His deep voice was demanding and caring. Like fire and ice. Complete opposites but exactly the same. He saunters through the foliage and begins talking to Zube and Jeremiah.

Zachary James- The Rise of Titanium

I spent my entire life calling that beautiful man Snow while he was a white tiger. He slept in my bed with me and played outside with me and I never noticed anything strange about him. I didn't even notice that the tiger sleeping in my bed was an immortal hot guy. I should've been more aware.

I step towards the break in the forest to try and hear what they are discussing.

"She couldn't have known about me because I was on strict orders to protect her from the Queen."

"You tricked her into thinking you were a pet."

"Someone needed to watch her and her father because…" A hand clasped over my mouth and I recognized the bony charcoal fingers. I could smell the carrion on the Dreag's breath as it began pulling me deeper into Elkwood. I thrash and pull against the towering creature but it holds firm. In a heavy shiver conjuring voice it says, "Shut up human." A fist slams against my skull and blackness takes over sending me into unconsciousness.

CHAPTER FIVE

I awaken in a bed of silk. I almost think that everything that happened was a dream but then I look at my surroundings. Over my balcony door a gust of wind makes sheer teal curtains flow like wisps. As I look around the room I see three doors, closed and two night stands are on either side of my bed. In a corner near the balcony sits a fire place and a small seating area. A long wooden table, along with a large bookshelf, takes up another corner by a large window. This place isn't anything close to my home. This air smells of lilies and jasmine. My home smells of burning wood and grass. Earthly smells that aren't ethereal like this place. Based on recent events, I can't help but think I may be at a Faerie Kingdom.

Two bustling maids barge through my chamber door. They move swift and fluently but what makes me lurch into the soft pillows is their blue iridescent skin and pointed ears. Their hair is as yellow as the sun. One of them turns to me and throws her hands in the air scowling. "You're going to be late for luncheon milady," she says rushing to my bedside and throwing the sheets aside. I am wearing a soft white night gown and I suddenly realize that somebody has changed my clothes; which means somebody's hands have roved over my skin without me knowing. A chill scurries down my spine.

Before I question why the Dreag took me here, the maids squeeze me into a corset and a white under gown. Whatever Faerie Kingdom I'm in the Dreag must be controlled by the High Fae. Even if the Dreag were being controlled by a Fae Lord, why would they take me, a mortal girl to their leader's Kingdom? Mortals weren't supposed to be in Elkwood from my understanding and now being brought here and being called milady confuses me more than it should. I am a princess but the Fae in Elkwood certainly wouldn't know that. Well at least I don't think they would know. The blue maids pull a sheer sunset-pink gown over my head and begin to lace flowers and garland through my braided hair. The whole attire makes me feel like a small child. These flowing gowns must be what Faerie women wear normally. Most of my gowns in Equadoria are made of chiffon or velvet never sheer or tulle.

The two bustling Faeries pull me out of my chambers into a large hall well-lit from the towering windows behind me. The walls and floor look like marble, but is truly created from seashells. I follow them down corridor after corridor until we come to the center of the castle and I see the door to leave and a staircase. The grand room must be the size of my castle at home. Crystal chandeliers hang from the ceiling and billowing curtains flow before me from the balcony. A salt smell fills my nose as we must be near an ocean, which means we are near a coast of Elkwood.

"Where am I," I ask as the maids push me onto the balcony. One of the Faeries mouths the words *"No time for questions,"* then bows deeply from the waist and leaves me to the glorious view. The air is pulled from my lungs as I witness the most gorgeous land of my life. Snow peaked mountains surrounded by hills and valleys of greenery, stretch before me. We are still in Elkwood, but I know I'm facing south because one of those mountains is the oversized Archaic Mountain. Archaic Mountain is where Elkwood is separated from the rest of the continent. Over the years my armies traveled through Elkwood and over that mountain to reach the southern lands of Solaria and Lunaria, the mean southern kingdoms.

Women with pointed ears and skin of every shade move about on the balcony under the canopy of lilies.

They talk of Faerie gossip and royal warriors they are interested in. A woman of onyx hair and a gown of golden sunlight seems to glow under the sun's rays. A crown of flowers and twisted vines sits atop her head symbolizing who she is. The High Fae of this Kingdom. She is the most mortal appearing Fae here as her skin is of the same paleness of mine. Her teeth gleam, and her sharp canines are too pronounced for a human. She grips a glass of sparkling pink liquid and I notice her fingers are sheathed in metal armor tipped with claws. She is something painted, ethereal, royal, and beautiful. Her crystal blue eyes, as blue as the sky above her head, lock onto mine and the stone of fear plops into my chest like a stone being dropped into still water, the ripples becoming the chills reverberating through my body. In a blink of an eye she has moved across the balcony and is before me, smiling that too white smile. Her strong voice of pouring liquid keeps me bound to this earth.

"Hello Ariadae, I am Queen Evaflora, High Fae of the Summer Kingdom," she says. She is the ruler of this Kingdom and now I know where I am, the Summer Kingdom.

"How did I get here? The Dreag took me," my voice is steadier than I thought but when I spoke of the Dreag many of her Courtiers gasped in fear.

"My Emissary witnessed the Dreag taking you- a Princess- to its lair and rescued you," she speaks of only the truth. Legends say that Faeries can't lie and all I have to go on is what I've learned from those novels I read. I can't shake the goosebumps that have imbedded themselves into my skin. My heart pounds so loudly her Fae hearing can most likely pick up the beat from miles away. "I wanted you to join my Kingdom for lunch." She smiles and everyone takes a seat around the large table.

Never eat a Faerie's food. Never drink Faerie wine. Never trust a Faerie. The rules in my novels always say the same thing and I can't help but put my life in the hands of some scholars. A Fae servant pours the pink sparkling liquid I saw Evaflora drinking before in a glass for me. I shake my head in polite decline, but the gentleman places the glass in front of me anyway. I won't drink what these ladies are drinking because their breed allows them not to be affected by the liquid. *Never trust a Faerie.*

"Cheers! To the power of the Summer Kingdom," the queen raises her glass in the air. The other ladies lift their wine in cheers and take joyous sips. I don't even dare to touch my glass and I feel the blue eyes of Evaflora glaring at me. "Why don't you cheer with us, mortal?"

"I'm not part of your Kingdom." *Lies.* I lied to a Fae only because I wouldn't even try to say I will never drink Faerie wine. She smiles and cocks her head in animalistic way. She is a feral beast staring at an injured doe. I certainly am the doe.

Before she can ask me anymore questions the first course arrives. They place soft chicken, green leaves, and bread before each guest and I can't ignore the heavy groan from within my stomach. I reach for my fork and knife and cut a piece of the chicken. The steaming breast sends tendrils of gorgeous scent into my nostrils. I freeze when I feel her eyes on me. *Never eat a Faeries food.* She wants me to eat this chicken to poison me. She wants to kill me before her Kingdom as a way to show her power. The other Fae would probably raise their glasses to my corpse slumped on the table. I place my fork back onto my plate and wait until Evaflora is focused on a young red haired woman beside her. I slide the sharp knife into my boot while 'I retrieve my napkin.' I can't help but feel proud of the trick I played on the Fae, now acquiring a weapon.

These ethereal beings around me have many different ages but I know that even the younger girls, who look to be near sixteen, are really several hundred years old. Evaflora looks to be in her twenties even though she was one of the six individuals Prometheus led to the Tree of Light centuries ago. Other Fae, who must be younger, have aged more than she. They bare the wrinkles and silver hair of an elder. It must be some sort of magic she uses.

A screaming young boy gripped by two guards is pushed to the queen. The table goes silent as all focus is on the boy and the queen. "Oh thank you so much Darwin. I am feeling quite aged," Evaflora purrs. The blonde haired boy with round ears is pushed to the queen who grips his face tightly between her metal clawed fingers. A growl escapes her lips as she looks at the boy's neck and face. The boy is a mortal, like me, and my heart begins to pound faster than before.

The stone vanishes and her eyes flick to me as she yanks the boys neck to her gaping mouth with sharp canines. Her teeth clasp onto his flesh and she begins to drink his blood as she keeps her bright eyes on me. Sweat beads on my forehead as the heat of the Summer Kingdom is now affecting me. My hand instinctively lifts to my throat. My hand is the only protection I have from the evil monster staring at me. Her slightly aged eyes pop and all age drains from her skin as she becomes young and beautiful. She now looks to be eighteen. Whatever power she has, she needs to drink the blood of mortals to stay young.

The blonde boy's hair falls from his head and row and row of teeth sprout from his gums. His flesh thins to his bones and he grows taller becoming something I recognize all too well. He is the same creature that attacked me in the woods. He is the creature that killed

Novid. He is a wendigo. He is a Forsaken. The stone thumps in my chest and I can't help but wish I was back in the forest and away from the wicked monster still grimacing at me. Jeremiah, please come and find me.

CHAPTER SIX

After the disturbing luncheon, I was told to go to the market and get some clothing and accessories. One of the yellow haired maids, who is on the plumper side, joined me as we walked through the cobblestone street. Fae of all breeds and kinds were twirling, singing, and dancing past me and I couldn't help but to deny the joyous behavior, they are too happy to have a blood sucking queen as their High Fae.

Seri, my maiden, wouldn't allow me to purchase the embroidered tunics we saw while under a canopy. I know she won't let me purchase anything that isn't ladylike so I pretend to look interested at the folded gowns before me in a large wooden cart. I look through shade after shade and nothing is even close to my darkened color palette at home. When I don't make a purchase she ordered the whole cart and said to have it delivered to the castle. I can't object only because I do need clothes and she is only following orders from Evaflora. I want to stay out of her way as much as possible so purchasing the gowns was needed. Accessories. I still needed accessories so I asked for the entire cart of ribbons and garland, and Seri made the purchase. All the money spent today was pulled from the queen's pocket so I wasn't scared to ask for prices.

"Today was a success don't you think?" Seri says excitedly looking at me, her auburn eyes bright. I don't smile as I look to her, and then turn away. "I know you don't want to be here, but your friends will find you." I flick my head to her instantly. I never spoke of Jeremiah, Zube, and Snow…err…Jax to anyone. I keep forgetting my Snow has been a shapeshifter named Jax. Her eyes widen as she notices the mistake she made.

"I didn't tell you about any friends." She grips my arm hard and pulls me between two manors. The crowd moves at either end of the alley not realizing we are hiding in here. Her eyes narrow in scold and she begins to whisper.

"This entire Kingdom is glamoured to believe that she is the best Fae to have as a queen. Don't trust a word that leaves Evaflora's lips and do not, I repeat *do not*, make a deal with her, or act out of turn, or else she will find and hurt you and your friends." I nod in understanding and she pulls me out of the alley and back towards the shopping carts. She smiles to passing Fae who I assume are her friends and she hands me a heavy sack of gold, "Don't spend it all in one place and be back before dawn." She leaves me under the canopy of a wagon and I watch her plump figure disperse in the crowd.

This entire Kingdom is glamoured by Evaflora. People must've rebelled when she sat upon the throne and ruled with an iron fist, so she casted the spell. She is a witch, a woman of wicked and twisted beliefs. I only trust the stone in my chest and Seri for the knowledge she gave me. If I am to live with a powerful witch, I will need whatever I can get to fight her. I am only a mortal but I don't recall how the mortals killed the Fae in the novels. I think if I can recall from what I read they used some form of wood to kill the Fae.

I wander around the square and I come upon a wagon littered in blades and daggers and arrows made of wood. The Fae merchant has a thick scar marring his handsome face. Short chopped black hair is atop his head, and scruff outlines his angular jawline. The yellow eyes in his head seem to glow from the shade of the wagon.

"Excuse me, sir-"

"Call me Lunan." He interrupts me but his thick heavily muscled form stops me from being offended.

"Well Lunan, what wood are these weapons made of?"

He leans in and whispers, "Mountain Ash." His soft voice sends a warm calm over my skin. I can't help but think of the hard chest beneath his strained tunic. His stomach must be sculpted by Prometheus himself. Every Fae I have seen is stunning. "Other than killing Fae, what would a mortal girl want with Mountain Ash weapons?"

"That's exactly why I want Ash weapons," my voice drops to a whisper. "The queen of the Summer Kingdom is keeping me here and I fear I will become her next meal." He seems to understand my fear but he chuckles my statement away.

"She is a succumbus Fae. She needs mortal blood to stay young and immortal, so there is a great chance you will become her next meal." His voice is a low chuckle. That explains why she drank that boy's blood at the luncheon. Why would he become a wendigo, although that may be a side effect to be drained by a Fae. "But," he stops laughing and whispers too. "I hate Evaflora so take as much as you want." He grins at me and I can't help but smile back.

I hid all the illegal weapons around my room in various places. A dagger is beneath my pillow so if anyone tried to attack me while I slept I could just wake up and quickly pull the knife. I placed a katana underneath the table, even though I've never actually used a sword before, and then I hid another dagger in the bathing chambers in a cupboard. I then placed my bow and two quivers of ash arrows in the closet that was now filled with dresses. I am beyond grateful for the weapons Lunan gave me because just having them around my chambers already made me feel safe.

The bruises from the wendigo were gone, along with the pain in my rib, so I assumed maybe I healed. But then I remember the hands that changed me from my tunic to the night gown. Is it possible they healed me while I was unconscious?

Evaflora needs human blood to stay immortal and young. If she was ever deprived of a mortal's blood she would most certainly die. What else would happen to the queen of the Summer Kingdom? She is the evil in Elkwood. She was the one who glamoured her entire Kingdom to seem like the perfect ruler. I may be trying to discover what is going on with my father, but if she is one of the six High Fae Lords in Elkwood she should certainly know of the curse on my father, especially since we are just north of her kingdom. She may know how to even fix a curse like the one binding my father to wicked evil.

I leave my chambers and head down the long corridor towards the room I saw the entrance in. The queen may not know who bonded the curse to my father, but she must certainly know of the magic used. After all, she is only a High Fae because of the magic at the Tree of Light. She should have great knowledge about the magic in that tree. I saunter down corridor after corridor, which I memorized this morning, and I finally reach the entry hall. I bound down the grand staircase and look for the throne room. Every ruler, Fae or human, has the audacity to create an extravagant throne room, so I assume Evaflora's must be titanic based on the size of the entry hall.

I dash towards the large floor-to-ceiling doors on my right. I grip the gilded knob and when I turn the handle tugging as hard as I can, but I find the door to be stubborn. Unmoving. Locked. I run to the other side of the entry hall and tug on the other oversized doors. They too are unmoving, stubborn, locked. I don't think every door in this castle is locked, but with Evaflora being the ruler, I'd say that she has a lot to hide.

Hinges creak from atop the staircase I notice the glass doors to the balcony open. I instinctively run and crouch beneath the marble stairs. The purr of Evaflora's voice is all I recognize. "The girl simply won't know."

A man's thick heavy voice questions the queen. He obviously lacks fear. "Why not tell her of the blood in her veins. If she learns otherwise we will suffer her wrath."

Evaflora snaps at his comment. "That is only if the prophecy is fulfilled…," they walk down the hall opposite to mine and their voices fade away. I lose a breath I was holding tightly. My chest thuds so loudly I fear they may have heard it. The man she was talking to wasn't Lunan. I remember the soft warmth his voice gave me.

We will suffer her wrath. There is a woman who is stronger than Evaflora, maybe the High Fae of the Spring Kingdom. Zube did mention a *she* when he talked of the Spring Kingdom. The way Evaflora snapped at him and said *only if the prophecy is fulfilled.* What prophecy? I decide not to follow the High Fae and her strange friend, but instead return to my chambers. I will talk to the queen tomorrow, or whenever I get a moment in private, hopefully sooner rather than later.

I crawl into my bed and I just wish Jeremiah, Jax, and Zube would find me already. Jax seems to know Elkwood so he should know that we must've been somewhat close to the tyrant Evaflora. They will find me. I leave my only hope to them as I lay fitfully unable to sleep. Even with the presence of the smooth sharp mountain ash dagger beneath my pillow, I can't feel safe enough to close my eyes.

I am running between the thick trees of Elkwood. Dashing for my life as Evaflora screams and sprints after me. Her razor claws reaching for me as her many fangs grow. They pulse at the urge to drink my blood. I can't stop from running, but the trees never break. It's like I'm running through a maze with no way out. Her pounding steps grow ever closer and the stone in my chest vanishes. I am about to die. Her glinting claws rake down my back drawing thick hot blood. She licks the blood from her claws and it forces her to push faster. She now wants my blood more than ever. A cry of fear and terror passes my lips and I fall to the hard floor. She leaps atop me before I can rise and sinks her fangs into my neck. All I can do is scream.

I awake from the horrid nightmare wailing, tangled in the sheets on the floor. Sweat soaks my night gown and I swipe the beads from my forehead. I can't get her eyes out of my head. The piercing blue eyes wanted to see me bleed, see me cry in that dream. If I can resist, I won't let her see me bleed or cry.

I draw myself a bath and soak in the ocean scented water. I let the soft beach scented bath salts ferment on my skin. I want to get out of this place as soon as the others arrive but if they don't know where I am, I must leave on my own. They are definitely looking for me, I feel it in my bones, but I know they are having trouble. The Dreag just grabbed me without a sign or symbol to signify where I had gone. I will leave as quickly as I can. *If* I can.

I know I want to leave this Kingdom but I still don't know anything about what is going on with my father. High Fae Evaflora may be one of the few people in Elkwood who can help me fix my father. No matter how much of a cruel witch she may be I need to trust her. *Do not trust a word that leaves Evaflora's lips.* Seri told me this yesterday in the market, but if I want to save my father I have no choice to trust something Evaflora says. Faeries can't lie, so whatever she says will be the truth unless she has a very good way of manipulating words.

I dress myself in a blue gown with white ribbons through my hair. I'm finished by the time the sun has fully risen, when Seri comes barging in, her face stricken with terror. She bows, sauntering behind her is Evaflora. Her onyx hair is bound tightly beneath a golden crown and a light rose pink lace gown pools to the floor. I expect her to kill me right here in my chambers for listening in on her conversation last night. "I wanted to escort you to Luncheon," she grins and her sharp canines glint against the sun behind me. I don't move and we all stare at each other in silence. Her blue eyes narrow and she says, "After you," gesturing towards the open door. I bow deeply and wipe my sweating palms against my bodice as I leave my chambers with the feral beast.

She walks swiftly through the corridors with an elegant grace. She is the perfect queen, but I can't stop my shaking hands and my beating heart. She needed to glamour her people to stop the fear she most likely caused. I wait for her to bring up a prophecy, or maybe say she knew I was listening, but she doesn't speak. The crushing weight of the stone in my chest is becoming something that makes me feel safe, even if the bone crushing pressure *is* constructed strictly of fear.

"I must be leaving," I say into the silent stone corridor. She glances sidelong at me and doesn't seem to acknowledge my statement. She seems bored in my presence like the human I am means nothing to her. Technically I do mean nothing to her, and she means nothing to me.

"Why," she growls seeming feral. A shudder rattles my body and I again wipe the sweat from my palms.

"I came to Elkwood in search for answers."

"About what may I ask?"

"A wicked evil that controls my father. He is a loving man but once he returned from a trip in Elkwood he was different. He attempted to murder me." Shock dances across the queen's face as she seems frightened for me. Her features change as she ponders what I have said.

"A curse." The words are fast and clipped. "A curse seems to be the cause of your father's wicked evil."

"How would I remove the curse from my father?" She looks at me and grips my hand in sorrow.

"There is only one way."

"What is it? I will do anything to have my father back."

"The Tree of Light can destroy any curse, so find it and take a leaf to your father."

"Where can I find it?" The Fae queen turns to me and grimaces. I should've known that she wouldn't give me the answers willingly. The witch before me only wants my presence here to torture me. Faerie scum.

"I do not know." We reach the balcony and begin another dreaded Luncheon. My father is cursed and I need to find my way to the legendary Tree of Light. Evaflora was there a long time ago, how does she not remember? Prometheus led her to the Tree of Light, but maybe he doesn't want the six individuals remembering its location.

A Faerie slams into me and spills her wine down the front of my dress. A string of curses escapes my lips and she looks at me, offended. "Watch your language mortal trash," she says. Her hand slaps against my cheek instantly stinging my face. The burning sensation causes an immediate headache. I grip burning skin and strike the Faerie woman across the cheek. She squealed in anger and blonde curls fall from the braid down her back. "This mortal must be punished. She has defaced a Kingdom Lady," the other Fae girls ran to her and pulled her away from me. I back away and slam into something hard. My vision flashes as the migraine worsens, I turn to see Evaflora who smiles at me in excitement.

"Now be nice Raisie. It's not every day we meet an above average looking human," She purrs a failed compliment in my ear. She grips my arms and I can feel her breath flowing down my neck, it is oddly cold.

The Faerie who Evaflora called Raisie screams, "How could you compliment a mortal bitch?"

My temper flares and I cover my ears to try and subside the pounding but it doesn't stop. "Release it," whispers Evaflora. Her grip fades away and I grate my teeth together trying to release the tension building. It pulls the edges of my vision and I become lightheaded. Raisie covered me in her wine and slapped me. The burning flares with my anger and my eyes whirl to the blonde Fae still gripping her cheek. *Release.*

I scream as the popping in my head causes blasts of light on my vision. The chairs surrounding the long table clatter to the tile and the glasses of wine shatter, spilling bubbling wine across the tablecloth. Evaflora grimaces at me and my migraine disappears, along with my consciousness.

I awaken in my bed and hear the sounds of Seri digging around my room. I rise and see my blue skinned maid placing fine china with- I'm assuming from the sweet aroma- tea on the coffee table by the fire. "Thank you. What happened?" I ask.

She doesn't even look back to me as she says, "You destroyed the balcony furniture, frightened the Kingdom ladies, and then fainted." Oh my, I certainly have stepped out of line worse, than I thought. "Come here." She stomps to me and pulls me from my bed and onto my bedroom balcony which I haven't used. The sky is sheathed in night, and I notice I'm still wearing the blue gown I wore this morning, but my hair is lacking ribbons and design. The copper waves blow in a slight breeze as Seri whispers to me, "What happened to not stepping out of line?"

"I don't know what's happening to me," I raise my hands in defense but now I realize Zube was right. I have some sort of power. "I think I have abilities, like a Fae power."

She shakes her head at me scowling. "That is impossible. No mortal can bare Fae powers," she scuffs. "You're as wild as the queen herself." That comment hurt. I doubt Seri realized, but the way she said that wasn't very kind. Seri is a Fae after all, why would she want to be kind to someone like me? "Evaflora won't punish you but there is an invitation to the Summer Solstice Festival next week beside your tea and I am preparing your gown. Do not mess anything up and I told Evaflora you will not attend Luncheon due to recent misfortunes." *Misfortunes*. That's all I can do in this Kingdom is cause misfortunes.

I speak softly as I take her advice wisely. "Thank you," is all I have to say, and she bows and hurries from my chambers. I'm beginning to notice Seri is always in a hurry no matter the day or time.

I head back into my chambers and take a seat by the coffee table where Seri placed my tea and the invitation. While sipping warm tea I read the invitation:

You are invited to this year's annual Summer Solstice.

Please wear appropriate clothing and be prepared to have the time of your life. Let the equal days grant you equal powers and enjoy the fun. Your time will be a wild crazy festival during the day and the night will be full of mischief and music. Be prepared to bring money as some shops and carts will be selling food and accessories and clothing. May the Solstice consume you.

Sincerely, High Fae, Queen Evaflora.

The flowery invitation is designed in pretty swirls and colors and is hand written in ink, I assume by a servant. Evaflora certainly doesn't have time to write invitations to the entire Kingdom and townspeople. Her perfectly manicured hand would be cramped for the rest of her immortal life.

This is an annual event so people will be aware of this party all over the kingdom. Maybe I can use this as my chance to slip out unnoticed. But if I leave now, I still won't know where to find the Tree of Light. I will search this entire castle for a way to find it. I need to know and if I catch up to my friends, they too will know where to go. I just need a map or scroll of some sort. Where would an evil queen hide a scroll that holds a great secret?

I finish my tea and leave my chambers with just the clothes on my back and determination in my head. I head back to the entryway, where I always seem to notice Evaflora. She likes the balcony so I head back into the dark night. The chairs have been neatly arranged and the table is bare of silverware or decoration. She is always out here, even when she is having meetings with unknown men. I search the balcony and I don't see anything other than the canopy of flowers and the table with chairs.

I turn to leave but then I see it. Beneath the ivy hanging down the side of the castle is a slim beam of flickering light. Moving the plant I peer into the slim crack and see flames from a torch mounted on the wall. There is a door in the side of the castle. I press against the stone and the slab, like every other damned door in this castle, it is locked.

I just want one door other than my door chamber to open in this place! I feel like all the secrets are hidden in this place by this wicked witch called Evaflora. It's preposterous. How many secrets are kept from me? There is a wicked evil controlling my father and I just want him back. I don't want to find the mysterious location of all the magic in the continent, but what else can I do to save my father? Evaflora being unable to lie even said there is only one way and it's to bring a leaf to him. I only fear Evaflora because she glamoured her entire Kingdom and she is like a feral beast, but even she fears the wrath of someone even more powerful than she and a prophecy needs to be fulfilled for Evaflora to be affected. Whatever is going on with Elkwood Forest is a lot worse than I imagined. I don't typically pray for, I have long forgotten most of the Gods' names, but please Prometheus guide me to the path that will allow my friends and my family to live.

I leave the balcony and head back to my chambers where I pull a novel from the large bookcase. The pages are yellowed with age and curled at the corners and the fabric over the hardcover is splayed and torn. The title of the book is *Nirvana.* It is the story of when Prometheus lead the six humans to the Tree of Light and how the Forsaken came to be. Three men and three women were guided by the winds that called their names. They all unknowingly wandered into Elkwood. As the forest led them deeper and deeper into the thick brush, they became more and more entranced. That must be the reason why Evaflora doesn't remember the location of the Tree of Light. Prometheus wanted the continent protected from the destructive mortals, but once he led these people to the Tree of Light, and gifted them with immortality they became the High Fae. The six Fae bred with humans and more and more breeds of Fae were born now creating the wild ethereal beings I see daily wandering the Kingdom.

Mortals soon began destroying the forest edge, slowly expanding their own land in greed and wealth. One mortal king even traveled to the northern most coast of Elkwood and plotted his land in hopes that would protect him from potential conquerors. His kingdom, Equadoria, became the largest and wealthiest kingdom on the continent of Abella, and the other kingdoms grew jealous. That would explain why we have been warring with Solaria all of these years. The Solarian king during that time must've been angered that he didn't think to go north instead of south first. *They began destroying Elkwood in an attempt to become wealthier, and the peaceful Fae Kingdoms were affected by the mortals' destruction. Faeries guided by dark shadows started to kill the mortals out of spite.*

A war erupted between the Fair folk and the humans, which lasted for a century, until The Book of Ash was developed. My father never had told me of the Book of Ash because I didn't know that there were wars between the Fae and humans. I have a lot of things to press my father with later. *The laws caused all ethereal beings to remain in Elkwood, but many Faeries didn't listen. The Faeries who killed the humans out of pure enjoyment become broken, damaged. The damaged Faeries became known as the "Forsaken" among the six*

Kingdoms in Elkwood, and because of the damaged Fae leaving Elkwood and denying the laws of the Book of Ash, the Tree of Light punished them by binding the Forsaken to Elkwood forever. The Forsaken must stay in Elkwood and cannot leave because of a curse placed upon them by the Tree of Light. If this tree is powerful enough to make curses of its own what power does it truly possess? To me this Tree sounds like another god or deity of sorts.

The evil abominations I encountered in Elkwood used to be Fae? What did Zube's mom do to become broken, Forsaken? *If the curse was ever revoked or lifted, the Forsaken would have free reign over Abella and could easily destroy all mortals across the continent. As long as the Tree of Light remains Prometheus made a deal that the dead Faeries, and all passing Fae, would be allowed to live in Nirvana, his Homeland and the location of all his siblings.*

I place the novel back onto the shelf as I think over the information bestowed upon me through a single novel. It was short, but by the time I'm finished the sun began to shine into my chambers from the open balcony. I was up all night reading that book. Hopefully I will sleep well this coming night.

I rise and head to the view overlooking the kingdom, and I can't help but smile at the glinting sun. Somewhere north is my kingdom, Equadoria, the place my ancestor placed thoughtfully on the northern peak of

Abella. Back then the location was perfect and peaceful but now…has only caused a great deal of unneeded anxiety and stress. If my ancestors never went to the peak of Abella and surrounded themselves with Elkwood than my father wouldn't possibly be a prisoner in his own mind. He may be stuck in his own mind, watching the world through his own eyes but unable to speak. Torturous, the thought is truly torturous. But I will do what I can to set my father free. If Tree of Light can place curses and turn humans to Fae than it will help me fix my father, I hope, but I need to find it first.

I head back into my chambers to my large closet, overflowing with glittering gowns. I remove the ice blue gown, which reminds me of Jax. His piercing eyes are so soft and caring. I want them to look over my body in even the most unladylike places. His posture, from what I remember, was straight and he held his shoulders in a king like way. Only years of training could possibly allow someone to be so mannered. I wonder if his dark curls grew shaggy in the three days I haven't seen him. I wonder if hard stubble has sprouted along his jaw like Jeremiah's had a few days after we first stumbled into Elkwood. I need to see him more and focus on his features when I leave. *If* I leave.

I squeeze into a green gown and lace up the bodice. It isn't a harsh lime green or a dark Elkwood green; it is a warm grass green. Something that reminds you of the summertime grass littered with morning dew from the humid air. I leave my copper waves flowing down my back, I am feeling airy today. A large full length mirror helps me place a pair of matching green flats onto my feet and I twirl, staring at the reflection of a fragile girl being slowly cracked from the harsh world around her. The green dress matches my eyes, but the auburn flecks shine a bit brighter today in some odd way.

Spinning into my room I hum the soft lullabies my father once sang to me when I was much younger. He would sing them to me when I was sick or woke from a nightmare, frightened of the monsters I once believed were real (which I have recently discovered *are* real.) He would also sing the lullabies to me when I was sick or upset at the world for ripping my mother from me. Elkwood took my mother from me soon after my birth and I no longer wish for her presence in my life. I don't miss her, I can't.

If I could make a wish right now, I would wish for my old life back. The way it used to be with just Jeremiah, my dad, and Snow...err... Jax. I am still not used to that.

The door flies open and Seri and I squeal in unison. I grip my pounding chest and she laughs in hysterics. She says, "You certainly love to get ready in the morning." Her auburn eyes flick to the soft waves flowing past my shoulders and her eyes widen, "You look very pretty milady but you may not have your hair unbound without permission from Evaflora." I head into the bathroom and Seri follows as I take a seat on the rim of the legged tub. She takes half my layers and braids them into a knot allowing the rest of my hair to flow down my back freely.

I finished an entire novel over the course of last night and I am constantly left to my own thoughts, which isn't the greatest way to wait for my friends. At home I would typically train every day with Jeremiah, but I doubt there is a training center nearby. My words are soft as I expect the answer "Is there a training room in the castle or a training building somewhere in this Kingdom?" Seri's eyes narrow and she nods questioningly.

"There is a Facility in the side of the ravine. Why would you want to know?" I lift my shoulders trying to dodge the question but Seri knows I'm up to something.

"If you want to train you must remain in the castle. If you head to the Ravine Center then the Fae warriors who are training will battle with you, or try to take advantage of you." Well there goes my only enjoyment and why would they name a ravine the Ravine? "There is a Garden Sanctuary in the courtyard located in the southern wing of the castle. I can lead you there if you'd like?"

"It's no building full of weapons and shirtless men, but I'd love to explore the Garden Sanctuary," I say grinning even though I'm slightly disappointed. I would've liked to learn how to wield a sword. Once I leave this Kingdom I will certainly ask Jax or Jeremiah to train me in the art.

We head down many corridors passing statues and alcoves which I could easily duck into and hide. We pass the entry hall and balcony and head down many corridors to the southernmost hall. Seri leads me into a stone room with glass doors, which open to the mammoth garden. I thank Seri and make my way into the labyrinth of hedges and flowers and plants. The only sound in the gorgeous sanctuary is the crunch of the gravel beneath my feet and the calls of distant birds. Stone statues of Prometheus and other Gods are placed intricately around the maze of beauty and a wide variety of colorful flowers takes my breath away. Pink lilies, yellow daisies, and many other flowers litter the large place making the gardens seem to glitter.

I walk under a large Elkwood tree and notice a large raven that perches on a high branch cawing into the summer day. Its black feathers gleam under the sun's rays and its dark eye falls onto me. The bird stops its caw and just stares at me. I stop walking. The air becomes thick and heavy as its beady eye remains on me. The wind seems to pull the air from my lungs as the garden, which was previously full of sound, is now silent. It has become mute. I pant heavily and the raven flies away. However, in moments the creature I thought had disappeared, comes back. The same being that called me into Elkwood and screamed my name. My ears bled from that call. My name is being called on the wind that wisps through my hair. I feel a pull in my middle like someone is tugging a strand of thread protruding from my abdomen. I let the invisible thread guide me deeper into the garden.

I have no idea where I am going but I feel the voice guiding me. I watch as the thick hedge pulls apart allowing me to enter, then seals me in a circle of tall plants. A small white pillar sits in the center of the circle, and a large stone bowl sits atop its flat surface.

"Look," the voice says pushing me, willing me towards the bowl. This voice wanted me to enter Elkwood and I can't help but think once I look into this bowl, the voice will be gone. It will no longer scream my name making me bleed and will no longer lure me to strange locations. This thought makes me peer into the thick liquid mirror completely full of liquid silver. The liquid is not clear, but is made of warm oil, like it was exhumed from the depths of the earth. I'm staring at liquid silver. I grip the rim of the smooth bowl and let my head slowly dip into the warm liquid.

Pain shoots through my skull shattering my mortal mind and the blur leaves my vision as I witness a woman running through a thick dark forest. Elkwood. Her white nightgown is stained with blood and her belly is swollen after the birth of a child. I can see her fear rippling off of her body and I can smell the stench of the sweat upon her skin. Her onyx hair flails behind her and I can't see her face. I want to shout for her to stop, but I am nothing. I am simply the air full of mist on a warm summer night.

She trips over a log and screams at the pain of her now broken ankle. She looks back at me. Into the dark, mist-filled air illuminated by the bright moon above. Her piercing blue eyes are glowing and gleaming with tears. She rises and tucks her hair behind her pointed ears. The thin nose and sharp features is a woman I know. This recent mother is someone that has haunted me. She is beautiful, just like her baby daughter whom she left home. Her tapestries and portraits hang along the walls of Equadoria. This is my mother.

She rips off her nightgown and begins running again on her fast healing ankle. The naked woman sprints even faster and deeper into Elkwood. I follow my mother and watch her anticipating her imminent death. According to stories from my father and others her body was found in our gardens, but only the onyx hair on her head indicated her as my mother. She was in ribbons. This was the night she died. Elkwood Forest wanted me to learn the way my mother died.

I wait for a creature to appear and maul her, but no beast comes. She is only running and I begin to wonder how long my mother survived in Elkwood until she died. Why was she running from my father and me in the first place? Equadoria is her home. No. I am wrong. She breaks through a clearing and stares at a deep ravine roaring with the crashing waves of ocean water. Across the screaming Ravine sits a large Kingdom.

She grabs a gown from the foliage and her fingers become covered with claws. She twirls a finger in the air and the wind twines her hair into a beautiful art. A crown falls upon her head. She looks back into Elkwood, and I recognize the piercing blue eyes and the too-white grimace. I am the air, and now I am mixed with the scent of metal, and magic. This woman is a High Fae. She is Evaflora. My heart stops beating as I realize that Evaflora is not only a monster… she is my mother.

CHAPTER SEVEN

After crying for six hours and then sprinting to my room and crying even more, night has consumed the kingdom. I lay in the ceramic tub with burning eyes and wet cheeks. I thought my mother to be a mortal, but now that I know she is Evaflora, my strange power makes sense. Zube was right about me having Fae abilities. However, he didn't know that Fae blood courses through my veins. I certainly am not immortal because I have aged as any typical human. I truly am sixteen, and I look sixteen. Evaflora- my mother- I really don't know what to call her. She ran from Equadoria because of my father. Did he banish magic because of my mother? Or did she run from my kingdom out of her own reason? What could that reason be? There are too many unanswered questions.

Upon hearing my sobs Seri comes barging into the bathroom looking panicked, "What is going on my dear?"

She simply wouldn't have known anything unless Evaflora told her Kingdom she had a daughter. Let's see how much she knows.

"Did Evaflora ever speak of having a child?" confusion flickers across her features as she immediately becomes puzzled.

"No," she says. "What would this have to do with your issue?" Her voice becomes concerned as she starts to pull me out of the tub. Stepping out, I decide to tell her.

"Evaflora is… She's…Evaflora is my mother," I choke on the words which seem very foreign to my mouth all of the sudden. Terror and horror is permanently pasted on Seri's face as she staggers back hitting into the wall and stumbles out of the bathroom. "Where are you going," I yell chasing after her. Her hand is already on the gilded door knob of my chambers and she looks back, angered.

"I told you things that are treason for anyone to hear and you, being her daughter, could just run to her and have me killed. I have a family to worry about," her words are venomous and accusing. Just like when she said I was no better than Evaflora.

"I would much rather trust you over the witch who has never been a part of my life," the words flow from my lips and I follow her into the corridor. "She gave birth to me and ran off to this kingdom, and now she is just a tyrant! No Kingdom should be ruled with glamour over the eyes of the civilians. I don't want to have her blood in my veins any more than you want to serve beneath her feet!" My statements became shouts in the quiet corridor and I couldn't help but have the feeling of someone listening.

Seri turns on me instantly stomping up to me with narrowed eyes and a furrowed brow. Anger seeps from her pores and she wraps her fist around my wrist squeezing extremely tight. Her words are a hushed whisper, "You will never speak to a Fae like that again! Do you understand me mortal," she is too angered to call me by my real name.

Her anger seems to feed into mine. I bare my teeth at her as I say, "Fae or mortal, what is your title to mine?" I instantly regret the words as I say them. Seri has been nothing but nice to me and in a moment of anger I have said something which truly means nothing to me. "Seri, I am so-," she releases her grip and relief floods into my bruised skin.

"Don't. Like mother like daughter," she spits the words viciously throwing as much hatred into one sentence as one could.

"Who is like their mother?" a questioning voice says from down the hall. The warm purr and voice of liquid gold signifies who it is. The graceful tall High Fae approaches Seri and I as my heart begins to beat rapidly and tears begin to fill my eyes. Seri faces her, and looks between us, glancing back and forth.

"What a family reunion," Seri growls grimacing at me. I bite my lip as I notice the realization in Evaflora's face.

"You're aware?"

"Very," I say bearing my teeth as a tear slides down my cheek. "Why didn't you tell me, why did you leave?"

Evaflora wails in laughter and smiles at me as she whispers, "You should've known all along, darling. And I left because your father was too focused on his friends with whom he trades, from the other continents. I left the night I gave birth to you. He didn't witness the gift of his first child being brought into this world. When I walked to the throne room to present you to him, he was too busy making love to a lazy prostitute." He wouldn't. My father would never cheat on my mother and especially with some courtesan.

"No, he would never," she shakes her head at me and begins to reach for my hands as all the tears have started falling from my eyes. "NO," screaming, I pull my hands away from her, "Don't touch me!" she looks offended as I push past her and run towards the entry hall. In my vision she was running and crying through Elkwood, but my father, the man who held my hand in the courtyard, sang me lullabies, discussed novels and politics with me, the man who mourned my mother's death the most, would not be so cruel. He told me he witnessed my birth and even helped the healer pull me from my mother's womb. *Evaflora's* womb.

I step on the front of my gown and begin tumbling down the marble steps of the entry hall crying out with each slam of my body against the cold hard stairs. Evaflora, who must've been chasing after me, screams my name as I reach the large open floor. She comes bounding down the steps and I scramble to my feet. She runs towards me and I begin backing away.

"Are you alright," she asks sounding concerned, but I can't tell if she is just trying to be manipulative or if she's actually caring because a monster like her wouldn't be truly concerned for the daughter she left. "Don't run I can help."

She reaches for me again and I can't help but think of the glamour she placed on her people, or the boy who turned into a wendigo when she drank his blood. I slam into the large doors to the castle and thunder booms shaking the stone kingdom. "Don't come near me you monster," I scream as my heart pounds heavily. Not only is there a storm raging outside but there's a storm raging within me. I can't trust Evaflora, but she *is* my mother. I should trust my mother, but I don't think I can. Not after she left me. Now it's my turn to leave.

I spin on my heels and hurl the giant wooden doors open. Slanted rain pours into the marble entry hall and I quickly become soaked. Lightning strikes, illuminating the empty courtyard. I run into the dark night. Evaflora screams something and a horn sounds from behind me. She has summoned her Sentinels to find me, or capture me, before I can get away. Suddenly I am aware that I am prey running from a predator and what makes my heart skip a beat is that I happen to be her favorite kind of meal.

I blindly run between wooden manors and my steady pace falters from the occasional tremors under my skin. Spiders crawl in my guts and I can't stop a hard convulsion that makes my body thrash. I find myself in an alley, full of large crates and boxes stacked high up the manor walls. Shouts and clanking armor begin to sound from behind and in front of me, so I quickly duck into the shadows of some crates. Sentinels' shadows scurry past the alley. Thunder rattles the sky and my thundering heart rattles my rib cage. My breath heaves in tendrils before me as two Sentinels start to head down the alley. Scrambling up the crates I climb to the shingled roof of the manor and look down as the men leave to join the other guards. I remain still and tense on the roof as rain pounds against the surface.

Zachary James- The Rise of Titanium

I need to leave the Summer Kingdom but I'm not actually sure how to get across the entire kingdom towards the ravine. Other than a few rooms in the alley and the square, I haven't seen this kingdom in its entirety. If only I brought one of my mountain ash weapons I could fight my way out of this Kingdom. I want to get as far away from this glamoured city and High Fae as possible…and now.

I rise and my pounding heart doesn't stop its hard steady beat. The stone is still as hard as brick in my chest and I am beginning to like the feeling of fear remaining with me. It's a warning before something bad happens. It just vanishes and I have seconds to fix whatever might go wrong. I begin to back up and my legs push forward, lurching me towards the large gap of the alley.
Three steps until I make a treacherous leap.
Two steps until my legs will push off the shingles.

One step and then the stone, fear, is gone, vanished. Before I can react, I'm flying through the air. I am falling towards the hard cobblestone, slick with rain, with no signs of stopping. Once my body slams against the hard ground, I will certainly die from the impact. I won't be able to rescue my father from the curse, Zube won't know of my Fae blood, nor will the other two. I don't even feel bad that the witch who is searching for me is losing her only child. Let her mourn me, I doubt she will.

I pass the shingles and something latches my elbow. Pain fires like lightning through my shoulder and arm. I am rising as someone or something unbelievably strong is lifting me. I have no idea who or what pulls me onto the roof, but I wrap my arms around a rock hard, rippled middle. His voice sends a warm calm over my skin, "Are you alright, Princess," Lunan asks.

"Now I am," the words leave my mouth before I can stop them and he laughs as I release him. "Can you get me out of here?"

"Yes but I'm not sure if you should," his voice is concerned as he beckons me toward the opposite edge of the roof. "High Fae of this Kingdom is scheming something and I am not sure what. She is keeping information and lying to the other Kingdoms. They aren't sure what to do because they don't know exactly what she is lying about."

I stop in my tracks as I question what he said. "I don't want to remain here and Fae cannot possibly lie, Lunan." He looks back and his yellow eyes glow with laughter.

"What fairytale did you hear that from?"

"Wait, Faeries can lie?" I can't help but hope he is joking only because now I certainly can't trust anything a Fae says.

He laughs and white canines glint the lightning that shatters the clouded sky, "Of course. Let's go." I turn over every word Seri, Evaflora, Zube have ever said. I even look into the few words Jax has said, but he spent his entire life protecting me from, I assume Elkwood, so I don't believe he would lie to me.

We leap from manor to manor making our way towards the ravine. Lunan never further explained why he thinks I should stay other than Evaflora lying. Every time I wanted to ask, his Fae hearing picked up on nearby Sentinels and he silenced me. He is leading me out of this nightmare. I want to leave the Summer Kingdom and get to the Tree of Light but I'm not even sure what direction to travel in to get to the hidden location. Even though it greatly burdens me, I must stay to see if Evaflora is hiding the location from me. She may have played dumb the day I asked her about the Tree of Light when we were headed to a luncheon.

"Go on without me." He turns to me with his finger pressed to his plush lips and I add, "I must stay to learn the location of the Tree of Light, to save my father, so go on without me. I do not want you caught. Evaflora will certainly kill you if she learns you attempted to help me escape."

He shakes his head and says, "We can pretend I caught you." I smile and climb down the manor front stepping on the windowsills and doorframes to reach the cobblestone street. Lunan lands silently next to me and I let him grip my wrists behind my back as we head back to the castle. Back to the place where a monster rules with a clawed fist. Back to the place my *mother* lives.

Thunder shakes the large looming castle before me and Lunan. Evaflora meets us at the doors and pulls us inside. Anger burns like flames behind her eyes and I swear I can see blue fire in her irises. She nods to Lunan and orders me to my chambers. I reach the top of the staircase and look back. Lunan smiles and winks at me. I return to my chambers where Seri certainly won't be lurking about. I was so rude to her, and she was one of my only friends in this seashell structure. I have chased her away with my horrid mouth.

My heart has calmed and when I enter my darkened chambers I notice a small light is illuminating my closet. When I enter it I see the most gorgeous gown my eyes have ever seen. This dress was what Seri was working on. I crumple to my knees before the gown, draped on a cloth mannequin and let hot tears burn my cheeks and fill my mouth with salt. I do not even try to cover the loud wails that have escaped my throat. My simple life has gone to hell because of Elkwood Forest.

CHAPTER EIGHT

I stay in the castle for the rest of the week watching as Evaflora prepares for the Summer Solstice. The help is always arranging large flowers and carrying flags displaying a seal of a golden sun surrounded by purple flowers. The Summer Kingdom's insignia is gorgeous, but the bright golden yellow and royal purple colors clash together. I wonder why Evaflora designed it that way. As I pass each bustling maid I look for Seri's iridescent skin, golden hair, and pointed ears. I can only assume she has left the castle. Hopefully she has stayed in the kingdom.

Before I knew it, the Summer Solstice was here. I awoke to no Seri, and I finally rose around noon, to gorgeous music. I walked to my balcony to watch the commotion.

Maypoles have been placed around the Town square. Purple and gold flowers decorate the kingdom, which gives the salt scented air a sweet aroma. I stare down on Faeries dancing to the ethereal music. The sounds of woodwind instruments blend together making a beautiful melody in the air, making your body urge to twirl. The music makes a flower begin to bloom in my stomach, and I can't help but smile to the tingling feeling. It's joyous and happy, like the children and adults I watch dancing. They are beautiful and grateful to be here, and I am not sure if it's because of the glamour or if they are truly happy. A part of me thinks they are actually enjoying this perfect Summer Day.

I still don't trust the Fae food, but when Seri's partner comes into my chambers with a silver tray of fruits and bread, I stumble to her. I eat the food savagely and the berries erupt sweet liquid across my tongue. I haven't eaten anything in almost three weeks so I sprint to the bathroom and the delicious breakfast in my stomach comes back up into the toilet. I need to slow down and slowly build up to eating more. Apologizing to the maid I nicely nibble on some bread before getting dressed for today.

I'm not really sure what I want to wear, but I don't know if I actually plan on leaving the castle. Being surrounded by Fae is not what I truly want to put myself through; I'm starting to hate this Kingdom. I hate my lying witch of a mother, and I hate that I don't know how to help my father. I've been in this Kingdom for three weeks, and I haven't been able to learn where the Tree of Light is. Evaflora said she didn't know its location, but Lunan told me that Fae can lie. She could have been lying to me to prevent me from learning how to save my father. She doesn't care what happens to him, she hates him, just as much as I hate her.

I lace up my corset and my lack of eating has given me a fourteen inch waist, there is nothing healthy about that. I pull on a smooth, bright, yellow dress that hangs with layers of silk to my ankles. Today is a day of life and happiness in the Kingdom, so I remain barefoot and let my long hair flow unbound. I can't help but keep looking at the dress Seri made me. It's extremely large skirt has at least several thousand layers of tulle. The dress is silver, like the moon at night, and the bodice appears to be made of a shattered mirror. A small oak box has some form of accessory. I am tempted to peak, but a knock on the door startles me.

"You are summoned to the royal Ball tonight, milady," says a maid bowing deeply. Facing her, I try to ignore the etiquette she has towards me. I don't wish to be called milady because that only makes it even more clear that Evaflora is my mother.

"When shall I attend the Ball," I ask through grinding teeth. I do not want to go and be with Evaflora's Kingdom. She will certainly make me a spectacle at this stupid ball and with my luck; Raisie who is surely still angry will be attending the Ball.

She responds coldly, "I will come to your chambers at dusk to prepare you before escorting you to the ballroom." She bows deeply again and leaves my chambers with a slam of the door. I need to control my emotions if I am to attend the ball. I don't want my Fae powers flaring up in the middle of a ballroom full of some of the highest officials in this Kingdom. I would certainly be punished but would most likely escape death because I am technically the heir to Evaflora's throne. If Evaflora did die I would never dare wear her crown. I am a human, so I must be considered illegitimate by Fae law. I think. I doubt the Faeries would allow a human to take their throne, even though I have Fae blood in my veins. Disgusting. It is truly a disgusting thought that I am one of these ethereal beings.

Wiping the burn from my eyes, I leave my chambers and head down the many corridors. I reach the entry hall, ignore the bustling courtiers attending luncheon on the balcony and proceed to head down the marble stairs. The large floor to ceiling doors, which are typically locked, gape open. I turn left and I see Evaflora's throne room. The walls are made of thick vines and trees, the ceiling is glass, and tall trees with green leaves scrape the skylight's panes. Silky white pedals appear from nowhere and fall elegantly from above to the floor, where they vanish. Large banners hang beside her throne, which is reflecting the sun into my eyes. It is made of some type of blue glass. Approaching the dais I stare at the blue throne, which towers above my head. The chair is completely blue and translucent; it's beautiful, hypnotizing, and luring.

A thread pulls in my stomach and I take a seat upon the throne and watch as maids walk past the door, ignoring me entirely. I feel like a true queen. If only I could rule a kingdom of my own and lead my people to a greater good. I want to protect them from Elkwood and release them from the banishment of magic. They can't have a queen who has magic in her blood sit on a throne that banishes such power.

I run my fingers along the jagged surface of the throne and realize it is made of some type of smooth curving sticks. Each stick ends in a sharp point. They remind me of large thorns. It resembles my father's crown. His new one, not his old silver and blue one. He had a cobalt crown of thorns on his head when he attacked me, his new creation since being under the curse.

"Diamond antlers," says a voice making me leap from the seat and tumble to the floor before the dais. Evaflora saunters to me at a steady pace. Her violet dress is made of chiffon and her crown matches the throne. Her black hair is unbound, and the translucent blue crown makes her eyes stand out more than before. She says confidently, "My throne is made of diamond antlers. Each antler was taken from the extinct crystal stag."

Not only does she glamour a kingdom, leave her child, and drink human blood, but she also drove a species to extinction to satisfy her greed. Every time I learn something new about my mother, I realize how much more of a witch she is. She walks past me and runs her hand along the throne.

"I loved their iridescent fur. I am wearing it tonight, their pelts," she says grimacing. I fight the urge to spit in her face. Faerie scum. She looks to me and asks, "You are coming tonight correct?"

"Of course, anything to spend quality time with my mother," I growl venomously. My words are like poison. "I can't wait until you skin me and wear me to your next Ball. Or will you make sure to drink my blood and turn me into a Forsaken?"

Her eyes lower and her features contort to pure rage. One by one she stomps her feet towards me. I scramble to my feet and start to scream, but the doors slam before I make it half way across the throne room. When I turn around her hands, wrap around my throat and my back slams into the locked doors.

"HOW DARE YOU SPEAK TO YOUR MOTHER LIKE THAT?" she screams. The whole Summer Kingdom could've heard her roar. I want to scream or say something back, but I can't even breathe with her strong grip on my windpipe, and I just know bruises are going to lace my neck as I die. My heart is pounding, and then it begins. The thud of my brain pulsing. I am aware, this time, of the power in my veins, and I can feel it building like a forest fire in the dry dead fall. She slammed the doors with her High Fae powers, and I realize now more than ever that I need to learn how to use mine at will. The thudding becomes all I hear. Her lips are moving too fast for me to comprehend. My lungs are burning and I know I need air. The pressure in my head is building now. Her grip slightly eases and my chest swells, my lungs are about to explode. I scream.

Her grip is gone, and she flies across the room slamming into the hard tree trunk wall. A loud smack bounces off the vaulted ceiling. My scream still echoes and I pant heavily. I rise to my feet and begin tugging on the door, which is, of course, locked. My head is still pounding.

"I knew you have Fae magic in your veins," Evaflora says laughing and rising slowly using the throne to stable herself. "You're a Telekinae, a Faerie that can control the world with their mind." There is a name for what I am, *Telekinae.*

"I am not a Faerie," I pant heavily.

"You are right. You're a half-breed." Green flames build at her fists and her crown falls to the floor with a loud clang. It sounds like two glasses clinking together, but much louder. Her hand snaps forwards, and I barely dodge the ball of flame, which explodes against the door. Scrambling away from the heat that licks against my back, I look at her. Another green fire flies at unfathomable speed toward me. I sprint like a deer in the wood as fire after fire is casted at me in an attempt to hurt, or maybe even kill me. She shouldn't want to kill me, I am her daughter. I reach the dais and scramble toward her. I throw my palm towards her as she did to me, and my power crashes into her chest, pinning her to the wall. Her body is stiff and her muscles are taught. The flames at her hands flicker away and she stares at me in surprise.

My headache is fading away and I have a strong gut feeling that once it vanishes my hold on her will too. The weight in my chest thrums heavily and I know the connection now. This heavy weight that sometimes vanishes before extreme danger is attached to my powers. It has to be.

Thud, thud, thud, thud, thud.

My head pounds as I start talking, "Why?"

"I was only playing with you," she whispers in a menacing tone. Yeah, right. She was trying to kill me, but for what reason?

Thud., thud., thud., thud.

"Why do you hate my father?"

"Because he was a cruel man!"

Thud.., thud.., thud..,

"He is not!" I repeat, "Why are you doing this? It's your last chance!"

"He is and once you realize that the better off you will be. If you could know the horrible tyrant he is, you wouldn't waste your time trying to save your father from the curse!" she screams. She is wasting my time. She knows I don't have much time left.

Thud…, thud…,

"I will do anything for my father, but what would you do for him? For me? Other than kill us?"

"I would enslave every last mortal in your kingdom and make them work their life away in my kingdom, rotting in the heat until they die!"

Thud….

My headache vanishes and she falls to the floor laughing and coughing. The doors open and I stagger backwards falling down the two steps of the dais to the hard marble floor. Blood lightly trickles from my nose and some drips from her mouth. I need to get out of here. I run for my chambers and don't stop until I slam the door shut behind me and the lock clicks into place. I retrieve the dagger from the cabinet in the bathing chambers and lock myself in the stone room as I cry in the tub gripping the Mountain Ash knife until my hands cramp. She wants to enslave mortals. This is no longer an attempt to save a curse on my father. This is something so much more. I need to save all the mortals in Equadoria. I need to save all the mortals in Abella before she tries to enslave the mortals. The entire life of mortals in Abella has changed and I don't know how to save it. How could I save the life of an entire continent? I need to wake up my father, so he can stop Evaflora. He will know what to do.

After many hours of crying under the silk blankets of my bed, I command myself to stop. Evaflora was lying to the Kingdoms about something, and I think wanting mortal slaves is her dark secret. Unless she also has something else hidden behind that secret door on the balcony I found when I first arrived here. She wants to use us for her dirty work. I will not let her enslave my people.

Equadoria would certainly be her first target to harbor slaves.

A knock sounds from the door, and I stifle a breath as Seri's partner steps into my gilded chambers. "Time to prepare for the Ball, milady," she says bowing.

"It's still daylight, why would I get ready now?" I ask in shock.

"Oh dear, it will take many hours to get you princess-ready," says a voice from the hall. Its familiar and my heart warms, as a plump Faerie with a threadbare gown steps into my chambers. Seri. I squeal in happiness and leap across my bed to greet her. Holding her tightly I ask, "What made you come back?"

She only laughs and strokes strands of hair away from my face, as she says, "A princess can never be pretty. She must be gorgeous." I laugh and spin with her. We step into my closet.

The corset tenses around my ribs crushing the ribcage beneath my skin. I can't help but wince as Seri yanks the strings.

"My you certainly have grown quite small, look at your waist! You're practically invisible," Seri comments in shock. Not eating for three weeks can do that to someone, but I don't give her an explanation, she knows I don't trust Faerie food. "The Ball starts at sundown," Seri adds.

About four different skirts of tulle make my dress pool around me in beautiful sways of fabric. I can hear the whispers of the tulle when I spin. As Seri fastens the bodice on me, which looks like a broken mirror, I feel it sliding around. I look at her, apologetically, and say, "I'm sorry I have shrunk down a few sizes." She waves my excuse away and begins tightening the bodice with a needle and thread. I have so much to tell her. So much has happened since the last time I've seen her.

"My mother tried to kill me this afternoon," I say it as unemotional as possible, and I try to ignore the burn in my eyes. The tightening bodice squeezes me just as tight as the corset and I wince.

"What?"

"In the throne room, Evaflora and I had a...incident," my voices quivers when I say incident. It wasn't an incident, it was purely an attempted murder on her part, and I for the first time somewhat controlled my powers. It was horrible in every way possible. Seri's eyes widen and then narrow.

"What kind of an incident," her brow furrows and her voice grows cold.

"She threw balls of green fire at me, and almost killed me, until I pinned her to a wall with my magic. Then she said something... something that I don't even want to comprehend right now."

Seri's eyes become fearful, and I can tell she is scared of what Evaflora may have said. She whispers, "What did she say, Ariadae?"

"She would like to enslave humans."

A scream escapes her lips and I expect all the glass in the room to shatter to bits but they don't. I add, "And if she does she will start with Equadoria."

She covers her mouth and shakes her head. Her words are clipped and quiet so nobody else can hear. "You must leave," she says as she begins running about collecting clothes to pack. I run to her practically tripping over my many skirts and grab her shoulders and making her look at me.

"I will, but not until I know how to find the Tree of Light. This place is the closest chance I have to getting there." I ignore the bustling maids preparing my makeup and hair equipment by the vanity and pull Seri into a hug. "I will leave as soon as I can. I promise." Nodding, Seri pulls me back over to the vanity and begins weaving intricate braids in my hair.

"Your dress has Faerie magic in it," she says changing the subject. I laugh at the statement.

"How can a dress be magic," I ask, playing along. She grins in the mirror and begins to tell me directions.

"At midnight make sure to head to the top of the staircase and twirl." Her directions are simple enough. I nod my head in silence while she quietly sings some Fae lullabies.

> *"We are we, now heading to your Tree,*
> *The Tree of Immortality.*
> *One by one marching on the soft earth beneath our feet,*
> *Only you will grant us the greatest feat."*

The sweet melody has almost a darker meaning. The song is about the Tree of Light and Prometheus, who guides the six humans to be gifted with powers and immortality. As she keeps singing I begin to realize this isn't really a rhyme for young children. It is a song for the angry Fae.

> *"Why, oh, why will you not let us die,*
> *For only I want to lie down and fly.*
> *I don't want your power,*
> *No matter what hour,*
> *Unless you let us die."*

She abruptly stops her song as the other maidens finish their task of applying makeup to my face. My porcelain skin looks angular and dark, with sharp black charcoal lines across my green eyes, creating a drastic contour along my cheeks. I look like a Fae with my gown and braided hair, woven into a large knot at the base of my head. Gold sparkles make sharp points that pull from the corners of my eyes at sharp angles. Ethereal. My look is truly ethereal and I can't help but feel quite excited to show off my horrifically beautiful look to Evaflora and her Kingdom.

Seri pulls out a golden pocket watch embroidered with flowers and leaves. I feel like I can almost hear the tick, synchronized with my heart beat. She smiles at her handy work and claps as I rise with a slow twirl showing her the beautiful attire she crafted with her own hands.

"You are truly a princess, much more beautiful than your blood sucking mother," Seri's partner says giggling. Seri nods in agreement and says, "I have one more accessory for you." She wanders towards a box. The same one I was tempted to open earlier, and removes a titanium crown of antlers. I shake my head in defense; I don't want to wear a crown from a dead animal.

"I'm not wearing that," I stammer and Seri frowns with remorse.

"Why not, milady?" she questions.

"It is from an animal and I think killing an entire species for jewelry and thrones is pointless and cruel. I am not my mother." she waves away my words with a dismissive hand.

"When the crystal stags became extinct as a result of Evaflora's hunting them, people created crowns of titanium antlers and committed treasonous acts, in a sort of rebellion. Wearing the titanium crowns was treason in its own right, but she didn't believe in execution so many people were arrested and the crowns couldn't be destroyed because they are titanium," she explains. Suddenly I can't help but want to snatch the crown from her hands and place it upon my head myself. I don't like Evaflora, no matter how much she tries to be nice. She is truly evil and always will be. "Do you want to wear it now?"

"Of course."

Lady after lady heads through the large ornate door on the second story to be escorted by Lords to the Ballroom floor. I hear the intricate, yet resounding, music of a fiddle and cello. Kingdom Ladies I recognize from my Luncheons wear gowns of lavender, rose pink, crème, and scarlet, but none of them are wearing tulle, purely made of silk. I feel a bit out of place but, I feel very confident as each Fae looks to my gown in envy. Seri did an amazing job with the gown, and for the first time in a month I truly feel like a princess.

Raisie, with her blonde curls bound at the top of her head saunters to me in a swooshing black and purple silk gown. Fae girls I don't recognize flank her and she chuckles to them as they look over me. Her roving eyes make me want to cross my arms, my confidence fights off the urge.

"You have a death wish," she says laughing.

"Why is that, might I ask?" I grimace and run my fingers through the whispering tulle.

"You can't wear a crown of titanium without being tried for treason. Don't take it off though; I'd love to hear your mortal cries as you beg for forgiveness."

Some emotion flickers through me and my body becomes hot with rage. "And I would love to wring your neck with my mortal hands, but certain things won't happen tonight. Sorry to disappoint you Lady Raisie."

Her eyes widen and she raises her hand to her neck in fear. I start to laugh as her and her little followers run off back into line. She shouldn't mess with me anymore, hopefully.

A Fae male announces Ladies as they head into the Ballroom where they will be escorted by Bachelors. I don't know which guy will guide me down the steps, but I am very nervous for what I will see when I walk through the doors. I am a princess, but my father never had royal balls. I don't know what to expect and I am the last Lady in line. I start to shake as, minute by minute, girl after girl is sent through the gilded doors into the glowing ballroom. Every monarch, Lord, and Lady in the Summer Kingdom will certainly be at the bottom of the stairs, greeting me with approachable smiles but black hearts. Courtiers are just predators hunting for prey, and I am just bleeding cattle in an open field once I walk into that room.

"Princess Ariadae Vox," says the man dressed in a black tailored suit. He opens the door and light floods the hallway, illuminating my silver gown which reflects the glistening chandeliers. The crowd gasps in awe, and I immediately notice Evaflora because she has a towering crown of diamond antlers. She must've pulled them from a crystal stag she murdered. She is a woman of her word as she wears the iridescent skin of the species she has driven into extinction. Her cunning eyes look joyous, but I can't help but see the splintering evil breaking through the blue. Evaflora is evil, wicked, menacing, and a pure tyrant born to rein darkness upon Elkwood.

I can hear her heels clicking like whips she would likely crack against mortal backs if she had the chance. I hate her. My mother is one of the few people who would like to watch my fragile body crack and fracture. She can hurt me in ways I don't understand yet, and I'm afraid for when she breaks me. That day will come. Soon. I can feel it coming like a thundering storm on the horizon. The air would grow thick and moist, and the sky dark, but she *is* the storm growing. She is on her way to destroy everything I love and won't bat an eye about the destruction she is planning. When her storm clatters down on me, I will shatter and crumble to the earth in a million pieces.

"High Fae, Lunan Berdu Walsh, of Day Kingdom," says the man who is announcing everyone. "He will be escorting, mortal Princess Ariadae Vox, daughter of Evaflora, and heir to the Equadorian throne." My chest concaves. He just told the entire Summer Kingdom that I am Evaflora's mortal Daughter. Lunan offers me his arm and smiles at me even though his eyes look truly terrified and angry. He is a High Fae. He has unearthly powers like Evaflora! His yellow irises seem to have flickering flames behind them. I force a smile, coldly grip his thick bicep, and head down the steps.

A clap begins in the crowd, and I see Evaflora with a sinister grin plastered across her face. Her singular clap started applause, and once we reach the final step, I don't get any relief. Everyone's eyes are on me. The mortal princess of the Summer Kingdom, these Fae must be furious with rage that a mortal is their heir. I would be beyond angry if the heir to my throne was a Fae. They must learn that I am not here to take the throne, and within this century I will be gone and, expectantly, Evaflora too. I couldn't imagine Evaflora remaining on the throne for another century.

Lunan pulls me onto the dance floor and we begin to waltz to the woodwind instruments. He glares into my eyes and I can see him trying to form words in his mouth. He is chewing on the perfect wording. His tan skin blooms pink with, I can only assume, anger and he asks, "Why didn't you tell me?"

"I didn't know until before the other night, in the rain. I found out that day," my words are hushed so no dancing couples can intervene or eavesdrop on our discussion. "And why didn't you tell me that you're a High Fae?"

"Please, I don't owe you anything." his voice is starting to get louder and I glare at him. "Sorry." I nod in agreement. He doesn't need an explanation from me and I don't want to press the subject. It'd be like poking a bear with a stick.

"Well I think I found out what Evaflora is lying about." His eyes widen and he looks around. He doesn't want Evaflora hearing our conversation, even though she is on the opposite side of the room talking to some Sentinels. Lunan pulls me to the tables littered with steaming food and frigid desserts. Small glasses of Faerie wine are poured and are neatly arranged on the table. Lunan beams at the boy arranging the glasses, and growls making the innocent child run off.

"Talk." A man of few words.

"She mentioned maybe wanting to enslave mortals," he flicks his eyes around and shock flickers across his face making the scar marring his stunning features twitch. "She wants to kill my father then enslave all of our people, and also enslave the mortals of southern Abella." Even as the words leave my mouth I can't quite believe them. It's preposterous, but sounds completely like an Evaflora thing to do.

"Has she started enslaving people or acted on her plan?" he asks in a shaky voice. It is very confusing to see such a large man almost cower in fear.

"Not that I am aware of, but Evaflora, being Evaflora, I doubt we have much time until she does. She knows my father is cursed too."

"Your father is cursed?" he questions concerned.

"Yes, but I need to find the Tree of Light to save him. Do you know how to get there?" I ask him, but already know the answer. *Nobody knows.*

"Yes," Wait WHAT?

"How? Why? Where? We got to go!" I start to beg. I pull against his arm and he stays firm and grabs my shoulders making me focus on him. His eyes. I will do anything to get to the Tree of Light and save my father. I want to be home with my dad and Jeremiah. Jax can even tag along. He grips my wrist in a large fist and tugs me from the ballroom and into the entry hall where it is quiet and nobody lurks about. We walk up the marble steps and take a seat halfway.

"Legend says that you need to cross the wastelands of western Elkwood and kill the Rune Witch with a dragon bone dagger. Once you kill the witch, find the Ravine of Wisps where the Oracle is located, along with many druids who protect and worship the object. Bring the Oracle to Prometheus, he and the other gods will find the location of the Tree of Light because they have now forgotten as a way to truly hide its location."

"That sounds like a story book," I say laughing. Where would I even get a dragon bone dagger? How do I even know where Prometheus is? Is there even a way to talk to the gods that created man and Fae and life? "First step: where can I get a dragon bone dagger?"

"Dragon bone daggers haven't existed for several centuries," he says frowning deeply. I assume there has to be one somewhere on Abella. "Find one and you can get to the Oracle."

I begin to think over all of this. My mother is a tyrant. My father is cursed. My pet is a shapeshifting Fae, and my best friend is in love with me. I've caused two people to be murdered, and I am now stuck in the Summer Kingdom where I need to get a dragon bone dagger, which may not even exist, to get to the Oracle, to give to Prometheus, to find the Tree of Light. My eyes burn and I begin to cry. I just want my father back. I don't want to do this anymore. I'm only sixteen I can't save an entire Faerie Kingdom from my mother and travel this enormous, horrific forest. Everything pushing against me, including my own sanity.

Lunan wraps his big arms around me in attempted comfort, but I quickly slip out form his grip. My words are broken and choked out, "I'm sorry, I just need a moment." I head back into the throne room and shut the doors behind me. Everyone bustles about as I wipe the tears from my cheeks, trying not to screw up my makeup. I blink away the burn in my eyes and smile at passing Lords and Ladies.

Seri made my gown, and I will make sure to show it off to everyone. A group dance starts on the tiled dance floor, and I join in as we all spin, dance, and lose ourselves in the music. I ignore everything and focus on the sound of the music notes that make my body twirl and I can't help but laugh in joyous happiness. Lords and Ladies glance in my direction, their faces turning sour when they notice the crown atop my head. Their faces make me smile.

The grandfather clock chimes midnight and I am in the center of the ballroom surrounded by watching guests. On the twelfth chime of the clock, a handsome Faerie boy twirls me and I watch as my dress transforms. The silver tulle is swallowed up by rising tendrils of glittering silver that leave my dress gold. Smiling I let the swirling fingers of silver rise in a ring around my body, changing my mirror bodice into a golden feather surface that is soft to the touch. I keep twirling even as people scream and shout in jealousy and wonder. I stop my twirling as my copper waves fall down my shoulders and the titanium crown remains silver atop my head. I bow and start to exit the silent ballroom but someone stops me.

"Ariadae, I like your dress," says Raisie smiling. She will not be my friend, but I will certainly guide her to the one person who deserves the biggest reward for this dress.

"My stylist was Seri, a wonderful maiden at the castle," I yell across the ballroom allowing all the courtiers to hear. Bowing I leave the silent ballroom and let my flowing curls and gold tulle skirts of my dress be the last thing they see of the queen's daughter tonight. It's already midnight, so I'm glad that this festival is almost over. I just need time to think and find a way out of here.

I am losing all expectation that Zube, Jeremiah, and Jax will find me. They probably have given up hope on me and went back to Equadoria to tell my cursed father that I am dead. He'd most likely only be angered he didn't kill me himself.

When I enter the entry hall expecting Lunan to be lurking about he is gone. He has probably slipped away somewhere to get a drink or seduce some Ladies. He is the High Fae of the Day Kingdom. I learned that interesting detail from the gentleman who announced our descent into the ballroom. If only he told me of his title. I wouldn't have been so trusting; unless that was part of a scheme he planned with Evaflora. However, I tell myself if he was with Evaflora he would've told her about our attempted escape and she would've locked me in my chambers until I became dust that needed to be swept.

I stomp up the steps and suddenly feel a wave of dizziness and nausea. It's no headache, but I certainly need air, so I stumble through the balcony doors and step onto the smooth tile in the warm crisp air. Music from the kingdom echoes to the back of the castle and the table for Luncheon is already adorned with silverware and flowering decorations. I simply breathe deeply, inhaling all the earthly scents of the Summer Kingdom.

My stay here has been anything but graceful or enjoyable. I long to be home, or in Elkwood, or anywhere away from this place. It's like I'm in the nightmare of Evaflora chasing me, attempting to drink my blood. It seems that she is closing in until she has the perfect moment to strike down to eradicate me and my kingdom. She can try to consume me, but I will assuredly go down swinging.

I notice something strange about the night air: it's not very dark tonight. I look to the stones beside me and see a thick beam of flickering light across the balcony coming from a place I have forgotten about. The secret door is gaping wide open and a torch with a feverishly burning flame is buckled to the smooth stone wall. My heart beat begins to flutter in my chest like butterfly wings flapping in slow motion. I approach the glowing tunnel and let the pound of my heart slam against my ribcage. This secret door could lead to another one of my mother's never ending secrets, and I don't think twice about going in. I yank the torch from its iron hook and start down the dark stairwell.

I've never been one to be frightened of the dark, but I do get scared of the shadows that lurk within it. Elkwood has only proven to me that monsters live within the darkness and are constantly hungry for flesh.

This secret place so far, has been a series of smooth-walled tunnels with an occasional winding set of stairs. The air is dry, but there are no cobwebs or dust. The place seems more up kept than my chambers at the castle. Many people must bustle about these halls for it to be so spotless. Nobody seems to be wandering the many hallways and corridors now, because the halls are almost silent and still, except for the strange constant draft that only sends goosebumps and chills across my skin. This place isn't meant for someone who doesn't know the corridors. I ignore all corridors I pass, laced with doors, because I don't want to get lost. I am in some kind of labyrinth that must run everywhere beneath the castle.

I wander past one particular corridor which is a bit darker than the others, and something stops me in my tracks. My skirts wisp from the abrupt movement but I couldn't ignore this sound. It was an animalistic wail. A shiver crawls down my spine, and even the torch brightly ablaze can't warm my icy skin. My thudding heart continues to hammer against my chest as if it's trying to break free. I am going make the most stupid decision I could probably ever make, but I head to the door in the hallway and, as the heavy oak door grinds open, not only do the hinges wail, so does the thousands of Forsaken monsters that lay before me.

Creature after creature looks to me as I wander past groupings of Dreag, Wendigo, Nymphs, and other monsters I've never seen. They all have thick iron collars keeping them chained to the wall. Teeth reflect my torch and monsters bigger than me click at me. Their skin is made of scales and their eyes are large black orbs set far back on the sides of their lizard like skull. Reptilian of some sort, I recognize these creatures. Troglodytes. I read about them in books. They are lizard men and women who can smell the warm blood of humans and mammals. They run and hunt and move like people. These aren't the only monsters I recognize. I notice big towering men which look like moving trees. Green skinned ogres also roar in my face blowing my hair back and I can't help but wonder if these Forsaken used to be mortals. These monsters may have been Evaflora's meals over the many years.

I think back to the first day I was here, Evaflora drank the blood of a mortal boy to survive but he turned into a Wendigo when she was finished with him. Was this on purpose or were these all accidents? Either way I can't help but feel bad for them. There must be some mortal consciousness screaming for help in those monster's heads. I may feel sorry for them, but I leave as quickly as I came. They may be Evaflora's mistakes, but they are also Forsaken who want nothing to do but murder me and eat me.

I head back to the main hall and start to head back the way I came, but I see a torch at the end of the hall.

"The door shouldn't have just been left open," says a deep male voice and my heart leaps from my chest in a resounding slam that makes me want to vomit. I immediately run the opposite direction, heading deeper into the chamber. My heels click against the tile and I throw my torch to the ground. The second sentinel hears the commotion and screams, "Hey! Stop running you're trapped!" I ignore his words and lift my dress so I can pick up speed.

Their clinking armor keeps me running and my breathing grows ragged. I can't let these two Sentinels catch me. I may have gotten away with other treasonous things, but my mother attempted to kill me willingly earlier today, so the order to kill me is obviously passed to all sentinels. I assume. Nothing would stop her after this. The stone in my chest has become a trustworthy weight, and it doesn't vanish giving me the only hope I have to keep running. I'm going to survive.

A flat wall sprouts before me and I abruptly stop. Dead end. There is only one hallway to my left and I bound down the stone corridor and open the double oak doors. Slamming the doors shut behind me I lean, panting, against the wood and look into a dark chamber illuminated by a skylight which beams down. The chamber is full of dust and cobwebs. The only dirty place I have seen in these secret tunnels. The moon shafts through the hole above and glistens upon a domed glass encasement on a dais surrounded by towering statutes. The stone people are depictions of Prometheus and his fellow Gods.

The statutes are creepily human-like, and I think their eyes watch me as I move up onto the dais. Lately the Gods have been a big part of my travels through Elkwood and even though I am not one to believe in Gods I'm beginning to believe the myths. There is always some truth to a myth. Some myths have more truths than others though. I should start to accept the thought of them because sooner or later I am to give them the Oracle to essentially locate the Tree of Light. Sounds easy enough, but I know it won't be. Prometheus will be testing me the entire time, and so will this goddamned forest.

Light grows in the chamber from beneath the door and I duck into an alcove, behind a God's robe as the door to the sanctuary opens.

"She had to have run in here," said a deep solid voice.

"We can't remain in this chamber, it's sacred," says an older sentinel. I just need to get out of here.

"How could this dust ball be sacred," asks the young Fae sentinel, obviously new.

"You see that pillar on the dais?"

"Yeah."

"Well inside of the glass encasement lies one of the last dragon bone daggers in all of Abella," the older gentleman claims. My heart flutters. This is *perfect*.

The two guys search about a bit but don't dare step on the dais. Maybe I have upturned some sacred ground, but if that encasement holds a dragon bone dagger, I would destroy this entire kingdom for it.

"Come on, let's go."

Several minutes pass before I dare move and I let a small pull in my middle lore me to the pillar. I didn't believe in the Gods, before but now this is too coincidental for me to ignore. *Thank you* is all I mentally say to Prometheus, but I lift the glass dome and reach for the bone hilt with the blade that's embroidered with flames along its edge. I am flying. This is the first step to saving my father. All I need to do is use the dagger to kill the Rune Witch located in the wastelands and get into the Ravine of the Wisps. I actually know how I can save my father from the wicked curse placed upon him. I don't know who placed the curse on the king of Equadoria, but I now know how to break it.

I quickly run down the hallway back towards the exit holding my shoes trying not to make a noise. With the dagger hidden in my lace garter, I feel comfort in the cold blade pressed against my bare thigh beneath my many, many layers of skirt. I don't see or hear the sentinels on my way back, but I do notice that the door to the room of Forsaken is open, so they must be looking in all the rooms.

I will leave the Summer Kingdom tonight. I need to just get to my chambers, pack my ash weapons, and get changed. Then I'll leave while everyone is still drunkenly partying. Evaflora is probably gobbling up all the attention of the party and the compliments on her horrid iridescent dress. Bile rises in my throat as I think about my mother being a High Fae witch.

I see the door that leads to the balcony and a replacement torch has been placed probably by the two sentinels. I head onto the balcony and place my heels back on my feet. The night air feels extremely cool against my steaming skin. I am beyond happy. Joy isn't a good enough word to describe the emotion I am feeling right now. Soon I will be with Jax and Jeremiah...if I can find them. And we will be on our way to save my father. I just need to calm down and go step by step. My first step is to get to my chambers and get dressed.

Right before I head through the balcony doors to the top of the stairwell, the stone in my chest vanishes and a hand grasps my unbound hair yanking me back onto the balcony. The glass doors slam shut and I hear the clicking of my mother's tongue.

Chapter Nine

Screaming at the sudden pain on my scalp, I fall to the ground holding my head. The titanium crown clatters to the stone. She is going to skin me and kill me right here on these stones. I try to thrash and writhe out of her grip, but her Fae strength keeps her bony, clawed fingers tangled firmly in my hair. Tears pour from my eyes until she finally stops dragging me across the stones.

"Did you like snooping about?" her wet angry voice asks. "You like being a thorn in my ass don't you sweet pea?"

"Stop, please," is all I say begging. "I am your daughter."

"No mortal will ever be my daughter," she screams louder than needed. The whole Kingdom most likely heard her. "The only mortals I take my time with are the ones I eat." Her hot breath beads against my neck and I squirm. I need to find a way free. I pull and claw at my skirts, lifting them.

"I am feeling quite aged," she growls. "I think it's time to eat." A sharp silver claw glides across my cheekbone causing hot thick blood to leak from my face. Her sandpaper tongue slides up my cheek. I yank my face away but she grabs my entire jaw, purposely pressing her glinting claws into my face.

"No, stop," I cry out. "HELP!" No headache is coming and I fear I may have used up all of my power this afternoon. It probably needs to build up and accumulate. Her iron nails pinch my lips in a tight, blood-drawing grip. She hushes me.

"Nobody is going to help you," she whispers into my ear and looks towards the secret door.

Now is my only chance. I raise my hand to my hair and I feel the taut hairs loosen and fall as I slice the blade clean through my copper waves. This was the only way I could get free. Evaflora screams suddenly holding nothing but long chopped hair. I let the smooth waves fall around my face as a tear slides down my cheek, mixing with the blood pouring from my wound.

I roll forward and stand holding the bone dagger in front of me, the sharp tip glinting towards Evaflora. She begins to have a hushed angered tone as she says, "How did you get your grimy hands on that?"

"I went into your sanctuary and retrieved what I needed," is all I say to my mother. I will not tell her how I knew what I needed to save my father. *Thanks to Lunan* is all I can think as I quickly throw my shoe at her before she pounces and I pull on the balcony doors. Evaflora screams in pain as I realize the doors are locked, and I use my other shoe to bash in the glass and run down the corridors towards my room.

"STOP!" I hear her angered scream behind me. My shoulder-length hair flies away from my face and I grip the dagger's bone hilt so tightly that sweat makes my hand stick to the handle. She knows I'm running, but she would summon her sentinels for backup before she came after me. I think. I push my legs harder and faster towards my room.

I slam through my doors and run straight into a hard sturdy chest. I look up and stare into the bluest eyes I have ever seen. I've only seen them once and that was right before I was taken by a Dreag.

"Jax," my voice quivers in question. He laughs and nods. He steps to the side and I see Zube sitting in a chair by the fire place and Jeremiah looking at the *Nirvana* book lying open on the table. No time for hugs.

"Ariadae," they all shout in excitement and run to me. I push past them and stop at the wild sight before me. Raisie's amber irises are full with sorrow.

"They came running through the front door minutes before Evaflora walked out of the ballroom. When they asked for you and I smelt him," Raisie drawls looking to Jeremiah. "I brought them to your chambers. I owe you for what I've said."

I saunter up to her and simply wrap my arms around her. She doesn't know how thankful I am. "I really appreciate this act of kindness, but we really need to be going." She nods and wanders towards the door.

"Always remember I'm on the inside." She winks and leaves the room to me and my friends.

"We need to leave right now." I head into the closet and grab my bow and two quivers which are already strapped across my back when I come back into my room. They barely moved from their spots and they all look at me puzzled.

"What happened to your hair," Zube asks sounding as stupid as I remember him.

Pointing to my short hair I say, "This is the only way I could escape from a pissed off murderous High Fae whose probably already on her way here right now." They immediately begin running about the room gathering the packs and some supplies they carried. I point out the locations of the mountain ash weapons for them to retrieve.

"You already pissed off queen Evaflora? You were only here for a month," whispers Jax with a panicked look on his face.

"A month is a long time, Jax. A lot more has happened than you think," I say to him as I head for the balcony. The three guys follow me and look to me for direction, their faces panicked stricken. I say, "We need to escape through the kingdom town and head to the bridge that crosses the ravine. There is where we can escape and begin to save my dad."

"How do you know how to save your dad?" asks Jeremiah sounding concerned. I miss his chocolate eyes worrying about me.

"I've learned a lot this month. I'll explain later."

Jax pulls a bow off of his shoulders and he tosses it to me. It's the recurve bow engraved with flames; a family heirloom. In return I give him the longbow I got from Lunan and a quiver of Mountain Ash arrows. I think we are ready to escape back to Elkwood.

I don't know how they found me in the Summer Kingdom, but I am so happy they did. I highly doubt they know she is my mother, and I don't plan on telling them yet. It'll only cause more issues later, and Zube may hold it against me. I can practically hear him now saying something like *'we can't trust the daughter of the psycho queen.'*

We climb over the railing and begin descending down the side of the stone castle. I'm trying to hold a tight grip on the ledges and windowsills we use as leverage. No sentinels have looked over the railing, but I can hear their clinking armor on the balcony above. The gold gown is extremely hard to move and climb in and the corset is still crushing my chest. I know the sentinels are going to let their ears and nose guide them. The sentinels can most likely hear my beating heart and they can smell the sweat beading on my forehead. I want to get as far away as I can before they realize we are but thirty feet below them.

Too late. The sentinel's shouts resound down the castle side. "Down there," they scream wildly. My muscles tense and the cords beneath my skin strain.

"Let go," Jax yells and I'm frightened to let go of the hard stone. I don't know how far up we are but I'm too scared to look down. I didn't come this far to die. Zube and Jax fall and all I hear is their body's crash into brush below. They are immortal, unable to die from falls or disease or age. When I look around Jeremiah isn't there and then the crash of him landing in the brush echoes through the air. "Come on, Ariadae! Let's go," Jax screams up to me.

I don't know why I say it, but I feel safer with them. "I am scared," my voice quivers into the night and I refuse to look down. I hear their gasps of distress as they fear Evaflora getting to us. Now I realize I have a great fear of heights along with the thousand other beasts in Elkwood.

"We're all scared but we need to go now! Evaflora is coming for us!" Jax yells up to me. "I'll catch you. I promise."

I place my faith in those muscled arms as I let my body fall back, releasing my grip on the cold wall. My heart, stomach, and the stone of fear rise into my throat as I am suspended in the air. The balmy night whisks around me as wind pulls my short hairs into my face. I scream as lightning strikes above me. Tonight is like when I first tried to escape with Lunan but now I will actually leave this Kingdom once and for all.

I collapse into Jax's arms. He has caught me just as promised. I pat his bicep in thanks and look to his glittering eyes. Ice, they are not the color of a cloudless day; they shine like the morning frost that layers the garden flowers and plants in the winter. Trembling I place my hand on his cheek and his angular face softens. He is beautiful. Lunan is gorgeous and Jeremiah is so handsome, but no other words can describe Jax other than beautiful. He is my best friend. He is my Snow.

I grow saddened as he places me onto the cobblestone ground because I want him to hold me forever. Dancing Fae scream over the vociferous music that erupts from fiddles and drums, as thunder reverberates through the city. We clash into the crowd of Faeries and I try to blend in, but my oversized gown makes it a little challenging. These stupid Kingdom dresses make it hard to escape.

"Try to remain hidden and look natural," Jeremiah whispers to Jax, Zube, and me as we get slightly deeper into the crowd. "We need to split up but if we get lost head to the bridge that crosses the ravine. We can meet near one of the spires there." I can't help but feel sad that I just got my friends back and we are already separating again. This makes my heart slam violently against my ribcage as I nod wildly. I want to leave the Summer Kingdom so badly. We wander our separate paths and I turn towards Northern Elkwood, the path towards my home and out of this death trap.

I stagger through the crowd on uneasy feet. My heels click loudly and I decide to remove them for the sake of stamina and speed. I want to get out of this bustling throng of festive Fae. Lightning strikes above and the Faeries scream again. Suddenly others begin shouting even after the lightning is gone. Looking towards the commotion, I see the Kingdoms sentinels pushing this way through the crowd. They are surrounding me and they don't even realize they are doing so. I duck my head and slink toward a wagon. The older gentleman looks at me with a gleaming smile that doesn't reach his eyes. His golden irises flick to my bow and quiver of Mountain Ash arrows and he nods as he looks away. Snagging a velvet cloak I fasten it on and I head back into the crowd. The broach gripping my cloak is the symbol of the Summer Kingdom.

I politely apologize as I push past Fae after Fae, moving through the crowd, not getting too close to the sentinels, who seem to be closing in on me. I will be boxed in and then everyone will see me get arrested. No, I will not be taken back to my mother, even if I have to hurt somebody I will fight to stay away from her. She, no matter what abomination attacks me is still my mortal, or should I say *immortal* enemy, I guess is a better way to say it.

A sentinel gets a little too close for my liking so I duck between two ladies.

"Excuse you," says a brunette Fae with skin made of leaves, absurdly bright; I can't help the shock that flashes across my face with the lightning overhead. "Why so long faced, mortal?" she spits loudly and I see a sentinel's eyes flick into my direction. I should've known the blaring music wouldn't drown out the conversation of

Faeries in Fae ears. I can feel his thunderous steps approaching as I completely ignore the Fae girl who is way too offended. His steps match my beating heart. And I cringe as I begin unstringing my bow from my shoulders. I don't want to hurt anybody, Fae or Human, but I need to save my kingdom. Reluctantly nocking an arrow, I draw my bow and take aim at the beast pounding towards me. Equadoria will wash this Fae's blood from my hands and forget that their princess murdered a Fae. I hope.

My muscles tense and my vision becomes a kaleidoscope. Everything is blurring together in one dotted picture. A tear breaks my lids and the fletchings escape my string. The arrow whistles through the air and a loud *thwack* echoes through the crowd. The arrow penetrated an eye socket throwing his body back to smack against the cobblestone. Blood immediately pools around his twitching body, and a cry escapes my throat as I bend over retching.

"MY GODS!" screams the Fae girl with skin made of leaves and everyone begins running. The throng of Fae screams in unison and the sentinels run to the body before they even notice me. I use the crowd to my advantage and run down a cobblestone street towards the roaring ravine.

He probably had a family, a wife, and friends. I took him away from people who loved him. I am no less a monster than Evaflora. *Prometheus, please, forgive me* I think, looking up to the turbulent storm above. He created Fae to be immortal, but he also created Mountain Ash to allow his creations to be destroyed. I willingly took one of his creations to destroy another. I am not just a monster. I am a *twisted* abomination. I can only blame this murder on the Summer Kingdom. The High Fae ruling this place may have her glamour affecting, not only her kingdom, but me as well. I can hear the churning darkness spinning within my gut. Hopefully I am just hungry.

I collapse to the hard stone and my jaw clashes against the cold rough surface. I scream in agony, soon to notice the dirt filled stones now patched with the blood from my bleeding cheek. Evaflora's claw cut me deep. This entire Kingdom and experience has cut me deep. No matter how hard I try to forget I will always remember what has happened here. The secrets. The lies. The truth. I have unearthed everything during my stay here. Elkwood is not only what I need to save my father, Elkwood needs to be saved from itself.

I hear a faint whistling- suddenly I realize an arrow is flying towards me. I roll, but it is too late. I scream into the night, thunder booms from the roiling clouds above me as a steel arrow tip grinds across my upper arm. The blade slices along the bone sending reverberations through my whole skeleton. This is the worst pain I've felt in my life. I need to get to the ravine before they kill me. I scramble to my feet and start sprinting up a hill. I can see the pointed tip of the spire. A flag flicks in the wild wind and hot, thick, plum-red blood starts to pour from my upper arm onto my forearm. It won't stop stinging! I think they laced the broad heads with poison to kill me if I get away? The stone in my chest holds firm so I can only trust that. I've learned that the stone will only disappear if I may die or if someone around me is going to get hurt or die. I don't want that stone to ever disappear.

Arrows whirl past my body, clattering against the stones on the hill's surface. I begin to peak the incline and below me lay the ravine and bridge. Jax, Jeremiah, and Zube stand next to the spire. Something is wrong. I can immediately tell by the lack of Guards on the bridge. I would've assumed that the only entrance into the Summer Kingdom would be highly guarded. I barrel down the hill, even as I hear the clinking armor of the sentinels peak the top of the incline.

"RUN," is all I scream and the shout rips my throat apart. The three boys look to me and begin sprinting onto the bridge. Jax stops halfway across and begins firing Ash arrows into the armored sentinels that are closing in on me.

Once I reach the bridge, Jax's quiver is empty and Zube and Jeremiah are halted by large tree monsters. The beasts are just like the ones I saw in Evaflora's secret tunnel, in the room of abominations. When I look back, all the sentinels that were chasing me- hundreds- just stare at me. I'm caught. Rain begins to patter along the bridge. I got so far and now I'm done. I can't save my father and I can't save my friends from imminent torture. I spent a month in this damned forest to lose everything. I didn't go through hell to lose my chance out of it.

Zube and Jeremiah join Jax and me on the middle of the bridge and the guards stay posted at both ends, just staring at us. I cringe as pain spirals through my arm and the entire right half of my body. I just want this all to be over. I want to drink poison or leap into the screaming ravine and end my life. My voice is ragged through panting breathes, "Just kill us already."

"Why would I ever do that?" a smooth voice purrs. Her voice will haunt my nightmares until the day I'm placed into a grave. "You mean so much to me." Evaflora saunters through the crowd and steps onto the bridge. I instantly have my bow drawn and an Ash arrow fixed on her heart. Sentinels unsheathe their blades in reaction to my movements and I smile as I ignore the growing pain in my arm and the cut throbbing in my cheek. The rain has now become a torrential downpour, completely soaking everyone head to toe. My vision blurs from both the rain and my own fury. Of course she would find her way down here to let me watch my friends die. Immortal bitch.

"Oh, stuff it. I mean nothing to you and you know it," My shaking voice is still stern and accusing, exactly like I wanted.

"Have you told your friends about our little secret?"

"What secret?" Zube asks dumbfounded. I'll be damned if she even speaks a word of her being my mother in front of him. "SHE'S YOUR MOTHER?" he read my thoughts. A wail escapes my mother's lips and I snarl not only at her, but also because the pain of my tense muscles is growing intensely. Holding the drawn bow is causing blood to cascade down my arm.

"Precisely," Evaflora grins. If she wants to play a game of telling secrets I am ready to join in.

"Have you told *your* Kingdom the great secret, Evaflora?"

"I don't keep secrets from my Kingdom," she states obviously lying through her pointed teeth. What a bitch.

"Well what about the glamour you placed on the Fae of the Summer Kingdom many years ago?" Her faces twists in rage and all her sentinels look to their High Fae in utter confusion. I simply chuckle as I listen to my friends gasp.

"You're playing the wrong game, mortal," She spits the word mortal with as much venom as possible. I don't know what comes over me besides pure rage as I grin at her deviously.

"I only play games I know I can win," is all I whisper to her and certainly every Fae nearby overheard it. Her pale cheeks grow hot with rage and I see her eyes begin to glow green. The stone vanishes and green flames erupt at her balled fists. The raging flames make her iridescent gown flicker a rainbow of colors. At the other end of the bridge lightning strikes and the tree monsters have become smoking pieces of bark scattered across the bridge. I keep my bow drawn through the haste and try to blink the water that's blurring my vision.

I let go of the string and the tension in my muscles immediately subsides. I hear Evaflora scream. Jax grips my wrist pulling me towards Elkwood and the sentinels don't follow as they now realize they have been betrayed by their High Fae. When I look back, I see Evaflora yanking the arrow from her abdomen as she hunches over, crippled. Her sentinels begin to head back towards the city, leaving her in the powering rain.

The rain and my own anger blinded me when I made the shot. A voice in the back of my mind tells me that she may not be dead.

CHAPTER TEN

We didn't stop running for three miles. Zube was leading us back to where they left the horses and supplies, near a den in a clearing. The golden gown is beyond irritating, for it only gets snagged and pulled on every stick within a five foot radius. The trim is covered in mud and the whole dress is soaked from the rain. Only a few droplets fall from the canopy of leaves above us but it's enough to still keep us wet. Jeremiah is pulling me along and I can tell he is angry. I don't know if it's how Evaflora is my mother or maybe that I didn't tell him, but I didn't know. What is really on my mind is why did those tree monsters block the other end of the bridge? Where did they come from?

"The clearing is up here through that foliage up ahead," Zube says pointing. I am just excited to finally get out of this cumbersome gown. I know I have some clothes packed with the supplies.

I am free. I am out of the Summer Kingdom and I am back with my friends. I will save my father and everything will be the same again. I will never forget though, never forget everything I witnessed and have been through in that Kingdom. My mother drinks blood to live. She is a witch who isn't afraid to kill to get what she wants. She tried to kill me three times, I think. Once was in the throne room. The second time was on the balcony tonight, and another time again tonight on the bridge. The stone keeps vanishing before danger will harm me and it went away seconds before her hands burst into flames. We wouldn't be alive if Prometheus didn't help us by destroying the tree men. It doesn't make sense why the lightning bolt would hit right on the monsters if it wasn't done by the gods. I can thank him, but I am so beyond done with magic and ethereal beings. I am sick of Elkwood, and I desire nothing more than for all of this to be over. For my father to not be trying to kill me. I just want to be home and siting in my library with a nice thick book in my hands, taking in the smell of dust and inked parchment. I drag myself back to reality and out of the depths of my thoughts.

Our feet pound in unison and we break through the sticks and leaves emerging into a large clearing. Knee-high grass covers the expanse of the clearing and small yellow flowers peak between the green. It's beautiful and quiet. It's *too* quiet. I peer to a den at the other end of the expanse of grass and when Jax and Zube head into the dark cave Jeremiah turns to me.

"What happened in that Kingdom, Ariadae," he asks instantly concerned. I know he only worries for me, but I don't want to tell him what happened to me there. It was so excruciatingly painful the first time and I've only been out of the Kingdom for maybe two hours. I don't want to start talking about it yet. I'm not ready.

"It's worse than you could imagine," is all I say to him and I can see the anger flare across his features.

"Who do I need to hurt?" he spits through grinding teeth. I roll my eyes at him.

"Nobody, I can handle myself, okay?" My mind flashes to the sentinel I killed in the town square. I shot the arrow into his skull in front of a throng of people. That's when I became a murderer. I rub my hands together feeling the ghost of his blood staining them. I grip the wound across my shoulder. He had family and friends. I ripped his life away from those who loved him yet Prometheus *still* helped me. If I kill the Rune Witch and bring the Oracle to him, will Prometheus help me again?

Jeremiah drags me from my mind and asks, "What happened?"

He at least deserves to know what I did.

"I…I," my stuttering is cut off by Jax and Zube coming back out from the cave. I will tell nobody about what I did. Not even Jeremiah. I don't care how much he presses and pries I will not allow my name, the heir of two thrones, be labeled as murderer.

Jax and Zube don't hold any of our supplies and their faces are grave. Something is wrong. I slowly walk to them and ask, "What's wrong?" Jax's ice blues flick to me and his frown deepens. My heart begins thudding and I slam into his solid abdomen, pushing past him into the den lightly illuminated by the rising sun's light. In a small pile, in the center of the cave, is a smoking mound of ashes. Somebody burned all of our supplies. They scorched our extra clothes, spices, medical tonics and bandages, *everything*. The weapons wouldn't have burned, so they must've taken our other quivers, daggers, and swords, and my family heirloom dagger. I cry out in frustration. I am stuck in this obnoxious dress and all of our expensive supplies are ashes. Anger bursts in blazing flames inside me as I storm from the cave in a rage.

"Where are the mares," Jeremiah asks as I approach the group. Zube just shrugs and looks to Jax.

"They were also in the cave," he whispers. I stomp up to them. They are so dumb.

"That ash pile is too small to have burned four full sized horses," I tell them. The mares must have run off somewhere. We need to find them and get away from the area. Not all of Evaflora's men heard me speak of the glamour, so there must be some who are still searching for us. I start to wander around the clearing. Near the side of the den, I see several drops of blood on some blades of grass. I begin to follow their trail along the hill of rocks. All over the foliage before me is coated with the dark liquid. Someone took the horses but they were stupid enough to injure them and leave a perfect trail for us to follow. I may be a princess, but I know how to track animals and I am familiar with plants that I can be used as herbal remedies or poisons. Reading teaches people a lot more than they think.

I push through the greenery and suddenly notice a large pile of blood splattered all over the forest floor at my feet. I choke on the air, all of the blood drains from my face. I approach the pile and cover my mouth, for the smell is vile. The bodies aren't anywhere in sight.

"Everybody, I think I found them," I shout behind me. My hands begin to shake and my eyes fill with tears. These poor horses were only here because we brought them into Elkwood and now some very good steeds are gone, dead. With this much blood they can't be alive. Where could the bodies have gone?

Drip, crimson liquid lands onto my hand. *Drip, drip, drip,* three more plop onto my hand and forearm. My eyes follow up a tree trunk and my pounding heart crashes violently against my ribcage. *Please, please don't be what I think it is, please.* I scream at the sight.

The corpses are skinned and hanging from their hooves. The vital organs are removed and the horses are just empty shells. Tight rope tightly squeezes the bloodied masses of meat that were once my mares. Jax, Zube, and Jeremiah crash through the foliage. The three guys tense in immediate shock. They just hang there and I can hear the groan of the rope that holds them as the mares swing in the breeze.

"Troglodytes," Jax whispers.

"What?" I ask. What could the reptilian people I read about do with the dead mares? "What about Troglodytes?"

He looks to me as if I'm stupid. He speaks slowly to make his point, "Only Troglodytes kill animals and people like this."

I sprint from the sight and lay in the clearing crying as my companions cut them down. I don't want to be there and see that. We will have to travel on foot from now on. It will take longer than I wanted, but I don't have any other options. We can't ride a wild animal, and I'm not heading back to any Kingdoms to steal some horses. Zube is banished from the Kingdoms anyway. We can begin traveling tomorrow, but I can't just walk through Elkwood with a dress and heels on. I need clothes, or maybe I could make some.

I wipe away my tears, reminding myself why I'm here and how far I've come. Nothing can stop me now. On that thought I remove the feathered bodice, exposing my black corset. I continue to remove the many skirts of tulle, leaving me in black tight pants. Anybody could see my undergarments due to the tightness, but I'm not running through Elkwood with a dress. The gown is only a reminder of the Summer Kingdom and… Oh no. I suddenly realize I left someone behind! I left her in the Summer Kingdom and I announced at the party she made my gown and Evaflora knew she gave me the titanium antler crown! The High Fae of the Summer Kingdom is going to murder Seri!

I fastened the cloak over my left shoulder and run to where everybody is. I crash through the foliage as they finish packing the dirt over the corpses.

"She is going to kill her," I whimper.

"Who?" Jeremiah asks running to me. He wants nothing more to know everything that happened. I push past him towards Zube who I know understands loss.

"My best friend, Seri, she was my personal maiden. She did traitorous things like giving me a titanium crown of antlers and-"

"She gave you a titanium antler crown? Oh my, this girl has a death wish," Zube interrupts, stunned.

"How do you know about that?" I ask. He was banished from the Kingdoms long ago how could he possibly be aware of the crowns significance?

"Every Fae knows of the Great Titanium Rebellion. Almost all of the Fae of the Summer Kingdom were brutally murdered in that rebellion and now Evaflora still sits on that throne. I don't know how," he explains to me.

"They're glamoured," I say interrupting him. "She glamoured the Kingdom to make them believe she's a good High Fae."

"No wonder she can rule with a sharp diamond fist and not be burned at the stake by her own people."

"We need to save Seri from the stake," I say. If we don't get her out of the Summer Kingdom soon she will be brutally murdered by my mother.

"We can't do that. Your mother will use her as leverage to get you in her grasps," Jax interrupts.

I look to the three of them. Even in our condition I know, I insist, to get her out of there and retrieve supplies. We can't head into Elkwood without other weapons, clothes and medical herbs and bandages. It would be suicide.

"We have to and you know that," is all I say to Jax. I look to Jeremiah and Zube. "Alright warriors what's our plan?"

Jax hunted several rabbits and deer to give to me as I begin stitching the pelts and furs together for some gear. I used the large amount of rope that snared the horses in the tree and I threaded a pair of rabbit fur boots and arm wraps. I used some soft deer hide to make fingerless gloves. The glove on my right hand wraps my index, middle, and ring fingers so the bowstring doesn't cut my fingers. Jeremiah and Zube got cloaks; Jax got boots and arm bands and gloves. Zube and Jeremiah wield swords while Jax and I bare bows and quivers. Our clothing, armor, and much needed gear differ greatly from warrior to warrior. We are preparing for war.

The sky has started to turn pink and the air becomes cool, night will be upon us soon. The bleeding in my cheek stopped hours ago and I braided some grass to stem the bleeding on my shoulder. I didn't have any more pelt or fur so grass was the next best option. We have our plan ready, and we will be back in the forest with Seri by daybreak. Jax and I squat in the green leaves, peering through to watch the bustling bridge. Courtiers are cleaning up the Summer Solstice festival and they run around like worker bees. I am waiting for the first sight of the moon to give the signal. We are going to cross the bridge. It was the original plan. We are going to sneak through the crowds and hopefully cross to the other side.

"Why did you hide from me all my life," I whisper to Jax. The question has been bothering me ever since I saw him shift for the first time last month. He doesn't look to me and I am not sure if I want to know the answer.

"I left my Kingdom and was searching for something to do, someone to be, and you were the first thing I found. Well your father found me, and on that snowy day he gave me to you," his voice was even and clear but then grows soft and slightly intimate. "You were unharmed, untouched, unburdened by the world and I wanted nothing more than to keep any harm coming to you. I wanted to keep you that way, but once I learned your father banished magic from Equadoria I never changed back into my Fae form until last month when we returned to Elkwood."

He was always protecting me. He sees me as innocent and weak and didn't want Elkwood or anybody affecting me or hurting me. My heart flutters. "Where did you go after the Wood Nymph attacked you?" I ask.

"I'll tell you some other time," his words were much colder than I would've thought and it kind of hurt.

He is keeping something from me. Probably still protecting me.

"I am not that little girl anymore. I can do things on my own," I try to stay quiet even though I want nothing more than to shout. I place my hand on his shoulder and he immediately pulls from my grip. How rude.

"No, you're not that little girl anymore, and I want nothing more than for you to become her again." I gasp. He was rude by pulling out of my grip but there is something more going on here.

"What is your problem?" I demand. I've had him around before I even met Jeremiah, but he shouldn't be so ignorant as to wish I was my younger self. He probably just doesn't want to deal with me growing up.

"My problem is I can smell your body heat, feel your pounding heart, and hear your aching body. I want nothing more to answer those calls but you're sixteen. I am immortal, and way beyond the decent age to enjoy you, but my problem essentially is I don't want you touching me because I can barely keep a safe distance from you without going insane." That answer wasn't what I was thinking. He wants to *enjoy* me? He can smell the heat and hear the ache my body has for him. He is attractive, and he looks eighteen, but I know he isn't even close to that age. He must be centuries old. Bummer.

What's even worse is I had a dream about him the other night. I dreamt we were in my bed in Equadoria and this time he wasn't a tiger. He licked every inch of my skin and my chest pounded against his thick soft lips. I still remember how he tasted, ginger and ice. His warm body against mine made the open air feel like icicles raking down my legs and back. I was letting him take me, and when I was fully exposed to him, he captured me in his grasp and I flew into nothingness. I was screaming and falling, but I let him fall with me. When I awoke the next day, I was upset. I was full of aches; more than I ever thought were possible. It felt real.

"Fine," is all I say as I look back towards the Summer Kingdom. I will save my friend before anything bad happens to her. Hopefully I will make it in time.

The silver disk begins to peak the horizon and I make the bird call. Zube and Jeremiah break from the foliage several yards away while Jax and I emerge ourselves. Our feet pull silently towards the ravine's edge and we duck along the stone side of the bridge. I look up onto the bridge still covered with people when I notice a large amount of guards at one end checking people. Panic flurries in my gut and I look to Jax and point. He sees the same thing and points on the side of the bridge. The bridge is covered in different carvings and statues giving us the perfect cover and climbing pockets. We are going to scale the side of the bridge.

Jax grips a pocket and steps up onto the wall. My heart is pounding and I suddenly realize I'm empty. We are missing something. *I* am missing something and it's important. The bone dagger is tucked tightly into the fur wrap I am wearing as a makeshift skirt. Jax is in front of me and Zube and Jeremiah are climbing across the opposite side of the bridge. My knees buckle at the realization. How did I not notice before? The stone in my chest is gone. It has been gone since we first left the bridge earlier this morning. I have a feeling it won't come back anytime soon. It's amazing how much I have relied on the stone and I feel like I'm walking into this blind.

"What's wrong?" Jax whispers to me. His long black hair gleams against the moon light. He is already at the first statue of a flower pouring water into the roaring ravine below. I barely hear him over the dark screaming waves.

"Nothing," I say. "I'm fine." I grip a cold stone and take a deep breath. The air reeks of salt water and it stings my naval cavities. Let's do this, I think to myself. I hoist my body onto the wall and I feel the weight of gravity pulling me down. I take my first step and with a trembling hand grip another stone. I step and now the water looms below me, calling me, pulling me down. The wall slips from grasp and my brain goes light as I lay back soaring towards the dark waters below. My vision is darkened and I am suspended as something tightly grips my wrist. As my vision clears I realize I am hanging above the ravine and start to scream. The roaring water drowns out my wail and Jax pulls me onto the statute. If it weren't for Jax grabbing me I'd be dead. And if it weren't for the roiling waves than every sentinel on the bridge would find us.

"What happened? Are you okay?" he presses immediately. I just lay into him. I hate heights more than I hate my mother. I need to rescue Seri; I want that more than anything in the world. I don't want anybody else dead because of me, I've already managed to kill Gaston, Novid, and four horses.

"I don't like heights," I coldly admit and squeeze my eyes shut. How else can I get across? "Is there any other way across?"

"I don't think so. Look, we only need to cross six more statutes and then we will be on the land again. We will be across the ravine. You can do it, I promise." His words are calming and helpful but I know he won't like what I am going to do.

"Alright," is all I say to him. He rises and quickly scales to the other statute almost effortlessly. I'm extremely jealous but I just get nauseas thinking about that. He gets a good position beckons to me. I have two choices I can either most likely fall to my death or I can take a harder but safer route. I flick up my hood and climb up the bridge wall and leap over the railing onto the tile. I land on silent feet in a potentially deadly path riddled with bustling Fae. I could be ensuring my own death right now but I don't really care. I hear Jax grunt and I see his fingers gripping the railing. If I get across this bridge he will surely kill me himself.

Sentinels saunter up and down the sides of the bridge and I look towards the commotion going on at the end of the bridge. I'll deal with that later, but I keep my distance from the passing guards. I can only pray they can't hear my pounding heart over the screaming ravine. If I am caught, I would be taken immediately to Evaflora who would delight in torturing me and my friends. She desires to see me suffer. I hope she died when I shot her with the ash arrow, but if she died I would be coming back into the Summer Kingdom for nothing. Seri wouldn't be in danger. The possibility is too great to risk.

The dragon bone dagger is safely hidden, but I notice a passing sentinel's eyes flick to my bow and quiver. I cringe. He stops walking and I keep heading towards the other end of the bridge using the hood to conceal my face. Right when I think he is gone a hand clasps around my arm and pulls me back.

He is older or maybe his work has worn him down for his beard is the color of ash and his eyes seem to be a sea-green? He looks like he has a family or maybe kids because he seems very fatherly even though anger is plastered on his features. His words are questioning, "Why do you have those weapons?"

I don't answer him. I simply keep my eyes down and let the rim of the hood cover my features. He becomes frightened, or fearful, or curious. I am not sure what emotion it could possibly be. "Answer me," he spits and his saliva lands on my chin. "Who are you?"

"I am the Queen of Titanium Antlers," before I can say anything else he falls back over the railing to the waters below. I scramble to the edge and notice Jeremiahs eyes peeking over the stone railing. He winks. He pulled the guard over the edge. I can only assume nobody else heard his screams from the water crashing against the rocks. Jeremiah saved me. I wink back and start walking towards the commotion.

Travelers and traders from other Kingdoms are gathered in small lines yelling and throwing things at the sentinels. They are angered at the sentinels for forcefully checking their supplies and the trading carts. They look for hitchhikers, wanted people, me, Jax, Jeremiah, and Zube. I ignore the crowds and run to the side of the bridge. Without looking, I carefully place my feet on a flower statue. I see Jax waiting below on the grass near the ravine's rocky edge. I am not ready for the inevitable lecture I am about to receive.

When I drop onto the slick rocks leaving the flower statue and the damned bridge behind me, Jax just glares at me. I ignore him. He can be angry all he wants, but I made it across the bridge without getting caught. The only person who recognized me is dead at the bottom of the ravine; his body's most likely torn apart by the raging current below. I don't know why I said I was the *Queen of Titanium Antlers*, but the title is very impressive and intimidating. I am no queen, but I would certainly like to be known as one. Equadoria would become the Titanium Kingdom. Magical. The thought is magical and beautiful.

Jeremiah saved me on the bridge, but I won't see him until later when we reach the castle. Our plan was to have Zube and Jeremiah walk the streets while Jax and I provide aerial cover. I follow Jax up the hill and onto the cobblestone street. We climb to the roof top of a small cottage and unstring our bows. It's my turn to take the lead.

"I have spent a good amount of time in the Summer Kingdom, so let me take the lead," I say to Jax. I no longer fear my voice being heard since the busy night streets below are chattering with people.

"Oh you are quite hilarious, Ariadae, but I have spent two centuries of my life in Elkwood and I know my way around the Kingdoms," he argues. He doesn't know me and Lunan have been on the rooftops and I know which houses lead straight to the castle.

"I've been up on the shingled roofs of the Summer Kingdom before and I can get us to the castle safely."

"Did anyone join you on the rooftops, princess?" Jax questions rudely. He can be as sobbingly stupid as he likes, but either way I will lead us across the houses.

"Yes, High Fae of the Day Kingdom. If you truly wanted to know," I say as I leap to the next roof and look into the street searching for Jeremiah and Zube.

Jax follows close behind and walks ahead of me ignoring the crowds along the street. He is extremely surprised and seems almost angered as he says, "Lunan Berdu Walsh?"

I spot their fur cloaks and I nod to Jax.

"Yes and I have sight of Zube and Jeremiah."

"Alright," is all he answers and I leap to the next roof as Jeremiah and Zube push farther up the street. The cobblestones below are littered in puddles from the rain that poured in the early hours. The shingled slanted rooftops are only damp in the areas that weren't exposed to the sun for very long, but otherwise I have a good grip to the roof. I don't like heights but being up here doesn't scare me much. I have been up here before. I have an advantage.

Jax and I leap from roof to roof for a while following Zube and Jeremiah below. We are getting closer to the castle and I notice an extreme increase in sentinels around walking through the people. They are handling, checking, and throwing back the hoods of the Fae and I can tell they are searching for us. They will see Jeremiah and Zube, and take them to Evaflora.

I unstring my bow and nock an arrow in safety. Jax does the same thing and we just watch the frisked throng of people below bustle about angrily. Jeremiah and Zube stay closer towards the wall and I watch them as they sneak between the crowds. They keep their hoods up and heads down. They should be safe and clear because the sentinels seem to have breached the center of the street. Even if they run into some trouble, Jax and I will help them out.

I feel naked, utterly naked without the stone in my chest. It seems fear has vanished from my body and no longer sits in my chest. I ache for love and I ache for fear. I ache for that stone in my chest and I want it to appear so I know when something is going to happen. I'm blindly wandering and I am trying to rely on every sense I have. I smell the ash of the burning torches below and the salt in the air. I feel the reverberations of my beating heart and the stomping of Fae on the street. I hear the crowds shouting in anguish and the sentinels barking orders. I taste my dry tongue and the salt water from the coast and the ravine. I see the bustling crowds, the looming castle, and the different manors that lead up the street. But when I leap over the ally, I don't see the sentinels stationed across the rooftops right in front of me, leading up to the castle.

Unwillingly, I draw my bow and squat low to the shingles. I stay in the dark shadows and my charcoal cloak makes me almost invisible even under the moon light. Jax stays on the other roof behind me and fires arrows into the skulls of unknowing guards. I choke on a breath and watch a guard as he hums a song. It's a child's song which I now know the meaning of.

> *"We rise and fall in the burning fire,*
> *Never ending and never growing tire.*
> *My mother spawns the life of a flower,*
> *Though it is no ordinary power.*
> *I create the sound of the wind,*
> *And I will be skinned.*
> *For only I'd love to die in the fire,*
> *That will never grow tire."*

The soft tune symbolizes the war between the Fae and the mortals. Great fires burned into the trees of Elkwood so the writer spoke of the fires in the song. My father sang that to me when I was young and told me it was about the spark of fire that pushes you and makes you brave and courageous and passionate about something. He lied about things, a *lot* of things. I learned the true meaning from the book *Nirvana* that I read while in the Summer Kingdom this past month.

I close my eyes and the bow groans in anger. The string begins to sting my fingers and my shoulder wound begins to tear again so I release my breath and the string at the same time. The arrow finds a home and I hear the *thwack* of it penetrating the singing sentinel's skull. His hums were immediately cut off by the arrow, and even though my eyes are sealed, I see the man I killed earlier this morning during the festival. Fear spikes through my body. I open my eyes as people scream in the street below. He was standing on the edge of the roof, allowing his corpse to fall onto the throng of Fae and sentinels below. Zube and Jeremiah were right next to them as well. I think I just blew our entire mission out of the water. We are like sitting ducks now.

I don't know how but Jax already has his grip on my arm and is pulling me back towards Elkwood. We leap over alley after alley and when I look down; I see Zube and Jeremiah running towards the ravine as well. I killed another person and I am numb. I am no longer my father's perfect daughter and I am no longer unharmed and untouched by the world. I'm not the only person to kill, Jeremiah did kill that sentinel earlier on the bridge, Jax killed a ton of guards who were on the rooftops and Zube fought in the war against Solaria. They will look at me differently. They won't see me as weak and will treat me as one of them. They will see me as strong and brave, like them.

Jax leaps from the roof and I stop. He barely reaches the next roof and he hangs clinging to the edge. He pulls himself up and yells to me, "WHAT'RE YOU DOING? We have to go now!" I shake my head. I will be strong and I will be brave.

My voice is a strangled whisper, "Seri."

My feet slam against the shingles and I don't even stumble as I leap from building to building. I can hear Jax sprinting behind me, but I ignore him killing sentinel after sentinel as I run. I am done being innocent, I am done being looked at as weak, and I am officially done being treated like the helpless princess. Elkwood hasn't broken me. It has taught me something. Elkwood has taught me that I can easily break and be fractured but each crack and broken part of myself will only make me stronger. I will shatter into a million pieces one day, and when I do I will be stronger than anybody could even prepare for.

After descending the side of a manor, I drop into a shallow puddle. Sentinels begin to run to me. Arrows flee from my quiver and I begin stealing Mountain Ash arrows from the dead soldiers to replenish my stock. It's like my quiver is never ending. Their bodies litter the courtyard of the castle. Nobody remains and I calmly walk up to the towering doors. My mother is certainly hiding behind them and happily waiting for me.

"Ariadae," Jax says warily behind me. He is worried, stunned, and not very brave at the moment. He just witnessed a presumably innocent girl murder around fifty to sixty armed sentinels. He should be shocked.

The doors groan open as I reach the stairs, only to see blackness within. I slowly move up the steps and nock an arrow. There is a slight commotion from inside, a body is thrown out the door and lands on the steps at my feet. The door slams and my heart begins pounding. I close my eyes and angle my head to the corpse. It won't be. It can't be. I open my eyes. It is.

Seri.

My scream sends reverberations through the stones beneath my feet. The echoing scream waves across Elkwood and I don't doubt that every Kingdom has heard my cry. My cries tear through my shredded throat and I choke on the air. Tears flood down my face and upon her corpse. Her blue skin is cold and littered in scars. My mother destroyed and mutilated my only friend in the Summer Kingdom. The world has stopped spinning and I am just alone. I'm surrounded by darkness. I am utterly alone on these steps.

Jax runs to me and tugs on my arm, but I won't move. I will never leave her here alone and dead. I would want someone to lay with me when I die. I want somebody to be there for me when life leaves my body, but I couldn't even do that. Evaflora probably laughed as she died, succumbing to my mother's torture. I am broken, but I am not shattered. I will not be easily repaired, and I will not let my mother get away with this. No matter what I will kill her one day and I will laugh as she lies dying, withering away.

All of a sudden lips are against mine. Jax. Now, the world is an imperfect place, but there isn't anything imperfect about him. No bad features. No bad attitude. I know that the world, Elkwood, my mother, everyone is against us, but I hear his name on the wind. His kiss sends me into oblivion. The dark abyss that seems to never end letting me fall, scream. I feel like I'm dreaming again.

I feel as if I fall until there is nothing left of me. I am broken, scarred, and torn to pieces. Maybe I *am* shattered. I won't be able to pick up the pieces. There is nothing left of me except for what's in his arms. The pieces I won't be able to put back together, every part of me, all of my imperfections, my dents, and my fractures. I listen, and stare into the glimmer of sparks that flutter through our hearts. This synchronized sequence makes flames kiss my skin. Not just my cheeks, my ears, and neck; but my whole body. This feeling is happening because of him, because of *Jax*. The only one who can put me back together.

Even after I've shattered into a million pieces.

CHAPTER ELEVEN

He guides me from the castle steps to an herbal shop near the lower bowels of the Summer Kingdom. We are only two blocks from the bridge, which is being guarded by every sentinel and guard the Kingdom has left. We aren't getting in or out. We came back because I insisted on saving Seri from my mother. We didn't make it in time, and now we're stuck. I lay behind the counter by an old wooden door while he sits on the counter of the shop. He organizes supplies across the surface.

"You shouldn't have gone back," He whispers. He is angered but won't take out his rage on me. I don't know why he holds back the words he wants to truly say. I deserve everything he has to throw at me.

"How was I supposed to know she was...," I say as my words die out in the dusty air. The wooden shops large windows are plastered with shelves and merchandise advertising to the streets outside. The rising sun makes the room glow orange, and it illuminates the swirling clouds of dust.

"There was no way for us to know, Ariadae. Stop blaming yourself."

"How can I *not* blame myself? She was my friend. She was my maiden. She did everything for me. She did everything so I wouldn't die in this damned kingdom," I scream at him. He recoils but he lets everything roll off his back. His resilience is beyond mine. I guess living through several centuries teaches you things like patience. "I guess everything she did was for nothing. We're still in this horrid place."

"We aren't going to die here. You're not going to die here," He says coldly. He lacks any emotion. He can believe anything he likes, but I haven't had the stone in my chest since the early hours today. I have just a strange feeling.

Without answering him I rise and walk to the counter to look over the supplies he laid out. There are jars full of powders and liquids. Some other plants are in small clear bags. A small pyramid of bandages sits next to the money box and a cluster of tonic bottles sits near a small box. The wood finish is glossed over. A jar stands out to me. Its silver lid reflects the lantern light above me. The jar is filled with a dark colored powder. It looks to be ashes like soot from a burnt out fire, as if someone scraped the ash straight from the fireplace into the jar.

I grab the cold glass and spin it in my hand shaking the dark powder about. A small slip of parchment is attached to the side of the jar with some sort of adhesive, it reads: Mountain Ash. The words are written neatly with dark ink.

"Why would anybody need mountain ash in a powder form?"

"I am not quite sure, but seeing as how we have an entire Fae Kingdom against us, I thought we could use it," Jax says to me. He's smart for thinking like that. He probably couldn't even touch the charcoal powder but someone like Jeremiah or I could use it.

"What's in the box?" I question, changing the subject. He looks to the box and begins stuffing everything into the satchel. "What's in the box?" I repeat louder.

"Doesn't matter right now, I can hear someone coming," His panicked words are clipped and fast. "Grab your bow and stay behind the counter." I follow his instructions. Nobody would be coming other than some townspeople. I watch as he places yarrow, passionflower, and ginseng into the satchel. The herbs are great for bruises and fevers but something is missing.

"Jax," I call to him as he finishes packing the satchel. "Have you got plantain?"

His eyes widen. He whispers, "No, it's okay, we don't need it."

"You don't need it," I correct his statement. Plantain is an herbal remedy for cuts, bruises, snake bites, and insect bites. It will help stop bleeding and flush out any bacteria in the body. Jax may not need it because he is immortal and can't die from an infection, but Jeremiah, Zube, and I will need an antiseptic like that.

I look around the room and search the tables and shelves for the big green leaves. I want to use it on the cut on my shoulder. Drawing back my bow earlier reopened up the wound. I even notice small drips of blood sneaking beneath the braided grass I had used to stem the bleeding. I need to get a better look around the shop so I slide over the counter and ignore Jax's hushed orders and shouts. I completely block out his attempts to grab my attention. It's on one of the shelves along the walls. The tables are covered in bandages and tonics for scents and internal healings. As I spin the world turns around me. I can feel the earth beneath my feet spinning and orbiting the sun outside. I am lost and I am gone, whisking away into an internal void. I feel the power beneath my veins and I can taste the vile venom on my lips. I taste metallic blood on my tongue and I can do nothing but let my mouth stick to the black tar that's sliding down my throat. If I don't leave Elkwood soon I am going to die. The forest is going to kill me.

Everything stops. The spinning stops. The horrible taste in my mouth vanishes and I can see the plantain on the shelf near the window next to some glass jars full of weeds and a rainbow of colored liquids. I sprint to the wall grab the sculpted glass and then I see it. The shadow ripples across the floor and I look to the outside windows. Glancing between the parsley I see a sentinel, not just any sentinel, Darwin, Evaflora's personal guard. He was the Fae who brought her the blonde boy she ate the first day I was here. If he sees me, smells me, or even hears me I'll be dead.

"Ariadae, come here, back away, slowly, don't make a sound," Jax whispers from behind the counter. My heart thumps. I fear Darwin may have heard his whispers, through the wood and glass of the store. Step by step I slowly place my feet slightly on a wooden plank, easing my weight, testing if they creak. Every five beats of my heart I step, making my way, excruciatingly slow, but safely away from the window.

Thump, that wasn't my heart, glass bottles rattle and I wince. I bumped into a display. Breathe, in, out, in, out. *CRASH*, goes a tonic bottle onto the floor. The liquid sprays along the floor and I cringe as my heart stops beating. The liquid might as well be my blood when Darwin is done with me. Darwin's head whips to the shop and I immediately run and leap behind the counter next to Jax who pulls me close. My breaths come out in strangled rasps and Jax covers my mouth as the doors little bell rings. He's here; Darwin is in here and will surely smell my fear. I quickly stuff the plantain into the satchel and I unsheathe the dragon bone dagger. He can get to me, but I will go down fighting any way I can. I won't let people know me as the helpless princess who couldn't save her father. Jeremiah wouldn't let the people of Equadoria have thoughts of me like that. My people will know me as the Queen of Titanium Antlers, though they may not understand the meaning, Evaflora will. She hasn't made herself present since I shot her with the ash arrow. Hopefully she is in as much pain as anyone could imagine.

A heavy inhale from Darwin signifies him trying to track me. Hopefully all the herbs and flowers mask the scent of the beads of sweat on my scalp and back. If he can find us from a few drops of sweat it's no wonder Evaflora chose him.

"I smell you," his deep voice groans. My fears are true and my heart begins to rapidly skip. "I am coming for you, girl. You may be Milady's daughter, but I am coming for you and your mother will make you scream." I squirm in my skin. I can't stop the tremble that is taking over my body and Jax can't hold me still. "I smell an Heir, a male. I can smell the ice beneath his skin." Jax's muscles lock up as do mine. We're caught.

I close my eyes and ignore the words leaving Darwin's lips. He is trying to torment me, but I need to use my powers. I don't know how to reach them, or touch them, or conjure them, but I dig down deep. I scrape through the darkest corners of my mind and soul. I am searching for something to grab onto, something to hold, to wield my ability.

"Are you behind the counter?" Darwin asks cunningly. He is teasing me in every way he can.

Just as I see his dark brown fingers grip the rim of the counter, I choke. A rope is taut across the darkness of my mind and I feel each thread writhing through my veins. I grab the rope as tightly as possible and twist and jerk the mental cord of my mind. The glowing braid is already becoming translucent and when a jar flies from a shelf colliding with Darwin's skull I run towards the back door. Screaming, Darwin curses towards me and Jax and I hear his muffled cries as we lock the door. The dark closet sized space is empty, except for a flight of stairs, which I instinctively dart for. When I reach the wooden door on the second floor, it is stiff and coated in cobwebs. I push and turn the cold knob but the door is locked. I hold tighter to the cord that's slowly vanishing in my mind and push against the unyielding door. The wood groans but right as I feel a hinge loosen the cord flies from my grasp and vanishes. I dig and search again but I only begin to panic.

"Move," Jax grunts pushing me aside as the door at the bottom of the steps begins to bang. Nails rake down the wood and I start slapping Jax's back in hopes of making him move faster. Darwin is going to claw his way through the door and I'm going to sit here and watch as he prowls up the steps. My heart crashes against my chest and the pain of the pounding hurts so much I think it may have cracked a rib. As Darwin's fist coated in fur busts through the lower floor door, Jax lurches his hand towards the door before him and a giant gust of wind makes the door explode from its hinges, inward to the room. The wooden door flies across the attic and slams against boxes of packaged merchandise.

Jax controlled the wind. It is clear to me his powers are bending and manipulating the air around us. What kingdom could that power possibly be from?

I look around the room and see an open window. A small, salt scented, breeze circulates the air of the room and I'm not sure if the flow of wind is from Jax or if it's from the window. We can crawl through the window onto the rooftops of the kingdom to escape.

"Through the window!" I basically shout pointing to the stunning view. Jax sprints to it and breaks the glass making room to fit his broad oversized body. I look to the stairs and Darwin stares up at me from the bottom. Jax begins to climb into the tight window and I realize I need to buy time. "Let us go."

"And let my High Fae's most wanted criminal escape? That's not how it works princess," says Darwin growling. His normal humane feature have transformed to a bear with horns and large wings. The wings are scaled like dragons and his teeth gleam yellow. I can almost smell the carrion on his breath from the top of the stairs.

"Can you pass a message to High Fae Evaflora for me?"

"Of course, what shall I say," he asks cocking his head like an animal. He knows I am buying time for Jax.

I draw my bow and aim the ash arrow at his heart. My words are fast and easy for him to understand, I say, "I am the Queen of Titanium Antlers and I will not allow her to enslave my people and use us mortals as slaves. I will make sure to shatter your Fae Kingdom and anything that keeps it going." I look to Jax who is safely out the window, so I loosen the arrow from my string and let it whiz through the air landing into the center of his chest. I just missed his heart.

I crawl through the window onto the thatched roof and let the sound of Darwin's body thudding on the floor confirm our safety. Sentinels had to have seen him walk into the shop and will surely come looking for him soon. We need to move. I look to the street below and I see the bridge, still covered in at least a hundred sentinels and guards. I think I have an idea how to get across the bridge.

"I know how we can cross the bridge," I say to Jax as I start to climb down the side of the building. I drop to the cobblestone and Jax follows behind me.

"How?"

"When I say so, direct your wind to the bridge," I say to him as we stalk towards the spires. We duck into alleys and under shop awnings to avoid guards. We reach the bridge and I hide behind a spire.

"What are you planning?" Jax questions and I ignore it. We don't have time to start asking questions.

"Just be ready," I mouth to him and he unsurely nods. I only hope he does what I ask.

I open the satchel and grab the jar of black powder. I nod to him and he scrambles to the opposite spire and I begin to open the lid. Jax can be seriously injured if this doesn't work right. His skin could be burned or maybe he could even be blinded or killed. Please work.

"Now," I shout and all the guards along the bridge turn to my shout. Jax rises and manipulates the air and strands of my hair pull into his fast flowing breeze. I open the lid and throw the contents of the jar into the pathway of his flowing wind. I can see the moving clouds of black powder swirling through the pounding wind. It's like the dust that floated around the shop but this time the swirls of powder are directed at the legion of Fae warriors that are stationed on the bridge. It is like toxic warfare.

The Fae warriors now coated in ash scream and wail as the dark powder burns their skin. I can almost hear the sizzle ringing in my ears. Welts and blisters bubble up on the exposed skin of some warriors and others cripple and wheeze. Sentinels who inhaled can no longer breathe. Guards who got powder to the eyes will be blind forever. Warriors who exposed their skin to the toxic powder cringe and blister on the ground. I may have started a war I will not be able to finish, but I will fight that battle when it's necessary.

Jax and I sprint across the tile, stepping over dead bodies and trembling guards as we charge into the dense green forest.

Zube and Jeremiah are waiting for us near the same den we left yesterday. We found them with blood shot eyes and swords coated in blood. Their night, once they made it to the cave, was filled with battling Troglodytes. Zube has four long claw marks on his arm and Jeremiah has bloodied scratches lacing his torso.

Later Jax and Zube sit outside the den organizing all the weapons and supplies for travel. Jeremiah lies on his back as I place the plantain on his bleeding wounds.

"You don't have any idea what I went through for the plantain," I say to him as he winces. "I'm sorry. Am I hurting you?"

"No," he grunts shaking his head into his arm. I know I am, but he won't admit it so I begin to work a bit more carefully. "I really appreciate it you know, the plantain, and you helping me."

"Don't over think it," I say laughing. I laid the leaves across the large cuts and I grab a roll of fresh white bandages. "Alright, sit up." He rises into the sitting position and it's hard to ignore the taut muscles of his stomach and back as I wrap the dry cloth over the leaves. He grabs my cheek and I look at him. His big calloused fingers scrape along my skin but I nudge into his touch. I need affection from a friend, someone I love dearly. I can tell he wants to ask about Seri but knows better not to.

"Hey, you're hurt," he says looking to the braided grass around the cut on my shoulder.

"I am fine; it's just a little scratch."

"No its not," he says as he unwraps the stiff braid from my shoulder. The grass sticks to some dried blood that hardened on my skin. "How are you still bleeding?"

"It opened up when I… I accidentally reopened the cut," I say not wanting to admit to what I did when I ran for the castle. I killed so many Fae, so, so many men, husbands, brothers, fathers, and sons. Hell, even a bear creature with horns, although I don't think he is dead. I murdered all of them and some part of me cringes for the murderer I am but another part of me almost smiles that I survived Evaflora's brutal warriors. I am not weak anymore. I even injured Darwin, the greatest sentinel of them all. Hopefully he passes my message along to my mother. I grin at the thought.

Jeremiah ties a small plantain leaf around my cut and tightens it with a bandage. He double knots the bandage like he does his shoes. There are so many things I know about him. He only wears the color blue during the winter; he refuses to address the southern kingdoms in Abella. Sometimes I catch him staring at the Courtiers wandering in their new dresses even though after his break up with a mysterious childhood lover he hasn't dated anyone.

"Thanks," I say to Jeremiah as Zube stomps into the cave. I look over my shoulder at him. "Can I help you?"

"Where are we going? You know how to get to the Tree of Light, right," he asks rudely.

"Yes, get Jax and I'll tell you everything."

Part Two
NIRVANA

CHAPTER TWELVE

They know everything. They know about what happened with Evaflora drinking the mortal's blood. They know about my power flares and they know about the plan. I told them about the dragon-bone dagger and the secret tunnels beneath the castle. We are headed to the wastelands. Jax says it's about a day's travel from our current location. Jeremiah was wide eyed and angered the entire time as he realized I was laying on the edge of a blade my entire month in the Kingdom, but he didn't give me much sympathy. He's being selfish, it wasn't my fault.

As we went through Elkwood, I look at Jeremiah who grips a pouch of water. Well I can only hope its water and not alcohol, but if it is I understand. I think I will need a drink once I'm back home.

"What was it like," Jeremiah whispers, confusing me. I look to him puzzled. "You know, learning that your mother is still alive."

"It wasn't a blessing from the gods," I grunt to him. Jax and Zube wander ahead sticking to a packed dirt path. "It's hard." My voice was quiet and cold. My words flowed away on a passing breeze. I don't think Jeremiah heard me. He doesn't quite catch things that I ever say, but I'm not really in the mood to discuss my mother.

I want to stop talking but the words just leave me lips uncontrollably, "Every night I used to dream she cared for me. But once I was in Summer Kingdom. Dreams of my mother changed. Suddenly they were of Evaflora trying to murder me. I didn't understand why. Now I realize, after losing countless nights of sleep, that I never stopped dreaming of my mother. My dreams just changed to reflect who….what she really was," my voice drops to a whisper. "A monster."

Jeremiah turns to me and grabs my shoulders. I try not to wince as he forgot about my injured arm and has gripped the healing cut.

"I feel sorry for you, Dae." He says using my nickname which he hasn't spoken in years. "Every night I thought of giving up and letting each different abomination tear me apart, but then I'd think of you. I knew I couldn't give up. Not until I found you." He pulls me into an embrace. He feels sorry for me because he knows exactly how I feel. He isn't just sympathetic. He is empathetic and he is my best friend. I wouldn't be so strong or moving like this if it weren't for him. I wouldn't even know how to nock an arrow if it weren't for him. He trained me every day, even when I was sick or tired he pushed me. He was always there, but so was my dad. My father isn't around anymore, but he will be soon. Soon.

"Are you love birds coming?" shouts Zube breaking the intimate moment. I wasn't ready to let go. As we separate I look to Jax whose features are slack and drooping, he is hurt. He saw me and Jeremiah hug. I can only hope he understands Jeremiah and I are only friends, I think.

"Yes," Jeremiah calls ahead and we run up the path and join them.

The air is growing cool and the sun is falling into the horizon. The golden rays split the sky and paint a canvas of pink, orange, and yellow. The smallest colors of twilight peak from across the sun. The moon mirrors the sun on the opposite end of the sky. I used to look at the moon from my balcony in Equadoria and dream of when I'd kiss a prince below the starry night but now, I want nothing more than to run from the darkness. The night is filled with monsters. Darkness is the place where dream roses bloom and nightmare thorns can cut.

I notice Jax is staring at me as I walk beside him. He shakes his head laughing and flames kiss my cheeks.

"What," I ask quite coldly.

"Nothing," he laughs waving me away like a gnat. "You're just too ambitious and I am a little jealous of that." He is a powerful immortal being and he is envious of me? I'm not like him. I should be jealous of him.

"Why? You have everything. Immortality, an amazing face that doesn't age, a decent personality," he wails at that. "I should be jealous of you."

"Don't be. You have your days to live and grow old and that's all I want to do."

"Jax."

"No. It's okay, I'm fine. I just don't think you should ever be jealous of immortals," he begins to explain. "Being immortal is like when a clock is ticking away and time is passing by but when the clock stops so does time. I am sitting on the axis of a clocks arms and I watch as they spin without me. I am missing out on the magic of growing old and experiencing a mortal life."

"You make being immortal sound like a burden," Zube says, butting into the conversation. I can't help but feel the ghost of Jax's lips on mine. My chest thumps and aches for him. I want him to kiss me, and feel me, and explore my curves and edges. I want to bite his plush lips. I shudder at the mental image.

"It is and-" Jax is cut off at the sound of a twig snapping in the darkness ahead of us. We don't light torches because we came to the conclusion that the fire attracts the larger abominations. When the Wood Nymphs attacked it was total darkness, but we had a fire burning when the larger and more dangerous Dreag attacked us at the river.

We all stop walking and stare into the swirling darkness ahead. The moonlight pierces through the canopy, illuminating the path. But about twenty meters ahead, where we heard the twig break, is just pure abyss of darkness. "Ariadae," Jax whispers under his breath and I can barely hear him. "Fire an arrow straight ahead."

I listen to him, unstringing my bow. My thumping heart clashes against my bones and my breathing becomes choked. I can't draw in enough air as I nock an arrow and pull the fletching to the corner of my lip. A shuddering breath breaks through a tremble and I let go. It whistles through the air and into the darkness where I hear the *thwack* of it hitting something. I begin to hear the drip of falling liquid and then a reverberating thud shakes the forest floor.

A roar so loud it makes tree bark peel. I cover my ears. The deep gurgling wail shakes the forest and I can see animals sprint across the path in fear. The *thud, thud, thud,* of running steps start as the wail ends. Jax is frozen in fear. I tug on his wrist pulling at him, but the reverberations begin to speed up matching the fast thud of my beating heart.

The gigantic sized beast breaks through the darkness and a cry of my own escapes my lips as I yank Jax from the path of the sprinting monster. It is at least thirty or forty feet tall, the trees are hovering about three meters above its hunched back. Large, jagged bones protrude from the grey dry, parchment looking skin. The monster reeks of carrion and feces. I gag as I crouch behind a tree, and Jax ducks into a nearby bush. It stops its sprint and wanders the path looking for us. My fingers violently spasm as my whole body trembles. This beast can tear me to ribbons in just a flick of its clawed fingers. The Fae can kill mortals easily but this thing...

The abomination is nothing I have ever seen. I peek around the cover of the tree and watch as large tusks scrape the dirt path. Fangs erupt from its mouth and its nostrils are bigger than one of my fists. It takes me a moment to realize it has the body structure of an ape, the mammals that inhabit the lower part of the continent. Its hind legs are shorter than the thick arms that drag along the ground. It snarls and I gasp. The slight sound makes the beast's head whip to my direction.

I hold my breath, nearly choking on the air. I can feel it approaching me. My pounding heart is skipping so that I think I am having a heart attack. The monster is going to rip me to pieces. Tears begin sliding down my cheeks and I cover my mouth as a whimper involuntarily escapes my lips. Hot steaming breath swirls around the tree and the carrion-scented air chokes me burning my nostrils.

Something glides softly against my shoulder and when I look down I can barely hold back the scream that wants to erupt from me. The creature's thick curved claw slides along my arm feeling me. I look to Jax who mouths to me "Don't make a sound." More tears fall as the beast heaves another breath. I can visualize my death. My blood will drip from the trees, littering the forest. The hungry Forsaken nearby will lick the crimson liquid from the dirt, soaking in my flavor. The beast's carrion breath will freshen as chunks of me slide from its teeth. *Please, let me save my father before you kill me* I mentally pray to the Gods.

Its claw shifts and wraps around my injury. A cry passes my lips. The wail was quick but loud as the monster roars squeezing my arm tighter between its claw and the tree. Something yelps far down the path and crashes through the forest. I barely see the shadow of a white stag as it dashes into the brush. The gods must have heard my prayers for the beast looks to the stag and sprints after it. I peel my bleeding shoulder from the tree and wince as blood soaks my entire arm and stains the fur wrapped around my forearm.

I can't stop the trembling throughout my body; I can still smell its odor. I ignore the pain in my shoulder as Jax crawls from the bush. I am instantly angered with him

"Why didn't you help me," I say in a hushed shout. The creature has only been gone for mere minutes and I don't want to risk it coming back.

"How could I have helped you, Dae?"

"Don't call me that," I coldly answer. Only Jeremiah can call me by that name. He would've helped me. Maybe he did.

Jeremiah's brown curls bounce as he runs to me. Zube follows a step behind.

"Are you alright," Jeremiah asks concerned. He is always worried about me, but he didn't witness what happened in the Summer Kingdom. He didn't watch me murder about fifty Fae sentinels who were armed. He didn't watch me use the mountain ash to kill a legion of guards on the bridge.

I am broken and scarred and alone. I feel utterly alone even with Jax, Jeremiah, and Zube I still feel alone. I need someone around to be with me. Whenever I call to them they need to answer. So other than being completely screwed up and the blood spilling down my arm I am okay.

"Yes, I am alright," I groan and start to apply pressure to the cut. "My cut won't stop reopening." The arrow did cut fairly deep when I left the Summer Kingdom.

"We should cauterize it," Zube claims. We all flick our attention to him and he raises his hands in the air defensively. My glare will cauterize his… "It will just stop it from opening up again and bleeding any more than you already are."

No. I will not allow them to burn me.

"He's right," Jax says. He looks to me. "We need to keep moving and I don't want you bleeding anymore. You look weak as it is." I do not look weak. I want to defend myself but I'm at a loss for words. What is my argument in the situation? They're right, I have to stop bleeding, but I don't want to be burned like some cattle.

"Fine," is all I say as I sit down on the path and cross my arms. Jax and Zube wander into the foliage and collect wood for a fire. I just want to leave the place. I want to be in my bed. I don't want blood or dirt on my skin. I want to just lay in a warm bath and think about everything. About what prince I will marry or what my first child will be like. I want human life back. I want to not worry about what creature lurks in the shadows and I don't want to see my evil, wicked, inhumane mother in my dreams.

This whole adventure is going to mar me forever. I will never be able to forget my scars or the blood I've shed. I may hate all of this but I need it. I needed to learn of the abilities I hold under my skin, and I need to know my mother who is still alive. I needed to know Jax was Snow. I could've gone my whole life knowing none of those things.

I've killed and murdered so, so many Faeries that no water, magical or normal can wash the blood from my skin. The dead soldier's blood and souls will never leave my body. My mind.

I look around at the dark night and down the path I see someone. It must be Jax or Zube now back from collecting fire wood.

"Hello," I call out to the figure. Jeremiah glances to me puzzled and looks to where I stare at the darkened shadow.

"Who are you talking to," he asks.

I look to him in confusion. "Don't you see the guy standing down the path?"

Jeremiah looks into the darkness, staring right at the figure and looks back to me as he says, "Nobody is on the path." My heart skips five beats and I choke on my air. Please be Jax or Zube. Do not be someone else. I've spent too many days in the forest experiencing deadly encounters.

I stand up and begin to unnervingly and hesitantly walk down the path towards the shadow. Each step in the dirt is four pounding beats of my heart. I stop about halfway between the figure and Jeremiah who just stares at me on the path. Drawing my bow I aim an arrow at the tall broad-shouldered shadow. The arrow whizzes and the figure disappears in a cloud of shadow, the arrow flying off into the darkness. The figure is gone but I suddenly feel the cold breath flooding down my neck. The heaving wheezes of the figure echoing in my ear. I shudder at the fear rattling through my bones. No beast or monster can be this evil. I can feel the darkness and evil pulsing from this monster.

I look to the aged and torn face. A gaping hole sits where his organs would have been. I cry out as Gaston looks down at me with eyes of pure darkness. No pupils or irises, just eyes flooded in black. Black veins spread and shudder like webs in the wind beneath his grey skin.

"You left me," his croaked and broken voice whispers to me. My pounding heart doesn't help me as I try to calm myself. He is just part of my imagination. It is my mind getting to me. "Novid and I are very alone in the darkness, Ariadae."

Help. I need help but I can't speak. My words are logged in my throat like a thick hairball. I might vomit at the horrid stench radiating from his deteriorating skin. It hangs in thick slabs that pull towards the ground. Why isn't Jeremiah coming? Can't he see Gaston?

Gaston's hand rises and he tucks a strand of my short hair behind my ear like a lover would do. His voice is like a passing wind on the night air. "I like your new hair."

"Dae, is anyone there?" Jeremiah calls. *Yes*.

Stop. I want to say the words but they are clogged and clinging to the bottom of my throat. A soft tear slides down my face and he whispers, "Don't cry. We will be together soon but I need to go now. Your friend heard your calls for help." He grimaces and as Zube grips my arm making me scream into the night, Gaston wisps away into the air.

"What's wrong," Zube questions as he pulls me into a hug. His blonde hair tickles my nose as I close any gap between us embracing his wide chest. I can feel his mental hands pulling and digging around my mind. The marred and torn face flashes in my vision. I open my eyes getting rid of the image. Zube saw the monster, Gaston, in my mind. He searched my memories for them. "You're seeing them too?" Suddenly I don't feel utterly alone.

I nod. "How long have you seen been seeing them?"

"The entire month," Zube whispers. I shudder. I don't want to speak I don't want to mention him or what had just happened. I don't even want to think of his words. He thinks I will die soon but I will not. I need to fight with all the strength I have. I need to train with Jax.

We head back to where Jeremiah sits by the fire. Completely choosing to ignore the recent situation. I watch as Zube heats a blade with the flickering fire. The heat causes the steel dagger to grow orange and molten in the flames. He pulled the knife from the fire as it brightly illuminated his face in warm light. Spitting on the blade it sizzles in response. I don't want that on my skin but I ignore it.

"Okay are you-," Jeremiah whispers but I cut him off.

"Just do it."

Zube wanders over and in a quick movement I feel the worst pain of my mortal life as molten steel is pressed against my soft skin and exposed muscle. The fire spreads from the wound throughout my veins into my brain, heart; heating my entire body. My scream echoes into the night and I could have sworn even the monsters shuddered at my wails.

We neared the wastelands by morning light. The travel was shorter than Jax initially thought but I don't think the night could prepare me for what might be ahead. I am to kill the Rune Witch in the wastelands. I'm not even sure what this witch looks like but assuming from all my other monster encounters in Elkwood I'm certain she's terrifying.

The sky is a belt of pink blending to baby blue. The day will be upon us quickly and I can only hope that we don't die from the Rune Witch but rather I kill her with the Dragon Bone dagger. I don't want to give her the chance to tear me to shreds before I step foot into the wastelands, whatever they may be. They could be a deserted span of sandy dunes or possibly a clearing of tall grass that reaches for the Gods above. Either way, it doesn't matter so long as I know them when I see them.

I look to Jax, his face set in a heavy glare; I follow his eyes as they burrow into the back of Jeremiah's skull. Jealousy? A Fae warrior is envious of Jeremiah? It couldn't be because I hugged him earlier. The embrace was quick and harmless, well at least I thought it was. Jeremiah did kiss me that first night in Elkwood, and he said he had feelings for me. I have feelings for him too but not in the same way he may be thinking. I thought I loved him, but I love Jax…Do I? I am not quite sure what love is anymore.

From what I've read throughout my years, love is something that makes you ache. It's a beautiful feeling that is given to us by the moon's power. We fall in love because we are connected to the other person. A part of us is buried deep within the other person and we love to see where it's hidden. What part of me is inside of my significant other? It's like a mystery game that doesn't give any clues. We need to travel and search for whoever holds the piece that completes us. Once someone finds their piece and the lovers are together they both can finally be whole again. I can't help but feel like a piece of me is within Jax, but he can't find it or he doesn't even know it's there.

"We're almost there," Jax whispers. I look away from him to the trees around us. They are grey, cracked, and splintering. The branches reach out like pointed claws and the leaves have disappeared from sight. Loud groans escape the swinging branches on the passing wind. Everything seems fogged, greyed over, in a never ending gloom. I can barely see the blue sky above through the dark, brittle canopy of trees above.

This witch could be anything. I wonder why she can't leave the Rune Yard. Maybe she is protecting something. She must be wicked and gangly, a torture to the eyes. My heart begins to pound as I whisper, "What is the Rune Witch?" I'm not sure if I want to know the answer.

"Her name is Irene and she is one of the three guardians of Elkwood," Jax answers. I've never read or heard anything about the three protectors of Elkwood. "There is Irene, Guardian of the Rune Yard; Ir, Guardian of the Gods; and lastly Irian, Guardian of the Tree of Light. They all are strong, and evil in their own ways. They can only be killed in three different ways"

"Why does Irene protect the Rune Yard?" Jeremiah asks. He is as scared as I am. I can see the fright in his eyes even though his face is in a firm stare.

"The Rune Yard is a prison where all of the worst beasts ever created by Prometheus live. They are buried beneath the Rune Stones, which look like head stones but have a glowing Rune. If a human lays a hand upon a Rune Stone, it can unlock the beast within and the abomination will tear apart Abella piece by piece. "

This path to the Tree of Light may be the hardest thing I've ever done. I don't know how I will kill her with the dragon bone dagger but I need to think quickly. I think we are walking into the Rune Yard now.

A large break in the trees releases us to a giant clearing made of slated rocks. All the jagged slates pile along each other and make paths over, under, around, and through each other. It's like a labyrinth.

"Well, let's try not to die," Zube laughs. I look to him glaring, stupid idiot. Who knows if the witch can hear us now? She could be watching from behind a slated pile of stones. I am starting to have the feeling something *is* watching us.

"Zube, do you have a Fae form," Jax politely whispers. Zube nods in answer and Jax press his eyes to him seeming to tell him to transform. I've never really thought about Zube having another form other than his human body. Jax whispers to all three of us, "Irene can smell human blood, so Jeremiah, Ariadae stick with either Zube or I." I go to move towards Jax but Jeremiah gives me a glaring look. His eyes are squinting in assumption. He will never trust Jax even after everything he has done for us. Jax has kept me alive so many times…, wait, has he? Suddenly I can't help to be skeptical. *I* saved us in the store at the Summer Kingdom and *I* rescued everyone from the Summer Kingdom during the Summer Solstice. There was the time when he used his wind powers on the bridge so I could throw the mountain ash into the gusts. I have put so much trust in him for thinking that he saved me, but it's been me saving everyone's asses over and over!

"Zube you're with me. Let's all split up and find the witch. We will take this step by step." I am resenting that I need to separate from Jeremiah and Jax in a prison for the most lethal killers on the continent, maybe even the world. I also need Jeremiah to trust Jax even though I'm not sure if *I* trust him completely. I know nothing about him now that I think of it. I will ask him some questions later, but right now I need to focus on what lies ahead.

Zube leads me up a slate hill to the top of a flat rock. A pillar slightly taller than I am is jaggedly cut and protruding from the grey stone. It looks like something from a temple ruin. The rune is two circles with jagged lines through it, and through the circles, faintly glows a warm orange. It pulses like a flickering flame.

What beast could be breathing and living beneath my feet, forever trapped within the rock surrounding it? This rune is like the lock on a prison gate. If the lock is opened, the prison gate can swing wide open releasing the criminal inside. No matter how tempting it is to run my hand along the carved rune, I make sure not to touch any pillar. I look around at the hundreds of slate piles, all topped with pillars, adorned in runes of all shapes, designs, and carvings. At the opposite end of the Rune Yard I see her hunched back, petting a Rune Stone. That slate pile is taller than all of the others and it is surrounded by slowly melting, glittering candles. It is a shrine of some sort.

"Over there," I whisper and point to the glowing shrine. "She is across the yard so you should shift now."

Zube nodding blinds me in a flashing light. His scars and rugged skin is now smooth and soft. His hazel eyes are blindingly bright and his teeth are pointed canines as he grins at me. Even with his strange pointed ears he is handsome, though not as good looking as Jax or Lunan.

"Well that's not nice," he croons as he read my thoughts.

"Prick," I spit venomously and he grins. I run in a crouch and leap over the small labyrinth path below and climb up the little hill. He follows, laughing, as if he thinks it's a game. I couldn't be more serious right now and I roll my eyes at his sly smile. That lopsided grin is something he probably gives every girl he wants to bed. If I wasn't a princess, or a person of morals, I may have let him take me there one day.

The witch only strokes the one rune and ignores the infiltration going on behind her. I thought she could smell the humans in the Rune Yard, unless Zube and Jax's Fae scent truly does mask my and Jeremiahs human smells. Irene doesn't seem to be protecting all of the Rune Stones. She is protecting *a* Rune Stone.

We leap from pile to pile ducking behind the pillars. We won't risk her seeing us. I try to be quiet when I take each leap, but when I land against a pile of slates, pieces break beneath my feet and clatter to the stones twenty or so feet below. Zube's Fae strength lets him make the leap and he helps pull me up. I get my feet beneath me and my pounding heart thrums a bit less than before.

"Thanks," I breathe letting the word catch on a passing gust of wind. He nods back and we look to the witch. She is facing our direction with a cocked head. I choke on my air and swallow my stomach, which has leaped into my throat. She heard the falling pebbles. Irene must be like the High Fae, being able to hear almost everything within a good forty foot radius. They can hear hitched hearts, and lies on tongues.

She straightens her stature and goes back to the Rune Stone adorned with candles and bones. Whatever she is doing seems much more sinister than we imagine. She is conjuring something. Zube leaps to a pile, which is right next to her slated pile, which is part of the mountain. There are two flat walls carved from the mountain, and the pillar is near the corner. I leap to the pile on the opposite side. Maybe Zube will come in and pin her down so I can kill her. Her hunched back is covered in thick white scars and her hair looks to be made of coral. It's a dark mahogany, and her skin is the palest of greys and pulls in odd places. She wears a dress of human and faerie limbs and I hold back a gag from her stench. Arms are the skirts and a ribcage is her top. I don't want to know who she killed to make her clothes, or what animal she got that big ribcage from. I just want to kill her and get to the Ravine of Wisps.

Slowly. I need to take this slowly and quietly. She mustn't see me. I crawl towards her slate. When I step on the flat, jagged edge of the hill, pebbles fall. Her body stiffens. I go taut and my heart beats like a running horse. Unsheathing the blade, I leap to her hill. My landing was silent. She relaxes and begins rubbing some form of plant across the stone. Sage, she is taking the soft green leaves of sage and dragging it across the stone pillar staining it green. The streaks remind me of someone wiping blood across a wall. Shaking the image from my mind I approach her. My beating heart pushes adrenaline into my veins and I feel more alive with each quick reverberating beat.

For my father. For my father. For my father is all I think as I lift the blade in the air and angle the glinting tip at her back. She turns before I can drive the knife into her skin. She grips my wrist, squeezing it with Faerie strength. I wince at the bone crushing pressure and her eyes are just some form of brown moss. She wraps her other hand around my throat. She begins to hiss words at me, "I heard you in my Rune Yard, girl." Her voice is like crackling wood from a burning fire. Every word gives you a shudder as she drags the vowels through the embers. It purrs like an army of spiders crawling through my nightmares and I know that not only Evaflora's liquid voice will stop Irene's crackling evil from filling my nightmares.

I pull against her bone-cracking strength and her body shudders like a chill rattled her bones, but it last too long to be a chill. It's more like a demonic twitch.

"Don't you dare fight against me, mortal. You're weak and shattered; I doubt that Fae boy will heal your broken heart. It's in too many pieces for even his calloused fingers to fix!" She brutally verbalizes my own fears about my feelings for Jax to me. Where is he? Where's Zube?

"Don't you speak of him like you know who he is," I manage to rasp through my clogged throat. I can't stop the impeccable fear that rattles my bones. We seem to twitch in unison.

"Who is the mortal that entered my home with the thoughts of murdering me? Of course it was you Ariadae," She whispers and her decaying breath heats my face. My pounding heart stops as she looks to the dagger in my white knuckled hand. "I know who your mother is and what things she will put into your mind. You came here for her bidding, didn't you child?"

I don't know why I say this but the words are passing my lips before I can stop the venom behind each one. "If you were truly smart enough to speak my fears, then you would surely be able to understand that I didn't come here for my mother." I smile at her devilishly, trying to duplicate Evaflora's wicked grimaces. "I came here to kill you, and get what I need to save my father, my kingdom."

If she has eyes beneath the clotted moss I would assume they widened but she only squeezed my wrist and throat until I was screaming and groveling on my knees for her to stop. I need to hold onto the dagger. I need to kill her, but I can't. I can't lose it and she will break my arm if I don't let go. I don't want to let go. I can't let go.

My fingers go slack as I lose the circulation in my right hand and drop the dagger; it clatters against the dark slates under me, holding a beast within. A monster with unruly strength and power beyond the stars is just beneath me and I don't feel it roiling or roaring from within the stone. It's almost quiet like the river I floated in until I was taken by the Dreag and was 'saved' by my mother.

I hold and wince at the crack I felt splinter through my forearm before my hand went slack. She broke my arm and my hand is limp. I deny the thought of resetting my bone. My thudding heart makes me move quickly. I drop to the stones and scramble for the daggers hilt. The shining blade glints the day sun off its silvery edge. Inches from my grasp, I reach with every muscle, vein, and artery, but when Irene grips my hair dragging me away, I cease my stretch and scream. I look out to the slates around me and notice Zube is gone, missing. He left me.

As I am pulled farther and farther from the dagger I see flashing memories of my mother dragging me across the patio, her cold hands gripping my beautiful, wavy, long… I grab the taut hair that's left on my head. How can I get away from Irene? She is so beyond evil and darkness, I barely feel that light inside myself. It's being stifled by her radiating night and I have nothing to stop it. She is breaking me from the inside out.

I can't let her win.

I can't let my mother win. She won't win.

I writhe and thrash with every bit of strength left in my core and I let her struggle as I flail about like a fish out of water. I never stop the scream and my vocal cords have strengthened since entering this forest. I have screamed and screamed so much that even my voice will no longer be hoarse from my wails. I am growing stronger, capable, and more influential with myself.

I dive through the flashing images of my mother and deep into the darkness I searched through in the medicine shop back at the Summer Kingdom. I dig and dig through the impenetrable night that is within me. Somewhere hidden is that twisted cord of my powers. The glittering thread, I need to find it before my blood spills down this slate hill.

My face is before the Rune Stone, its surface still stained with the green sage. The rune on its surface is four triangles meeting at a rhombus center point which is encircled. The symbol is black and empty like the abyss I mentally dive back into.

Burrowing deeper into the oblivion inside myself, I dive for what I need. I need some small shining piece of thread. Even something as tiny as a toothpick can save me. I so easily gripped the glowing cord of my power in the herbal shop but now I am having trouble.

Irene grips my jaw and forces me to look at her, pulling me from my mind she says, "I want you to touch it." Gesturing to the Rune stone I shake my head. I will never lay my hand upon one of these many Rune Stones if it does what I was told. "Lay your hand on the rune you naïve child!" I am not some imbecile. She acts like I don't know what happens if I touch these runes. She wants me to release a beast into Elkwood that would destroy Abella. Nobody could stop it, not even Prometheus. I won't go down in history as the girl who caused the destruction of the continent. "We need the Akuji back, Ariadae." What the hell is an Akuji?

Irene presses her hand into the back of my head and grips my broken forearm. Light flashes across my vision and it's not the cord of power hiding within my mind. It is part of the pain and explosions that make my body want to coil into myself. I pull against her as she further tries to place my hand on the stone. Water burns my eyes and I barely see through the pain and roar in my ears. I'm screaming, but I don't care. Let my mother hear my wails and come running to watch me die. I would allow the witch to kill her if I could get away from this; get away from the pressure along my cracked bones. Get away from the building weight clouding my skull in a storm of explosion and torment. Get away from my fingertips getting closer to the Rune Stone.

I feel the cold rock of the rune's surface and I wince, a tear falling, and I see it, feel it. I can touch the dagger lying behind Irene and the warmth of the hilt rises into my mind. I look into my oblivion and floating there, suspended in darkness is a glowing white thread. A star in the night, but the star is as thin as a fine hair. I take my chance and tug on the warmth of the thread, the hilt of the dagger, and when I pull the cord of my power, the thread vanishes. My fingers are splayed along the Rune Stone and I choke on the sudden pause in the hammering rhythm of my heart. I let go of the stone and Irene releases me.

A cry escapes me as I slump to the stones and let the cool slate flood my hot skin with chill. I am enjoying the feeling of the crisp stone on my shuddering body. I did it. I killed Irene; Guardian of the Rune Yard. I will now be known as Ariadae the Fae murderer, guardian slayer, and Equadorian savoir. My only priority is to save my kingdom, whatever has been happening in Elkwood isn't part of my problems.

She isn't dead, she is mumbling something, Irene, and her words are gurgling. I just lay there and then I hear her hacking cough. I sit up and look at her body shaking along the stone. The dagger's tip glinting between her breasts. She is as limp and frail looking as the many decaying arms she uses as a dress. She was created by Prometheus for a reason, to guard the Rune Yard and she was breaking the rules. She tried to release a beast into the world and I'm glad I killed her. I am glad that a thread of my power came to me before she placed my hand on the Rune Stone. the ground is still but I am waiting for a rumble or reverberation of the beast leaving its prison.

"Get...get...," Irene gargles as more blood trickles from her lips. "Get him...,"

"Get who? What are you saying," I asked panicked. I am not one to care for dying beasts but she is trying to say something and if it has to do with my father then I will listen. I can see the life slipping from her every passing second.

"Get. Him. Back," she chokes on her last words. Get who back? Who was she trying to get back and where to? I want to shake her back to her life but every part of her skin and looks repulses me. Her chest falls and caves into the ribcage deeply and stops heaving. She's gone.

She wasted her final breaths on giving me directions to something I don't know. I don't know who she was speaking of so how can I do anything to help? I shouldn't help her it isn't important. Irene's reasoning is evil, demonic, and ritualistic. She's dead. It's not like I could help her even if I wanted to.

Boots scrape and grunts come from the three males rising along the slated stones. Jeremiah runs to me but stops to walk around the dark pooling blood. I hug him and wince at the pain in my forearm.

"She's dead?" he questions. I nod to him and we both look away from the body, to each other, our eyes meeting. His warm chocolates meet my open garden. His brown eyes have flecks of gold and tiny bits of orange glowing near the irises. His eyes are beautiful, like the chandeliers at home, and the views from the Summer Kingdom balconies and the Fae males that always seem to find ways to be around me. I miss it, everything, home.

"She wasted her last breaths on asking me to bring someone back," suddenly it clicks. When she was forcing me to put my hand on the stone she said she needs to Akuji to come back. "What's an Akuji?"

Jax climbs up the hill. His face pales from my words. "The Akuji is a monster that Faerie parents tell children about to make them behave."

"Then why would Irene need the Akuji back?" Jeremiah questions.

Jax's eyes grow wide. "That beast that attacked us last night...I knew I recognized it. That was the Akuji." I think of the giant talons and ape like body. If my father told me about that as a child I would definitely behave. "I didn't know it was real." Jax adds.

Zube climbs up onto the hill. He was right near me when I last saw him. He should've helped me or tried to rescue me in some form instead of letting that smelling guardian hassle me.

I march up to him and as he rises above me I slam my palms into my chest and he falls from the slated pile onto the flat stone below with a loud thud. Jeremiah and Jax scream from behind me as I shout accusingly, "And where were you?"

His brows knot together and he glares at me as he tries to get wind back into his lungs. I wait impatiently for his most likely obnoxious answer.

"What is this about," Jax runs to me and looks between Zube and I. Zube was supposed to help me, save me if I needed it and back there I did need his help. I even feared she may make me touch the stone before I could kill her.

"Our friend here, left me for Irene," I grunt and spit, the salvia landing atop Zube's head of tousled blonde hair. What was he so busy doing that he couldn't get the princess of Equadoria out of Irene's filthy grasp? Rage is all I can feel as flames burn beneath my skin. "If it weren't for my powers, which I can barely control, I'd be dead and a giant beast would be wandering Abella."

"WHAT," Jax screams making fear bubble in my stomach. "Why didn't you help her?"

Now we are all waiting for answers and Zube just glares at me like I'm some kind of monster who took his toy. Apparently he has gotten his breath back because he sits up.

"I was looking for you," he claims, looking to Jax. "I thought you would stab her and then we could leave. I didn't know you were going to get attacked and have the knife thrown from your hand."

"It wasn't thrown you bastard, she cracked the bone in my forearm and I lost circulation in my hand." I am only just now able to move the first joints of my fingers. The veins aren't full of blood yet and they feel like pins and needles along my skin.

Jax's finger brush mine in warning and my heart begins to beat. Jax just whispers, "Your heart fluttered when you said you were looking for me. Explain that to me, please." Fae know when people are lying by the beat of their heart and Zube lied. He lied to Jax, Jeremiah and especially me. I have trusted this kid and he even fought in my father's army against Solaria. Why is it now, after all of this, he is lying to us, to *me*.

Fear crackles along Zube's features but disappears as quickly as it came. I unstring my bow and draw an ash arrow, aimed at his heart. I have killed so many faeries and I am at the time now that another one wouldn't hurt.

"Five seconds."

"Until what," Zube asks confused. He is so unintelligent it almost pains me.

"Until she fires the arrow and kills you," Jeremiah breaks into the conversation. I don't appreciate everyone being a part of this although they do need to witness this. "She is saying you have five seconds to explain yourself."

"How can anyone explain something in five seconds?" The whine almost sounded like Evaflora's purring voice.

"Five," I groan.

"How can you blame me? I needed the money," Zube erupts immediately into explanation.

"Four," Jeremiah hisses and Zube coils into himself.

"I have spent my entire life suffering and she made the greatest deal."

"Three," I say. The string is pulling forwards and my fingers are itching to release the arrow.

"She said if I don't help you she would pay me an unfathomable amount of money."

"Two." My voice is almost not audible. The wind is taking my sound and I don't want to say anything, but sulk at his betrayal.

"Please don't kill me. She promised to end my banishment in the Kingdoms," Zube begs now pressing his back into the slate hill I leaped from to kill the witch. "I made the deal with…"

"Who did you bargain with, Zube," Jax growls like a feral animal.

"Evaflora."

"One."

I roar as I let go of the string. I wasn't going to shoot the arrow only because I need to trust people. I wanted him to be a part of my Kingdom one day. He could've stood beside me on the Equadorian throne as a military leader, but once my mother's name left his lips I forgot everything other than rage and blood.

I fall to the ground as the whole world shudders. Zube screams but only for the arrow that protrudes in the stone beside his head. The ground is rumbling beneath me and I think it's because I touched the Rune Stone. The beast Irene made me summon is now crawling from its grave below to destroy Abella. It's my entire fault.

The slated stones begin to shake pebbles from the stone surfaces and thunder booms through the Rune Yard as the slate hills crack and separate. A very dark jagged line cuts through the ground and splits the stone beneath us. Zube scrambles up the hill to us but I just look away. He can die for all I care.

I need to find a way out. There doesn't seem to be anything other than the flat stone walls before me or the separating land behind me. A beast, anything, the worst abomination imaginable, will crawl out of there and I won't have anywhere to hide. I dash around in panic and my beating heart crashes against my chest harshly. The hammering rhythm is painful.

"Ariadae!" someone shouts from behind me and I ignore them. I fall to the stone as another ravaged shudder shakes the earth beneath me. I grab the dragon bone dagger before the ground splits and sheath it in my boot. Right as I slide the blade into the fur I am flying.

The slates have vanished and we are falling, plummeting down into the dark abyss. Wind squeals in my ears and I scream as the light of day above starts to become a small sliver of light. It leaves me alone and diving into darkness that will swallow me whole. This ravine will devour me and any power I have left. I am losing what is left of me from Zube's betrayal and this killing darkness. Its pressure builds in my chest and I think I might regurgitate my innards.

Other howls billow around me like singing angels but we are all plummeting and not flying. Jeremiah, Jax, and Zube all fall around me and I can't help but wish Zube doesn't die when we splat against whatever lies below. I want him to die slowly and painfully.

The ice cold water was a punch to the face. Icicles seemed to jab against my skin and when I look around we are all in a world of sparkling bubbles. The water glows like blue stars in a liquid form. I didn't see the water until I was beneath the surface with no air in my lungs. Rising to the surface as quickly as I can I see something magnificent.

It's like washing away the film over my eyes; this place had a glamour casted upon itself to look like a dark ravine. It's the complete opposite. Temples carved in the mountain side have arching bridges high above the water we are submerged in and the grass is littered in dancing glowing stars, wisps.

I am in the Ravine of Wisps.

CHAPTER THIRTEEN

I pull myself from the glowing river and lay on the silken grass, the soft green fingers tickling my wet face and arms. If this wasn't the entrance to the Ravine of Wisps, than I would be splayed out in a pile of blood. I mean Jax, Jeremiah, and Zube- which I wouldn't mind- would also be piles of gore. This isn't the beast that should've come from the Rune Stone. The rune on the pillar was dark unlike the others. What if that was the Akuji's prison? That would explain why she was trying to bring it back and nothing came out of the stone when I touched it.

I truly thought the ground separating was a monster escaping to Abella and I would have gone down into history being the Abella destroyer. I'm glad I didn't.

Coughing and gurgling makes me look to Jeremiah, sodden with glowing droplets, crawling from the river. I yank off my cloak, heavy with water, and run to him. Gripping his thick biceps I pull him to his feet.

"You're okay, right," I press. I want to make sure he is okay before I help Jax who is swimming towards the shore, up river.

"Yeah…How about you?"

"I am perfectly fine, I think," is all I grunt before a fist connects with my jaw. I fall to the ground and pull the dragon bone dagger from my boot. I swear I am going to gut Zube, even in front of all these peaceful wisps.

"That was for almost killing me!" he yells.

Jeremiah pulls his blade from his golden scabbard and Zube copies. They begin a raging sword fight. Men are always quick to pull out their swords. Rising, I march up to the two and start pulling Jeremiah away from Zube.

"Coward," he shouts absurdly. Why won't Jeremiah just let me fight my own battles?

"Because you're a Lady," Zube yells above Jeremiah as he twirls his blade in a wicked taunt.

"Didn't stop you from punching me, prick." He is truly an ass. A mule looking, rude, and absolutely disrespectful ass. I hate him.

"You deserved it," he fires back and the comment only makes Jeremiah try even harder. Their steel blades scream against each other and they keep moving in a stupid scrabble.

"For what," I retort with vicious anger. "You were making deals with my mother!"

I run to the two boys and I push Jeremiah away. He stumbles to the grass as I press the blade against Zube's throat. "I am sick of blood being spilled from my hands." Jeremiah needs to stop doing this for me because Elkwood has destroyed me, mentally and physically. "Now I have killed many trained faeries, surely killing a banished, outcast lesser faerie wouldn't be too hard to do." The threat was truly primal and I don't know why I spoke like that to him but I want him to fear me, Jeremiah to stop protecting me, and I want Jax to start fighting for me. "Now if we weren't inside a holy place your blood would already be staining the grass."

Easy enough. I think I got my point across. I sheath the blade and leave the three boys behind me as I head towards the purple stairs that lead to a temple's entrance.

Wandering the halls of the temple is only making me worrisome. I know the Ravine of Wisps is a sacred place and nothing sinister would happen here, but the corridors are empty and quiet, *too* quiet. Lunan told me of the sacred temple back in the Summer Kingdom. Each step echoes through the hall and I stare out the gaping arches along the wall that open to the ravine's stunning view. Far up ahead, a waterfall dumps beautiful tendrils of the blue water into the river. The flowing water looks like the diamond antlers, light blue, translucent, truly ethereal.

Trees with pink pedals are scattered across the green banks below and the air throws wind currents through the open tunnels of the temples. Up ahead, I can see a bridge connecting this temple to another one on the opposite side of the ravine.

Jax moans from behind me, "Where do you think the Oracle could be." I almost forgot the whole reason why we were here. We just need to get the Oracle and find a way out of this worshipping place. They call this place a temple but I haven't seen any monks. I'm starting to even think what if all of the holy has left? Although I would imagine it being protected what if everyone left or died?

"Better question," Jeremiah says, his voice echoing into the ravine. "What does the Oracle look like?" He's right; we don't know what it is. But what we do know is that we need it for Prometheus to find the Tree of Light. I don't know where to even look between the two palaces. It's like trying to find a single flower inside a rainforest. The odds of discovering the Oracle are small, but at least they are here. Hopefully the Oracle is still here.

"Let's split up," I say to the three wandering aimlessly as we breach the arching doorway to the bridge. "Zube and Jeremiah," Wait I don't want those two together after their quarrel before. "Zube and Jax go to the other temple." I clarify. "Jeremiah and I will search this one. If you find anything meet on the bridge. Be on the bridge, Oracle or not, in three hours." They all nod in agreement and Jeremiah saunters to me grinning as Zube and Jax head onto the wooden bridge.

I look to him as we duck into another corridor. He laughs as I stare at his humane features, untouched by the Fae and magic around him.

"Why do you really think Zube made a deal with Evaflora," my words are stale and dry like the air that seems to constrict my breath.

"I'm not sure, but his reason seems understandable in a very strange way," he mutters. Water drips somewhere in the hall filling the silence with something other than tension. "You like him don't you?"

Does he truly believe I would like him after his possible betrayal? Who does Jeremiah think I am, some unintelligent imbecile?

"I hate Zube more than you know," I retort violently, letting the venom sink in.

"No," He fires back looking to me. His words are now a mere whisper that is almost drowned out by the dripping water and roaring waterfall at the other end of the ravine. "I mean Jax."

My heart flutters at his name. Of course I like him but not in the same way I like Jeremiah. Jeremiah is something special and different that just floats on the surface for me to always grab. Jax is something far beyond that, deep and mysterious, appearing and disappearing into the darkness that lurks below the surface, alone, quiet, unexplored. I want to just dive in and explore the surface but always have an anchor, Jeremiah, hovering above me at the surface. I need him more than he knows so.

"I don't know," I lie. I don't want to lie to him but sometimes I have to. Now is one of those times.

I see a large door up ahead that reaches the ceiling. Once we reach it the stone seems to be carved of the different Gods. They are granting powers, answering wishes, writing Abella's Codex. It's the ancient book which holds all the rules, laws, and stories that made Abella-Abella.

"What do you think is inside," I say, my voice flowing into the ravine.

"Scrolls, old manuscripts; anything you would find in a holy sanctuary, I guess," he whispers. A large hole in the wall beside the door seems like a way to open it. I push against the carved stone and it is firmly locked. I don't want to stick my arm into the hole. Who knows what could be in there, it's surely a trap that will sever my hand.

"Jeremiah," I whisper. "There's a hole in the wall. I think it's how we open the door." I don't want to do it but I know Jeremiah wouldn't. I doubt he even cares about what could be behind the door.

I graze the rim of the dark hole. It looks like a gaping mouth waiting to take a bite of its next meal. Hopefully it isn't my arm. My heart thumps in my ears as I slide my arm into the cold tube. Its jagged walls scrape against my skin as I feel the end of the hole. A small divot in the stone on the floor of the tube has small holes along its surface and is damp from water. Where is the water coming from this deep in a hole?

Feeling around I feel nothing but the sharp stones. It's pointless, how could this be a way to open the door? I don't see any other levers or handles so this has to be it. I look to Jeremiah and say, "Look around for another way to open the door." He just nods and begins searching the hall like a hound tracking an animal on a hunt.

Something taps on my hand making it moist, wet. Water is somehow dripping inside the hole? That would explain the dampness of the small bowl carved in the stone and the dripping sound I heard when walking down the hall. The water dripping doesn't answer how to open the door. The small divot had holes in it so if it is some form of pressure plate the water is leaking through.

I tap on the pressure plate and it doesn't budge. It is unlocked through water, but the dripping didn't work. May be a large amount of water needs to be poured on the bowl at one time. I simply cup my hand to the slowly dripping tap and wait as it fills. Droplet by droplet my hand begins to fill but slowly, way too slowly. It's as if every drop that breaks from the top of the cave pocket falls in slow motion landing in a rippling still pond.

Jeremiah stumbles back to me, gazing in confusion. His brow furrows and he says, "It's been almost an hour, Dae. What are you waiting for?" It's been an hour? It couldn't have been an hour unless I truly was in a daze. I would only guess minutes passed by, not an entire third of our searching time.

I try to answer him but I can't breathe. The air leeches from my body and my hand full of water spills into the divot making a loud clank. My chest has tightened so heavily that I grovel to the ground in a heaving mess. What is happening to me? I think the water has poisoned me or possibly some form of magic is controlling me like it did my father. Will I become an evil tyrant like him and kill people.

No, it can't be that. Jeremiah runs to me and helps me try to stand. He keeps asking if I'm alright but I don't hear him. I only see the movement of his soft, thick, caring lips, cracked from the ravines chill. I wheeze a bit but I do finally catch my breath and realize what happened. The pressure hasn't vanished because I have forgotten about it. I lost this stone in my chest so long ago that my body doesn't recognize the foreign feeling. This weight, pressure, constriction in my chest is the senses of an emotion. It is a warning sign for my mind which can't see anything coming until it happens. The hard, cold, and heavy stone is back. My *fear* is back, but what is it trying to warn me of?

A loud series of clicks and scraping comes from behind the stone door. Water trickles from the hole in the wall in a small river and slides to the floor where it pours into a gutter. Following the water that travels up onto the door, rising, the water is rising and filling the carving. This is a magic I've never seen, controlling the elements isn't something average people can do, unless they have immortal genes, immortal abilities. Unless they're *Fae*.

I take a step back as the doors slide open and the water leaves the carvings and pours onto the floor. Jeremiah was right; the room is filled from floor to ceiling with scrolls and manuscripts. It reeks of aging parchment and dust. I wonder how many religious and sacramental works have been inked onto these pages and scrolls. I want to devour the words and stories that are written within.

Somewhere, buried beneath this history is the Oracle, but we need to learn exactly what it is we're exactly looking for. We came here on a story of a legend and so far the story has been true, hopefully it remains that way.

"Wow," is all Jeremiah says and I couldn't agree more.

"Let's dig in," I say and the words carry on the acoustics of the open chamber. Its vaulted ceiling is domed in glass and the sun peaks through. How could light even reach this deep into the ravine?

Jeremiah starts on a basket of tightly rolled, yellow scrolls but I don't move a step. The stone is heavy and dormant. I need to look around this place no matter how dangerous it is.

Stepping forward the stone begins to beat like a thrumming heart pounding beneath my collarbone. We can't be in here.

"Jeremiah," I call to him and something scurry's deep within the chamber. "We need to go."

He looks to me, puzzled and reading a scroll of some ancient language. "Why?"

It steps from behind a pile of leather bound books. Its robes hang in swaths of brown fabric and darkness covers most of the body. The stone is now punching my insides. Jeremiah turns slowly toward the robed being and drops the scroll he was holding.

"Hello, Ariadae Vox. Have you come to me for pleasure or for your own benefit?" The groveled being moans, its voice deep and masculine. I take a step back, a step towards freedom, and a step from the druid before me as a scream pulls from my lips.

CHAPTER FOURTEEN

~Jax~

I didn't want to leave her. She was supposed to search the temple with me but now she is with Jeremiah. If he even lays a hand on her, or kisses her, I will tear him from the… I'm not jealous; I'm protecting her, always. Never will I love her the way Jeremiah does, I can basically smell his flushed body from the opposite side of the ravine. Lust is a smell that floods your nostrils with the scent of flowers, which need to burn in acid.

"Jax," Zube says uneasily. A growl ripples in my throat and he puts his hands up in defense. "Sorry, kitty." A laugh erupts from him and I drag his body and press him against the wall. His soft human flesh is barely aged against my immortal strength. His neck veins throb against my fingers and I grin. Oh the scent of fear is so rejuvenating.

"You call me that one more time and I will rip out your tongue," I whisper and the metallic tang of fear rises into my nose. "Zube, if you ever hurt Ariadae or betray her again and I will help her send you to Evaflora, who will surely drink your blood and turn you into what your mother became."

Sadness consumes his features and twist abruptly to anger. Snarling in my face, his breathing heating my cheeks, Zube spits, "Don't speak of my mother like you know what happened!"

"I watched you run from that town house," I voice quietly. Some nights when Ariadae was deep in slumber I feared potential threats from Elkwood so I would leave her chambers and the castle to wander the streets. I knew that the Forsaken couldn't leave the forest but even worse monsters, like Evaflora, my father, any High Fae, could just wander from their kingdom into Equadoria. So I couldn't help my instinct, to protect. One particular night when I was near the outer slums I heard screaming so using my sense of smell I found the hut. Blood was pooling from the door and a small boy came stumbling out in fear and watching the inside. I watched him stare into his home, soaked in his family's blood. His sister, father and baby brother were murdered by an abomination. I didn't help him for I feared that he would know what I was. I could smell his heritage from beneath his human form, I can smell it now, and what makes it even worse is I can smell it on Ariadae.

I later tracked down Zube's mother and left her Forsaken body in ribbons at the back of the castle. Everyone thought the ruined corpse was Ariadae's mother but even guilt couldn't bring me to tell the magic-hating king what I am and what I did. I won't even tell Dae.

I drop Zube and leave him to the wall rubbing at his throat. "You were there? You didn't help me? Fuck You!"

I recoil from him. "I killed your mother and protected the kingdom. *You* weren't my responsibility."

Zube just rolls his eyes. "We'll discuss this later. There's something up ahead."

We run down the hall to the door which is wide open. Zube follows in pursuit and I ignore his presence all together, I need to focus on finding the Oracle. I can only assume it would be some form of object or map that can only be opened by Prometheus. People only get directions from maps.

The room is littered in moss and ivy that twine up the walls and along the ribbed surface of pillars. This place, before the abandonment must have been beautiful. It may not be abandoned yet. The thought makes my heart jump; I hope Ariadae hasn't gotten into any trouble in the other temple. Suddenly I am aware of the distance between us.

I walk to a wall that is engraved with a mural which is also painted. It's a depiction of some war. A male Fae is wearing orange robes and is surrounded by red flames. This must have been part of the Kingdom wars. Kingdoms were battling against one another and surprisingly only one of the original six beings, who were guided to the Tree of Light, died. The High Fae of the Day Kingdom had been torn apart by Evaflora on the battlefield. Lunan has taken the dead Fae's throne and is now an even better ruler than Giordain ever was.

Across from the fire wielder on the mural is a depiction of a girl with snow white hair and robes of the bluest night. Bolts of blue lightning crackle around her and along the ground. The red fire and blue lightning clashes together, but what doesn't make sense is the third Fae. Someone of unknown gender wearing only a cloak of purple is floating above the two elemental wielders. This center Fae has some form of magic around its body in swirls and curling power of the darkest shade of violet. What kind of power are they conjuring? It isn't anything I have seen in my lifetime.

"Jax," Zube calls from across the chamber. He beckons me to him and I saunter over. "Do you think this is what we are looking for?" He points to a small dodecahedron made of glass on a pillar. A small glow pulsates from the center. It is openly sitting in a chamber with open doors, something seems a bit off, too easy, but I will let him grab it if it's a trap.

"Looks like it," I say gesturing to it. "Grab it and let's head to the bridge." My stomach rises in my throat and my heart begins to pound in my ears as he grips the delicate prism. I hold my breath and I can count the seconds between my heartbeats. Zube even hesitates before lifting it like he might not do it, but then he pulls it from the pillar, hugging it close to his chest. One second passes and we don't hear anything. Ten seconds soon becomes thirty and thirty soon becomes a minute of pure silence. It wasn't a trap, we can leave now. All we have to do is get to Ariadae and Jeremiah than leave the Ravine of Wisps. I am not even sure how we can leave this place. We will find a way out when we need to but right now I just want to go and see Ariadae, make sure she is alive and okay.

We head back through the hall and to the bridge. She isn't there so maybe she is still searching for clues. Or in danger?

A scream erupts through the ravine and I know it's hers. I've heard her scream one too many times and I sprint toward the sound of her vocal cords. I smell her fear before I even round the corner and see her in the hall with Jeremiah backing away from an illuminated chamber, before them is a figure in aging robes. Drawing my blade I pull Dae behind me. Her fingers on my shoulder send tingling sparks through my pores and veins helping the adrenaline pump quickly.

"An heir to not only a mortal throne but also a Fae Kingdom," the druid speaks to himself excitedly. He looks to me his golden eyes careening over my body, his stare only infuriates me. "Two heirs of Fae Kingdoms are in my presence."

I ignore his statement. "Who are you," I ask with wrath in my voice. Ariadae's fear doesn't rejuvenate me, it burns me and I will do anything to make her feel safe. I step forward, angling my blade toward the druid.

The man only laughs and says, "I am Croterra Samsara, the last druid in the Ravine of Wisps." Well that was easy enough. This mortal is way too gullible and easily persuaded.

"What is a druid," questions Jeremiah. How shocking.

Croterra wails in laughter and points his attention to the ignorant mortal, "A druid is a human who wields nature's abilities to protect the land. I know it may be hard for you to comprehend but you will learn of my kind."

Stepping around me Dae approaches the druid cautiously, still keeping a safe distance from the man. "Can you help us find something we need greatly?" Her voice is loud and tenacious like a queen's would be.

"And what is that my dear," He responds and his eyes seem to glow like he knows what she is going to say next. "The Oracle?"

My heart shutters. How could he have possibly known that? Well he did know Ariadae was a Fae just by looking at her and he knew of my origins as well. Croterra is smarter than we expected.

Ariadae quirks her head in question, she seems to wordlessly ask how.

"I have seen, read, and created many legends my girl. It's not every day a mortal slays one of the three guardians of Elkwood and enters the Ravine of Wisps. You're after something. Answers I assume."

I sheath my blade as I realize the threat this man poses is not violent. He wouldn't allow a battle to happen down here with the peaceful wisps floating about.

"What answers do you need?"

"It's not answers we need, Croterra. We need magic," Ariadae explains, and his eyes widen in shock as he looks at us all.

"What magic do you need, exactly?" He asks as a blue smoke begins to coil around his fingers and palm. What does he think we are going to take?

Ariadae looks between me and Zube and recedes a few steps, "We only need the Oracle, so we can take it to Prometheus. He will guide us to the Tree of Light and we can save my father."

She doesn't tell him everything but that's the gist of what he needs to understand. Ariadae looks to speak more but I grab her wrist stopping her. I don't want her revealing anything that will anger Croterra. Shaking my head the druid power vanishes as quickly as it came.

"Alright then," Croterra says becoming cheery. "Let me tell you the story of the Oracle."

~Ariadae~

We sat around the chamber filled with towering scrolls and manuscripts. I felt as if I were conversing with Gaston and Novid around a pit of fire in the forest. It was only a month ago which feels so long ago, but also so recent. I am losing time and we need to be home within a week. I can't waste any more days, or weeks for that matter, dallying about Elkwood. We have a path to follow, so we have to do is take the steps, but in big strides, no more baby steps.

The legend behind the Oracle, Croterra explained was that the Oracle was created by Prometheus's friend, Sapientiae, who made the object because Prometheus, after creating the Tree of Light and guiding the six individuals, planned to destroy any memory of the tree's location. Sapientiae knew that one day the Tree of Light, would be needed again so he made the Oracle to allow Prometheus to remember.

Sapientiae, being the god of wisdom, is very smart in doing this. I'm not sure how he could've known that one day the Tree would be needed, but I am glad he did. If he hadn't created the Oracle over a millennia ago, there would be no hope in saving my father. In the millennia that passed since its creation, I have been the only person to actually reach the Oracle. Heading to Nirvana where Prometheus dwells is a whole other adventure.

Once Croterra finishes explaining the creation behind the Oracle, we sit trying to make sense of it all. It explains a bit why Prometheus needs the Oracle to find the Tree of Light, but how could someone not come in search of the Oracle? How come Evaflora hasn't attempted to murder the Rune Witch? I did take the dragon bone dagger from her Kingdom. Something isn't quite adding up.

Zube flicks his attention to me and he nods in agreement; it was a slight bow of the head probably not to attract too much attention. Bastard, he read my thoughts but I'm glad someone is just as lost as I.

"Well it is getting late," Croterra starts, rising from the floor and dusting off his robes. He begins to shuffle towards the door. Gesturing to the chamber he says, "There are no accommodations so you all can sleep here in the monastery or even the grass outside, but I warn you. The wisps like to play games with the sleeping." With that creepy last statement he winks and exits the monastery leaving the carved doors wide open.

After he is safely out of earshot I walk to Zube and pull him aside. Pushing down the angry boil in my blood I ask, "Can you please avoid reading my thoughts?"

"I may have lied to you, Ariadae, but I am still a Sentinel for *your* Kingdom. I swore an oath to protect all those in right for the throne. I may not be your friend, but I am certainly not your enemy."

Something ripples in my skull. He knows every way to irritate me. My words spit out like acid, "You say you're not my enemy, but you did a good job working with my mother."

He steps back. A heavy thud presses against the back of my eyes and each beat sends darkness across my vision. My heart begins to pound in synchronization to the thud of my head. I need to control my power. I search in the void of my Ora and find the glowing cord, braided and glowing, and throbbing as if it will burst. Caressing the cords the throb slaps my mental fingers. My power is angry. The braid flares and light flashes through the darkness.

"What's going on," I choke out through my ragged breaths. My air is coming too fast and I can't breathe. I fear I might suffocate. "Help." My knees tremble in weakness.

Jax and Jeremiah run to me. "What did you do?" Jeremiah screams at Zube.

Help. Please. Stop the heavy pounding. My vision is almost black, but I see Jax jump into Zube's face, but the pounding is too loud. All sound is gone. All air is gone. Everything is about to leave my body when Croterra barrels in and scoops me into his arms. His lips move as if he is whispering to me.

The braid takes over the darkness. Light, glowing smoke fills the darkness and everything inside of me is on fire. My organs burn and the heavy thud makes my vision go away all together.

It's not even a minute and I feel calloused fingers drawing symbols across my skin in a wet substance. Runes. Croterra is painting runes on my body. Why? To stop the bubbling power? My organs no longer burn but when I look in at the braid of my Telekinae powers, it is a soft warm glow. It is still white, but no longer angry, pulsing, smoking. It's as if nothing has happened and the oblivion surrounding it has returned.

"Slowly open your eyes and sit up," Croterra's soft voice whispers to me. Listening I follow his directions and look around as I sit in a chamber in a temple on the other side of the ravine. I see Jax and Jeremiah through the open arches waiting along the railing beneath a bow.

"What-," I start, but Croterra presses his hand to my mouth then hands me a bowl of glowing liquid.

"That water is from the ravine's waterfall. The water can heal you," He says. "What happened to you is what we call a Flare," He explains and I quirk my head in question. "When a Fae's abilities haven't been used enough, or if they have let's say an excess buildup of magic, it will Flare. The power will sear you from the inside in an attempt to leave your body."

Gagging on the repulsive drink I nod in understanding. He further explains, "You being a mortal I question how your abilities could have flared because typically mortals have more trouble using their power than actually losing control of it." He looks about and wanders the room thinking to himself. His expressions show an extreme internal battle.

"You aren't a mortal."

The bowl clatters to the tile and I jump up. "What?" I squeal hoarsely. My throat is raw, was I screaming?

"You can't be a mortal, but you are a mortal. Something is different about you," He speaks as if I am some sort of alchemy project.

"I think that's more than obvious," I snap. I'm starting to feel as if everywhere I travel I am judged and questioned. I just want to be home.

"An immortal in a mortal's body... But that means...," His internal battle has become a verbal one, great. "The prophecy!" My mind immediately wanders to the prophecy I heard Evaflora talking about the first night I was in the Summer Kingdom.

He runs to me and drags me over to the far wall where a mural is painted and engraved in the stone. Three Fae using abilities in battle. One is surrounded by flames, the other is a woman with white hair and blue lightning bolts and the third a hooded figure surrounded by some swirling purple ability. Jax had been talking to Jeremiah about a mural he saw in the temple and I can't help, but wonder if this is the same one. From his description it sounds like it.

"This is the Prophecy of the Fae Druid of the Void," He says gesturing towards the depiction. "As it is told an Immortal born as a mortal, that'd be you."

"I got that." It's like I have a Fae trapped within my human body.

"Once connected to their Immortal genes, the being will become the Fae Druid of the Void. The most powerful of all druids."

"Why would the Fae Druid of the Void be the most powerful," I ask nervously. I don't want that to be me, I don't want to be an immortal. "Why would you think that's me?"

"All three Fae Druid's are the most powerful druids because they cannot be injured or affected by the magic they use or conjure at their own will."

"What do you mean affected, Croterra?"

He pulls the hood of his robe down revealing warm auburn eyes and a head full of shoulder length golden hair that is missing large patches where scars now litter his skull. Rolling up his sleeves I see the rippled torn skin of different injuries. My stomach turns at the sight of his marred skin.

"What happened to you," I question in fear. What monster of Elkwood could have destroyed him? How did he survive?

"Every time I use magic this is what happens," he whispers. "Druids are just humans who have trained to wield Fae like powers. Our bodies aren't made to have powers, so every time we cast a spell a cut or burn will adorn our skin."

I want to say I'm sorry, but I don't. He did that to himself and allowed the continuance of his own use. That is his fault, I don't feel bad. I don't. I also am alone with him and I don't even know who he is. He did save me, but I don't know if I can trust him. He thinks I am some Fae trapped in a human body. I do have powers, but it's only because of my mother.

Backing away I head for the closed door and push against it. He calls after me but I ignore him and run across the bridge to Jeremiah and Jax. I want to go, I want to leave and never come back.

Grabbing my bow and quiver I make sure that the dragon bone dagger is safe within my boot and I head back to where Jeremiah and Jax are standing near the corridor that leads out of the temple.

"What're you doing," Jeremiah asks with a furrowed brow.

"Leaving; do you have everything?" I say walking past them down the long hall towards the stairs we entered the temple on. Jax and I almost died for the supplies that we got in the Summer Kingdom so we don't want to forget all we have.

"Yes, we didn't have much anyways. Why are we leaving so suddenly?" He asks following me.

"Where's Zube? He has the Oracle correct?" I ignore Jeremiah's question and all of the sudden Zube comes around the corner of the railing and waits for me to descend the stairs before wrapping the cloak I dropped earlier across my shoulders. I don't say anything out loud but I mentally thank him. He knows I am not in the mood to talk with him. I am sick of everything I know changing and being ripped from my grasp.

"The Oracle is right here," he claims pulling the glass object from a satchel he had taken from the monastery.

"Let's leave," I groan and stomp towards the waterfall. The water is coming from somewhere so there is probably stairs or a way to climb up to the top.

"Why," Jax asks from behind me but I ignore him and let the billow of my cloak be his answer. My whole life is ruined from Elkwood and the quicker I get to Nirvana and then the Tree of Light, the sooner I will leave this damned forest.

"Why?" he pesters again. He doesn't need an explanation. He doesn't deserve one because he probably lied to me too. What if he had something that he never told me about or what if he is helping my mother too? I know it's an outlandish thought, but I didn't think Zube would betray me. I was wrong.

"Why?" He presses, now shouting. I turn on him. He wants an explanation? Fine.

"I am sick of wandering around this forest blind. I am tired of my friends dying and people stabbing me in the back," I look to Zube and his face flushes. Prick. "I want this to be over. Everything, I want to be home. And most of all I want you to get out of my damned business!"

Turning on my heel I keep heading towards the waterfall. I don't care if they follow me or not, I'm heading home. My bed is just calling me and my aching body is itching for it. Silk and velvet cushions full of cotton, perfect for a heavy head like mine.

Standing next to the roaring water I can't hear anything. Not even the whispering between the three boys behind me. I don't care what secrets they keep for themselves, they can stuff it. I keep searching the area for stairs or a ladder or anything to exit the ravine but I don't find anything. Even the surface of the wall is smooth as slate, probably from the water eroding the rock.

I can't be trapped down here because Croterra said that he was the last of the druids. They could've just left; I hope they left because if they did than there is a way out. I keep searching but again find nothing. When I look to the guys they haven't even moved.

"Will you all stop being Kingdom ladies and help me find a way to leave," I ask nicely but they just look at me and keep whispering. Idiots! Fine, I will find the way out on my own. I drop my bow and quiver on the grass and stomp off towards a tree adorned with rose hued leaves.

Looking around the tree I begin to climb its branches. My cloak snags and pulls on twigs but I just yank it free. It is honestly the least annoying thing going on currently. If I climb high enough I may be able to see all through the ravine and maybe find a pathway out.

Not even Jax is on my side, he knows how much I hate what's going on. But I guess that still doesn't give me a right to yell at them. A pang of guilt rattles in my gut, but I ignore it. I will apologize later if I remember. I don't doubt that they'll remind me of it.

I reach the peak of the tree and I can see almost the entire ravine. Wisps dance, pulse, vanish and reappear all around the temple and the ravine itself. I notice a small silhouette of Croterra standing on the bridge between the twin temples. I can see so much, but yet so little. It's as if the only way out is to fly out. I wonder if my powers would allow me to fly. I highly doubt it, but it would be nice.

A blue flame appears before me and I see a tiny wisp smiling. Jumping back I fall from the branch and tumble down the tree. I seem to hit every trunk and limb and pain immediately fills my body, when I finally land my rib cracks, again. Through a painful scream I hear Jax and Jeremiah sprint to me instantly forgetting why they were ignoring me. Pricks.

"Don't touch me," I shout as I push away from them, gripping my waist. That stupid wisp startled me. It appears above my bow and quiver for some odd reason, but they do say that the wisps lead you to where you desire, and for me that's home. I string my bow and head to the rushing water of the glowing river. Croterra said that the waterfall can heal people and I just want the pain to go away.

I slowly step into the water and let the cool ripples glide along my skin like chilled fingers on sunburn. It's an orgasmic feeling. I face the waterfall and the pounding water looks to come from nowhere, falling from an abyss of sorts.

The water rushes heavily past me but it presses down on my body hard. I look to the guys and I'm not moving with the river, I am moving against it, towards the waterfall.

Panic sets in.

"Help! Help me," I scream through a raspy voice towards Jax, Jeremiah, and Zube. They don't have to help me if they hate me, but they run for the river. I reach but I begin to be pulled down under the surface. The bubbles rise up and my scream is swallowed by a mouthful of water. As my body twirls and spins beneath the waterfall I am caught in an undercurrent, the vortex whipping me around like a doll. I never got air; I didn't have time to take a breath and my lungs already burn. They are too filled so I release the only air I have left. Relief lasts for only seconds before the pressure builds again.

I see through a fogged haze Jax dive into the water. He will be sucked into the current too! Jeremiah follows Jax and I want to cry. All my friends are going to die and I didn't even have time to apologize to them for being a bitch. I had screamed at them for no reason other than my own attitude. I am disgusting and Prometheus will smite me for this. I'm sorry.

The vortex pulls up and I start to rise in the waterfall. I am being lifted on a current that flows opposite of gravity. Right as I feel my lungs open I close my eyes and take a breath.

Air fills my lungs as I cough out water into a small stream that flows into the Ravine of Wisps. I am alive. The way out of the ravine was up.

CHAPTER FIFTEEN
~*Ariadae*~

The three boys rolled up and over the edge of the waterfall into the creek. They all choked out water. I wring out my cloak and hair as they rise and put themselves together. We made it out of the Ravine.

"We start moving as soon as you all are ready," I say steadily. My rib is no longer bothering me thanks to the healing of the ravine's water. I think the fracture is healed. "I didn't get to say this before, but I'm sorry. I am sorry for screaming at you because my own problems are pressing down on me like a rock."

Jeremiah smirks, "It's alright," He groans through cracking knuckles. "We all know what you feel like. We want to be home as badly as you, Dae."

Jax brushes past me in a heavy saunter. Anger radiates from the wind that passes through my hair. What is wrong with him? I apologized. I would've assumed him of all people would understand.

"Now that we're done apologizing, let's leave."

Jeremiah runs past to follow pursuit with Jax. I want to stop him because Jax's anger may be directed at me and I doubt he won't lash out at anyone, but I don't stop Jeremiah. I let him run to the wolf…Or white tiger I should say. Jax hasn't been in his white tiger form since he revealed himself to me. It must be a relief for him to stop keeping his true self a secret. My only question is why did he even come to Equadoria? He claims he was on orders from the person he bows to, but why did he get those orders?

Zube walks up to me and I look into his green irises. My glare is colder than ice as he whispers, "I can't apologize more." He becomes suddenly sad, his features sagging in thought. "How you felt in that kingdom is how I feel everywhere I go and Evaflora offered me the lift of that burden. For a minute I felt as if I wasn't banished from every Fae Kingdom in Elkwood."

He is apologizing? He betrays me and still has the nerve to serve me. We left the Ravine of Wisps so killing him sounds like a good idea. But I don't want to kill him. It's better he be a friend rather than an enemy.

I drop my voice to a soft innocence as I whisper, "One day, when I rule the kingdom of Equadoria and I sit on the throne, I will lift your burden. You will be in my kingdom, Zube."

He smiles at that and I join in at the thought. I could sit on the throne with him standing beside me as a Lord of Equadoria or maybe he can be my knowledge and eyes. He could tell me what is happening throughout the kingdom each day and attend my Kingdom meetings with the other Nobles of Equadoria. It would be magical.

His lips part like he wants to say something but he is cut off by Jeremiah calling for us to hurry up. We turn and head into the expanse of trees. The trunks aren't as thick here and they are wider apart. The limbs are thinner and longer, completely removing us from a view of the sky. Morning pink slightly peers between small holes that are amidst the leaves.

Jax says we are heading towards the Night Kingdom which is the center of Elkwood. Apparently the Night Kingdom has both day and night, but is buried beneath the ground in crystal caves. The tunnel's dirt appears black and the crystals illuminate it like stars. Zube tells us all of the different stores and places beneath the ground. A whole city is down there and it is named Twilight because when the crystals glow, the illumination causes different colors to blend together and it looks as if the whole ceiling is covered in a pulsing, glittering, fog. The city's buildings are carved from obsidian and the streets are crafted of a black soil from deep within the earth.

If I wasn't so inclined to return home and save my father and kingdom, I may have spent a day or two visiting. That's also if the High Fae would allow me to reside there. Although I have Fae powers I am still a human and I don't think he would want a human in his Kingdom and the other five Kingdoms had to have heard of what I did at the Summer Kingdom last week. I killed over fifty soldiers just trying to get to the doors. Imagine how many I have killed throughout my stay there.

The number is immense, and I don't want to think about it. Many Fae have died at my hand but now that I think, how many mortals have died from them? That number would put my death list to shame.

"Where do you think Nirvana could be?" I ask to nobody in particular. I assume either Jax or Zube will answer. Jeremiah is as lost as me. I hadn't even thought about how hard this must all be on him. All of this is tough to choke down.

Like I expected, Jax answers, "My mother would tell me that Nirvana is night and day, darkness and light, the moon and sun, but she always said it was always in me. Nirvana is a place as perfect as the eye of the beholder.

So basically my Nirvana is completely different from, let's say, Jeremiah's."

"So how do we get there," Jeremiah asks what I was thinking.

"We follow our center."

Jeremiah looks to me and his brows knot together. I don't understand what Jax is saying but it must have some form of double meaning.

That was also one of the few times Jax has talked about himself or his family. I have the urge to question him further but I don't want to push a sensitive subject. The last thing I need is him losing track of his 'center'. So I just follow Jax and let him guide us through the trees and grass of the forest floor.

Foliage from the trees becomes extremely thick and tightly woven together. We are forced to stop and slowly cut through the brittle sticks. After cutting through a foot or two of branches a moor opens before us. Large grassy fields are open and look like waves to an ocean of green. Large animals lying down are scattered across the fields and massive rocks are piled on top of each other at the opposite end of the moor.

It is so peaceful and quiet but the clouds seem to cover the sky which must be blue by this time. It is almost noon, I assume but the large grey puffs are low flying and seem to gloom over the beautiful grass. I smell the sweet prairie flowers of summer vegetation and something else…something that stings and makes my nostrils flare. The stench is repulsive.

"Prometheus be damned what is that foul stench," Jax spits covering his nose and mouth. I search the space of the fields. I don't see any of the Forsaken, although they smell bad it isn't the smell of carrion. It is the stench of…

Not ten meters from where I stand I see it. I see the rotting corpse of cattle. Not stopping the gasp that passes my lips I step back, away from the dead being before me. The beast's innards are missing and all that is left is a husk. What monster could have done such a thing?

My pounding heart and heavy breathing keeps me from staring at the body. Staring across the moor I notice that the cattle that looked to be lying in the grass are just bloody husks.

I realize that my heart isn't pounding, but the ground is moving. The reverberations make me think of the monster we encountered before we got to the Rune Yard. Whatever is making these trembles in the earth is very large. I don't want to battle another monster or have anyone else get injured so I look to Zube.

"There are three guardians of Elkwood," he starts reciting what Jax told us. "Irene, Guardian of the Rune Yard; Irian, Guardian of the Tree of Light; and…"

A monster larger than the trees surrounding the moor crawls from behind the piled rocks. As if on command it rises onto its legs and stares at us through the armor it wears. Each plate of the dark armor peaks in a glinting point and it raises a large battle axe.

"Ir, Guardian of the Gods," Zube finishes. Ir roars and lurches on big heavy legs into a sprint.

What have I gotten myself into?

CHAPTER SIXTEEN

~*Ariadae*~

Run, *is all* I can think, so I listen to my conscience. I run and run into the forest behind me. If Ir is here, then that means Nirvana is nearby and I still need to get there. He was hiding behind the rocks, so there is possibly a way near those boulders.

I run in the trees letting each one pass by as I try to stay on my feet. The forest floor is quite clear of twigs but the grass still hides small rocks and other obstacles that could trip me. I'd get hurt if I fell at this speed.

"Where are you going," Shouts Jeremiah following in step behind me. His voice is drowned out by the thunderous boom of Ir's heavy steps.

"We still need to get to Nirvana," I answer. "Head towards the rocks where Ir was hiding!"

Jax sprints by in a blur of wind and speed. His Fae body gives him faster agility and endurance. If only I could be a Fae, just for the benefits of the body, nothing else.

A bright light flashes next to Jeremiah and Zube shifts into his Fae form and catches up to Jax. The two of them are many meters ahead but I can still see their black silhouettes weaving between the trees. They are running slower so Jeremiah and I can keep up.

Suddenly remembered of this, it's almost as if Jeremiah and I were kids again. We used to run in the streets, racing each other to see who was the fastest or running from imaginary beasts, but now it's not our imagination. There *is* a giant monster chasing us.

The ground's reverberations become so violent I stumble on my own steps and the trees shake wildly as if they are scared of Ir. So am I. A giant shadow approaches the tree line that I am running next to and, surprisingly fast, Ir's blade starts cutting through the branches. I scream and jump away from the blade and the trees fall atop one another and clatter to the earth. Dirt flies in the air and Ir keeps swinging his axe towards Jeremiah and me.

Sprinting, pushing my legs harder than I ever could I scream and run. Wisps of my shortened hair fly around my face and my cloak whips in the wake of my dash. The ground begins to tremble again and I don't want to look back at Ir, who is sprinting behind us. He created a clearing by slicing down the trees and I leap back into the maze of Elkwood. Leaving the ruined clearing behind me, Ir seems to keep up. Loud cracks cut through the air and as I look back a whole tree flies past me less than a meter away.

Tumbling into a roll I dash deeper into the woods. He may only be able to run through so many trees. Maybe the trunks can be a barrier against him. The bigger they are the harder they fall. Maybe we could buy some time if we were able to make him fall.

Through the haze of falling dirt around us, I see Jax and Zube reach the rocks and start searching between the boulders. My ears perk at the sound of something whirling and spinning through the air. It is loud and heavy. *MOVE* my mind shouts and I stop running and roll to the left. Sparks fly with dirt and grass as Ir's axe slams into the ground, exactly where I was running. This may be harder than we thought.

Ir stomps his feet and the only visible part of him is his glowing red eyes. He roars at us and grabs four trees at once and throws them. They arch through the air; I look to where they will land. Jeremiah stares up at them dumbfounded. The trees are going to land on him!

"RUN!" He looks to me frightened and then the trees land. The large trunks pin him down and pile onto each other. The leaves and limbs create a dome hiding him from me and Ir. "Jeremiah! No!"

I dash to the dome of leaves and push through the foliage. Branches snap and break as I climb through the piled trees and head down towards the ground. His crying wails help me find him almost instantly.

One of the tree's trunks lies across his shin and blood trickles from his lips. A large branch is pinning his chest to the earth. I dive down to him and begin to move the branch.

"I am going to get you out of here, okay," I blindly talk before I begin to panic anymore than I already am. "It's all going to be okay. You're fine." Lifting the branch he coughs up more blood and sits up. If he didn't insist on coming then none of this would have happened. It's not like this was an outcome any of us expected.

A tree is yanked from the pile and thrown away. Ir is digging his way to me. Without thinking I unstring my bow and nock an arrow. The bow is drawn and the arrow head is aimed on his eye as he pulls away a second tree, exposing us to the heavy gloom above. The string snaps and the arrow ricochets off the plate of armor covering his forehead. I missed.

"I need to go," I shout to Jeremiah and I leap from the pile of branches before he can respond and before Ir can chop me down. His axe swings and wind slams into my back as if it was inches from cutting me. Dropping back into a sprint I bound for the boulders which are only meters from me. Ir is distracted by me running and ignores Jeremiah to follow me. Thank the gods.

Jax jumps out from behind a boulder and shouts, "Duck!" So I listen and dive to the grass littered with rocks. A jagged stone cutting into my knees and cheek makes me whimper.

Roaring winds howl above me and spiral into Ir. The reverberations become slow from his failing attempt at running. "Help," Jax spits. How could I help him? I don't have the same powers as him.

Rolling away from the tunnel of torrential wind I dash to him and face the giant who is forcefully trying to run but is stopped by an invisible howling wall. Looking within myself I find the glowing braid of my power but I don't grip it like I normally would. I brush and glide my fingers against it until it glows and I am taming it at my will. Forcing the power out I project my hands towards Ir and his armor is gripped by a fist of my power. Lifting into the air, Jax's wind pushes him back and away from us. The glowing braid is vanishing and becoming translucent the longer I use it. Before it disappears I do one last yank on the cord and the armor that holds Ir flips horizontally and he drops. The bigger they are the harder they fall.

We didn't use trees to trip him, but our powers did the job. This seems like a feat but he isn't dead, just lying down. He may take a while to get up, although we aren't sure how long it will take.

"Help me get Jeremiah," I say to Jax who pants heavily. How did his power take such a toll on him? Is it really that hard for him? I understand feeling weak because now that the cord is gone and slowly forming I feel weaker but not to the point where I can't breathe.

Through heavy pants Jax says, "Zube ran to him when you dived on the ground."

Stumbling through the forest Zube drags Jeremiah like a large doll. Although Jeremiah is extremely muscled Zube doesn't seem to have a problem carrying him. It must be the Fae strength.

I run to them and Zube places Jeremiah into the grass. His skin has paled and his eyes have become dark and seemed to have sunk into his head a bit.

"How did you get the tree off his leg," I ask through strangled gasps. Tears burn the back of my vision for my friend who is so badly injured. Why does everyone that has followed me into Elkwood get hurt? This is my fault. It's entirely my fault. "I am so sorry for leaving you,"

I whisper to his unconscious body. He could still hear me, I know it.

"It was a lot of grunting and weird body angles but I managed to lift it enough for him to drag himself out from beneath it and once his leg was out he fainted," Zube explains and I look from him back to Jeremiah.

"We need to move," Jax starts. "Who knows how long it will be until Ir gets up."

"That's *if* he gets up," Zube clarifies. Jax's black hair gleams as he looks to where the beast has fallen.

"*When* he gets up, he won't be happy." Nodding, Zube moves to grab Jeremiah and I rise, following Jax into the maze of boulders.

Grass is between each of the ginormous rocks. The stones are onyx in color but they aren't shining like obsidian would. The boulders are a matte, just like stone. It's strange how things in Elkwood are completely different from the rest of Abella. It's almost like Elkwood forest is it's own continent.

Each corner we round I look for something, anything that could lead us to a way to Nirvana. It's almost as if Ir was just wandering around for fun. The way to Nirvana couldn't possibly be here. Nirvana is the afterlife, maybe we needed to die to go there.

I share my thought to the others.

"We weren't supposed to die nitwit," Zube fires back with attitude. I don't know what his problem is.

"Okay, then enlighten me. Where is the door *'nitwit'*?" I spit, using his insult venomously.

"Will you two stop being children?" Jax shouts. His skin is flushed with anger and frustration sits behind his eyes. I understand how he feels. "I am stale of listening to you two squabbling with one another."

A laugh passes my lips uncontrollably. Stale? Squabble? Who would speak like that? Something is really bothering him, I wonder what?

"Alright, sorry I miffed your bliss," Zube chuckles rudely mocking Jax. I did want to snap back with a mocking comment as well. Jax rolls his ice eyes and they flick to me. His blues ride up and down my body and they settle for a second on my corset. Instantly, a chill rattles my body and I become uncomfortable. Pervert.

I turn on my heel and head between two boulders. Jax calls after me but I just wave him an obscene gesture and saunter between more rocks. Men are always the same. They only focus on the physical aspect of the body instead of what is beneath that surface. I would have expected Jax to be a little more obedient but I guess all males have it in their genes. It may even be harder with the Fae because of their very primal ideals and rules.

The sun beats down on the boulders through a small break in the gloom above and I notice the sting on my face from where the rock cut me. Wiping away the blood something blinds me. A light reflected the sun's blinding beam into my face and I stand at the sudden redirect of sunlight.

I generously approach the silvery object and ignore the fact that I may be heading straight into danger. Ir was claimed to be the only protector of the Gods so I don't think anything else dangerous could be here. Rounding the rock I see the surface is painted in shimmering runes that glow against the onyx stone and a large thick silver slime pours from an unknown sore. The door-sized column of mirror-like liquid ripples and makes rainbows of light bounce off at odd reflections. The liquid stays within the large dome of runes surrounding it.

"Zube! Jax! Can you guys come over here? Bring Jeremiah," I call to them. I completely forget my anger towards Jax and focus on the pouring mirror. They run around the corner extremely fast and stand next to me before I even blink.

"What is it," Zube asks. I am wondering the same thing.

"Do you think it is a blight of some kind," Jax answers. That wouldn't make sense. Why would a blight be surrounded by runes that someone had to have placed.

Zube has read my thoughts and I can tell he uses this to his advantage. *You're an idiot.* I look to him and he smirks silently saying *I know.*

Zube reaches forward and places his finger against the flowing mirror and instantly he is dragged into the liquid and vanishes as if he was never there. I'm left completely stunned. It's a door. I hope to Nirvana.

"Put Jeremiah through," I say and Jax does so. "It's the door to Nirvana." I still hope I'm not wrong, but it would make sense.

"After you," Jax whispers gesturing to the door. I take a deep breath and suck myself into the moving tunnel that leads me to Nirvana. Jax follows me through and we land on white quartz stairs next to Zube and Jeremiah.

CHAPTER SEVENTEEN

Ariadae wasn't expecting the sheer size of Nirvana. The god's home is a whole different world than the place Prometheus created with his fellow gods. The home of the gods is made of glittering white quartz and is a large throne room that all the gods sit in and stare at a pillar that holds a visual orb of what they created. The world.

Zube grabs Jeremiah and violently shakes him awake. Coming to his consciousness he is first terrified than he is in awe at the outstanding sky of exploding color. Rising, all four of the travelers head up the stairs towards the throne room, towards the gods, towards Prometheus. He was expecting their company.

"Hello my child," Prometheus purrs from his throne. The other six Gods smile as they hear the pounding hearts of the travelers. "I have been waiting for your arrival."

Oh how small she is compared to them. She is only the size of one's foot compared to the rest of the creators. Her fragile voice quivers in the echoing chamber as she asks, "How did you know I was coming?"

"We know everything," answers Amare, Goddess of love and beauty. Her golden waves are coiled atop her head. The crown of red roses off sets her violet eyes as she stares at Ariadae. She isn't the prettiest mortal that Amare has created but she did gift this child with a form of grace.

"This is truly amaz-," Zube tries to say but Prometheus cuts him off.

"How dare you speak without being spoken to? No manners do you have!"

"I apologize, Prometheus," He bows deeply. "I didn't mean to disrespect you." Prometheus could feel the heavy thud within Zube's brittle boned chest. Oh, he wonders how quickly his brain would explode from Prometheus's power.

"I am here because I need something, desperately," Ariadae speaks, her voice barely above a whisper. "My father is cursed and I need to head to the Tree of Light and retrieve a leaf to lift the curse binding him to evil." Fair enough, but the power of the Tree is valuable Prometheus thinks.

Bellum, God of war, shifts in his seat at Ariadae's words. Ariadae doesn't know what she is doing. "And how do you expect to find the Tree of Light, mortal?" he voices. His red eyes glare down on the weakling at his feet, although she isn't completely weak. She has abilities like the Fae that Prometheus gifted. He could easily take away her power at the lift of a finger.

Zube steps forward and pulls the Oracle from an unknown pocket. Sapientiae perks at the sight of the object he created. *Yes, give it to Prometheus mortal*, He thinks to himself. It has been many centuries since the Oracle was created and to see it now gives him excitement, contentment, happiness. This day has finally come and he can't stop his translucent irises from raking over the girl and her friends.

Prometheus points to the object and steps from his throne. "What is that?" he asks in a shaking voice.

"I can guide you to the Tree of Light with this powerful artifact. How did the druid allow you to have it?" Sapientiae says from his seat. Prometheus' eyes dart to the god of wisdom.

"What is this?"

"I had created it, so one day when we needed the Tree of Light it could again be used."

Prometheus looks between his brother and the Oracle. "Well if the druid was protecting it why did he give it to you?"

"I don't think he knows we have it," Ariadae whispers visibly nervous. "But if I may ask, will you guide us to the Tree of Light?"

Bellum looks to Sapientiae and shakes his head, eyes in a glare, Bellum has grown angry. Who cares? He is only the God of War, the world could do without him, but Sapientiae, God of Wisdom is something special and needed in the world. Ariadae is someone special in this world, although she has killed many of the Fae. She will learn from her mistakes and the Gods can see the hassle she has taken, the journey, the death, and the love that will come of this, so they take pity on the mortal.

"You have done many spiteful things, child," Prometheus starts. "Those things aside you have been a kind, sweet hearted girl, and we believe that, although you have killed many it is for the greater good of your kingdom. There is kindness within you and it sits beside a strong powerful magic that still hasn't awoken." The girl seems to be scared of smite and beaming with bliss. "We have decided to allow you passage to the Tree of Light."

She drops to her knees and tears gleam in her green eyes. The poor innocent child is so broken. When she finds her mate, Kane Archaeminza, things will be different. He is waiting for her, in the Winter Kingdom. And her brother, Lunan will always be around for her, but he needs to stay leading the Day Kingdom. Evaflora will be given her smite soon, her sins are beyond comprehension, but there are many others like her in Abella.

Odi looks uncomfortable, his black hair slick with sweat and his black eyes flick around vigorously. "Ariadae," He shouts looking to her. He is the God of Hate and Death. "I fear your future. Be careful."

"Why," asks the Fae, Jax Lycus Archaeminza. He has been protecting the mortal for some unknown reason. He may have imprinted on her, but he is not her mate, no matter how hard he tries.

"Death will come of you, but never fall into the abyss of darkness. That is where Novid and Gaston had gone and now they wander and haunt you because once you're on the bridge between life and death they will come for you. Run, just run for the light and don't allow them to get you."

Ariadae's heart flutters in her chest like a snare drum as she stands dumbfounded. He is the God of death and hate but how could he have known what will happen on the bridge between worlds? The God's power is too powerful for even a mortal or Fae to understand.

Pacem, the God of Peace and Health looks to Jeremiah who is lying on the ground unconscious. "For all of your trouble, child." Pacem waves his hand and suddenly Jeremiah is awake and his leg is healed. He looks around, stunned and rises to his feet.

Jeremiah notices Ariadae obviously distraught and pulls her back. He lowers his hands to the small of her spine and leads her for the steps.

"Thank you," Jax bows. "I speak for them as well. You just seemed to have frightened Ariadae. That's all."

"She will learn of her fate," Bellum moans loudly. "Leave my presence."

Following the God's order, he walks back to Ariadae and her obnoxious friends. They will soon head to the Tree of Light and then be back in Equadoria before Abella Day which is July 4th. It celebrates the creation of Abella.

Before, the four travelers could head back through the passageway, which will talk them back to Abella, Prometheus shouts from behind them, "Follow a cord of yellow gold. It will take you to the Tree of Light."

"Thank you for your kindness," Jeremiah calls and deeply bows before running through the door to follow his friends. In a bright blurry flash of colors he is pulled away from Nirvana and is standing back in Abella, surrounded by his friends. Glowing faintly before them is small, thin cord, glittering like the warmest fire, wrapped around a rock and is gently draped over boulders. The cord rolls off into the distance and winds around rocks heading towards what is most likely the forest.

It's time to finally finish this horror.

Part Three
TREE OF LIGHT

CHAPTER EIGHTEEN

I am going to die. Why would he tell me this? I thought I was going to die so many times, but now I *know* I will. The only information he gave me didn't tell me when or how I was going to die, but he did tell me that Novid and Gaston will take me once I enter the darkness. I won't allow them to, nobody would want dead decaying hands over their body. A chill runs down my spine, making my whole body shudder.

"It will be alright," Zube whispers to me. He needs to stop reading my thoughts. "I won't let you die."

My fear warps into flaring anger and he is standing in the line of my fire. My words are harsh, angered, and accusatory as I growl, "You would most certainly let me die if my mother created a large enough wager!" I wouldn't be shocked if he was working with my mother right now.

"How dare you," Zube spits.

"How dare *you*," I correct him. "Who was it that left me for dead when Irene was trying to use me? Oh right, it was you." I poke his chest making him back away. "You are an arrogant, selfish, insufferable PRICK! So before you try to correct me focus on what's important."

"And what's that," He groans and rolls his eyes.

"The prick that is smaller than a bean sitting in your jocks." Jeremiah and Jax laugh at the insult as Zube chews on his tongue and spits his saliva onto my forehead. Oh he is going to regret that.

I unsheathe my knife and hold the tip of the blade against his groin and he shutters and tries to pull away but my power grips him to the ground. Unable to move, he quivers like a cold kitten in the rain.

"You're quite frightened now that I might castrate you, huh?" I purr making me think of my mother's voice. I hate her but I can learn a thing or two from the witch. "Spit on me again and you lose your cock."

With that I sheath the dagger and follow the looping golden cord. Let him shake in his boots, but I plan on saving my father and never looking back at this forest again. Jax hasn't trained me with my abilities but I seemed to have gotten a fair grip on willing it as I please. My Telekinae genes once frightened me, but now I almost feel at peace with the immortal blood running beneath my mortal skin. It's like my own treasure, but these powers are my secret weapon. Nobody will expect the princess of Equadoria, although mortal, to still have powers.

After wandering through the forest making sure not to stray too far from the golden rope, I notice that the forest is quiet. Not the kind of quiet that I should fear because the trees still speak. Birds chirp loudly and wind howls through the leaves, sending the branches dancing and swaying. There is no Forsaken around and just the thought of the Dreag and the Nymphs, along with the Troglodytes, sends a chill along my spine, there is too much to fear. Too many enemies of mine are just waiting around the next corner and who knows; maybe Ir is running behind us on soft heavy feet. We never saw him when we headed into the tree line because the cord traveled the opposite direction of where he fell. I still pray he doesn't get up.

The sky is still blue, but the sun is falling towards the west. I only wish that we find the tree before nightfall because, although we haven't heard or seen the Forsaken now doesn't mean I want to run across them later. They are just not what I need at this moment. Jeremiah, although healed is limping around, so Jax keeps calling him a "gimpy", which is driving me nuts! I need to focus on the sweet birds and rustling leaves.

"Gimpy!"

"I hate you," Jeremiah shouts. He stumbles over the roots that are half buried beneath the ground. "Are we almost there?"

"I'm not sure," I moan and roll my eyes at his childish whine. "I hope we can get there before any of them show up." I don't say the name of the Forsaken in fear it might summon them. What if they come to get us after someone talks about the Dreag or the Nymphs?

"How many different breeds of them are there?" Jeremiah asks to Zube, but he only shrugs.

"There are a lot," He whispers. He looks around like they heard him.

Jax begins to speak in a low monotone voice as if all emotion leaves his skin. "Supposedly there are four clans within the Forsaken race; Nymphs, Dreag, Troglodyte, and the Arbor. All four are extremely deadly and have their own ways of tearing you bit by bit, but the clans I fear the most are the Demised and the Umbra."

"I thought there were only four clans," I question. He even started with saying there are four clans.

"Those four clans are the most renowned and popular. There are also two smaller factions that don't fit the four clans. Those that are in the factions were originally exiled by the Forsaken. The two factions are the Demised; shapeshifting beasts who can take any animal form. And the Umbra; monsters of shadow and terror which can conjure ones worst fears to harm them," Jax finishes explaining and I barely heard the last words over my pounding heart.

The Forsaken seem to have their own form of caste system and political standards. This is just too much to think about right now. I need to strictly focus on what is before me and if we encounter any of the other clans than we'll cross that bridge once we reach it. For now I lock my eyes solely on the rope before me and saunter ahead, moving slightly quicker than before.

After trekking through the woods, for many hours the sky has changed from the billowing, colorful palette of oranges and pink, and is now a darkened blue-gray. The trunks and leaves of the trees have become black and it is getting harder and harder to see in the approaching night.

My legs burn and ache as I take step after step and I eventually become like Jeremiah, having trouble walking along the roots and branches of trees. The uneven terrain is easy for Jax and Zube, who still hasn't shifted back to his mortal form. The pointed ears, muscled bodies, and almost glowing skin of the Fae make them ethereal, but unlike Jax, Zube's other form is not an animal and is a human body. He must like to have the advantage over Jeremiah because

Zube is smaller and weaker than him, well when he is in his human form.

"We should stop for the night," Jeremiah whispers as I take a step forward and feel a heavy pang in my chest. It thrums like my power flare but when I look inside myself my braided cord isn't pulsing but it has grown almost double in size. My heart pounds and squirms to keep going. "Should I make a fire?" Jeremiah quirks.

"No," Jax says looking as adrenaline filled as I must seem. "It's near."

"What's near," Jeremiah questions. He wouldn't feel it. He doesn't have the same Fae genes pulsing through his veins and power in his mind.

"The Tree of Light," I whisper barely audible over the rustling trees. My blood pumps and seems to push me forward like my body is in a trance.

Jax shifts into his white tiger form and I mount him like I once did.

"Where is it," Jeremiah presses. He rises and steps toward me as Zube grimaces next to him.

"Up ahead. Try and keep up," Zube moans seductively. The magic from the tree makes a tingling feeling dance along my pores. It's not the sweet, respectful dancing, no, it is the hip swaying, and body grinding dancing that is taboo at royal balls. Oh how I just want to dance like that. All of the sudden I notice Jax's heavily muscled fur body between my thighs, so I hit his side making him pounce and run faster than any animal could run. His legs seem to move faster than a hummingbird's wings as we dash between trees and branches. Elkwood passes by in a blur and I look into the darkened woods, something glows next to me. Not the golden glow of the rope, but rather a white light of something running alongside us.

It is the white stag! Its powerful legs propel it just as fast as Jax. Smiling at the stag I look forward and a colosseum rises before us. The stone is a darkened grey and carvings are littered across every tile and stone that makes the walls, arches, and opened walkways.

Jax stops his sprint and the stag wanders into the center of the colosseum. It looks about. Sitting on a small dais in the pit is what I've been looking for. What I've needed for almost two months. The Tree of Light is before me and it isn't even close to what I imagined. The dark trunk is large and twisted. The roots are thick and digging into the soil. The twisted trunk erupts in a large circular space of leaves that are as white as a winter snow, or Jax's pelt, or the sunlit clouds from this afternoon. The leaves glow and shimmer like a silk gown, glittering beneath a chandelier's lights.

"It's beautiful," I whisper. I step over the railing and climb down the uneven stones on the wall surrounding the pit. Jax shifts and follows me down. "We made it. We have gotten to the Tree of Light."

Rubbing dirt off my black pants and golden corset Jax drops behind me and says, "Remember we still need to get a leaf to your father. The adventure isn't over just yet."

I know. I don't say anything, although I want to, I can't. Awe has taken over and I watch as the white light fades and pules from each illuminated leaf. The dark trunk off sets the magic of the glowing leaves. If only someone could paint this, it couldn't be captured so beautifully. Only a Fae aristocrat with an extraordinary talent may come close, but nothing could compare the real thing.

"This isn't just a regular tree Jax," I start. He saunters to me and I look at his blue eyes. Unyielding, powerful, ethereal; all those words define his eyes. "This is something only six individuals have seen and they don't even remember it. We will go down in history, Immortal history to be exact Jax." He just stares at me with contentment. It is true, all the Fae children will learn of this discovery in their schooling, if Fae actually attend schooling.

"I know, Aria," He says. *Aria*? Why did he call me that? I like it. "It's just, why have we found the Tree of Light, but haven't been attacked by the Guardian of the tree? Doesn't that seem a little suspicious?"

Zube runs into the colosseum and Jeremiah clings to his back. "We made it. We're actually here," Zube laughs excitedly. A flutter flickers around my chest and I get excited as well. His green eyes lock onto the tree and they widen in shock. "It's beautiful."

"That's what she said," Jax chuckles gesturing to me.

"Let's grab a leaf and leave," Jeremiah steps in. He looks about like a frightened animal. "This place gives me the creeps." I find this place amazing and stunningly beautiful, but I can't help but agree with him. This place has a strange silence, and echo, darkness and light, a ying and a yang. It makes me uncomfortable and uneven.

I approach the tree and the pulsing leaves blind my irises as I remove three leaves and place them into a small leather sack. I'm not sure how many of them I need to lift the curse on my father so it is best that I just remove some extra just in case. I keep plucking the branch until the sack is about half full. That is when the stone in my chest vanishes and my heart skips a beat.

CHAPTER NINETEEN

An arrow flies past me as I duck and roll down the dais onto the tiled stone in the center of the arena. Jeremiah and Zube draw their swords and Jax unstrings his bow and is firing arrow after arrow into the Troglodyte archers.

How did they get here? How could they have found the Tree of Light? Then it hits me. They followed us here and that would also explain why the forest was quiet but still felt safe because they were around just not going to attack. How could they have known that we were heading to the Tree of Light?

More beasts come flooding into the colosseum and I start to notice the clans. The white Wood Nymphs leap and crawl along the arches while the Dreag claw up the walls and ceilings like spiders. The brightly scaled Troglodytes fire arrows and bare swords and are clad in iron armor lined with fur. Then four Arbors drop down into the arena's center with me, Jax, and the white stag that just stands awkwardly watching it all. I need to get out of here. I need to save my father.

A primal instinct takes over and I stop thinking as I fire ash arrow after ash arrow into the dark, thick bark skin of the tall beasts before me. I thought that the clans would be separated, not work together. What could this planning be the outcome of?

One Arbor from my right sprints making me miss the one on my left before it grabs my arm and throws me into the wall of stone. The rocks crack against my back and I fight back a scream as the hulking monster roars in my face. Odi said I was going to die, but I have a feeling that I am not going to die just yet. I will die soon, just not today.

Jeremiah drops from above and lands on top of the sharp jagged bark of the Arbor and drives his sword deep into the beast's skull. He saved me but at what risk? He left Zube up top alone to fight against all of those abominations.

"Thank you," I shout over the whistling arrows and clashing blades. He nods in answer.

"Not today," he says barely audible over the noise. He won't let me die today.

I draw the dragon bone dagger and angle it out as I keep my back pressed against the spider webbed stone. We are in a giant arena and since my bow is across the circle of the colosseum, this is all I have. I need to keep my back safe as Jeremiah always told me because an enemy will try every time to get an advantage on you. My current enemy already has the advantage of numbers; I better not give them anymore.

Zube leaps down in front of me and gives me a smirk before he, Jax, and Jeremiah surround me. They made another protection circle which I don't need. I am perfectly safe, well not perfectly.

I look to the stag and it stands uncomfortably. Shifting on its hooves the animal, although in the heat of danger seems very relaxed and serene. I start to wonder if it's even there and then I notice the small patch of blood on its stomach. The blood partially peeked around the side of the animal, but it isn't acting injured.

From a blinding flash of light I shield my eyes.

"That run reopened my wound," a voice purrs devilishly. I know that voice anywhere because it haunts my nightmares and I think of it when I am frightened. It's my mother's voice. "You shouldn't have shot that arrow into my stomach, Ariadae."

"Sorry I missed your throat, Evaflora," I snap. She laughs, throwing her head back in an ugly wail. She is sick. "Have you been following me?"

"Ever since you saw me in the woods that second day you entered Elkwood."

"You bitch," I growl. I saw the white stag before Gaston was killed. She has been watching me and following me.

"Don't speak to your mother like that," she moans as she cracks her neck. "I just needed you to get me to the Tree of Light, so I could lift the curse binding my children to Elkwood."

What children? I am her only child unless she means the…The Forsaken. I look to her. How could I have not noticed that once she drank the blood from the mortal boy's neck that he became a Wendigo. He became another beast in her army. She has been creating an army all her life and keeping them in that secret room off the balcony. That was why so many Forsaken were chained up because she was keeping them hidden until she was ready, and now I led her here. I brought the antagonist to my hero story straight to what had to be protected most. I will go down in history for leading a monster to a sacred land and being one of the few mortals to ever find the Tree of Light.

Evaflora stalks around one of the Arbors and adjusts the raven feathered skirt of her gown. It is stunning, but makes her look like her true self, a villain.

"The only way I can let my children leave Elkwood is if I lift their curse and the only way I can do that is with this tree," She starts. She saunters up the dais and begins stroking the branches and leaves of the tree. Her skin is poison to the life of this place. "There are so many Forsaken in my army that if a leaf only saves one individual than I will need to take…This entire tree." *No. no, no, no, no, no, no.* I can't let her take it or ruin it. I need to stop her from taking the Tree of Light.

Leaping forward I dive for the dais and sprint past Jeremiah and Jax who don't move. An Arbor lurches for me, but I quickly surge to the side dodging its tremendous hands, made of twigs and branches. I throw the blade and Evaflora lazily lifts a hand and her green flames turn the dagger to ashes. Another Arbor grabs me and throws me to the ground. Pain fires up my side and I groan at the aching soreness. What a bitch. I can't do anything to her right now without being killed or severely injured. We're surrounded by her army, and I assume this is only the smallest portion of it. Only one Dreag killed Gaston and only one Wendigo killed Novid. I shudder at the thought of what hundreds of Forsaken can do.

Her green flames swirl around her fist like coiling snakes.

"Thank you, Ariadae," She points her attention to me, "For everything." Her green flames slice into the trunk of the tree and in one clean chop the whole damned Tree of Light collapses. A pain stabs into my chest and something lifts. When I look to see if my braided cord of abilities is still there, it is no longer growing big, it is back to its original size. The curses of Elkwood have been lifted, my dad is saved, but what she just did can't be forgotten. Evaflora lifted the curse that keeps the Forsaken from leaving Elkwood. She turns around and begins to head out of an arch that leads into the darkened forest. She looks back at me and says, "It's time to pay a visit to your father.

CHAPTER TWENTY

~Fayla~

I feel it. The Tree of Light has been chopped down. I don't know how, but the stab of pain has erupted in my chest and I just know. Abella tremored and I felt the shake because the soil and dirt of the continent surrounds the cellar I am in. The dark musty air fills my lungs and the scent of mold and my own piss and feces has become a common aroma. I have forgotten what it feels like to be self-conscience because Duke Rywell took that from me. He took my innocence, my happiness, and my virginity. The people who gave him gold to take me, stole the only hope I had, the only drive for wonder. But I won't let that define me. I will not be a broken, weak, dying Fae girl.

My father was strong once, until Duke Rywell visited our manor in a mortal kingdom I don't remember. The plan was for him to become acquaintances with my father, but after three days with the mortal in my home, my father lost everything that made him sane. I sat at the dinner table with my mother when he sliced her throat for talking too loudly. I never spoke and never said a word, but I remember her blue eyes fall on me as her blood sprayed onto my gown of the palest pink. He sent me to bed and I learned, from a maid screaming, that my father had leaped from the fourth story bedroom window. When Duke Rywell set the house into flames he grabbed me and made sure to walk past my father's unrecognizable body.

That happened thirteen years ago when I was only seven years old, although immortal I have been stuck down in the cellar in his home and have been used as a play thing he forgets about every once in a while. He only comes down to greet me when he is drunk and angry. I have thought of murdering him so many times that my thoughts are consumed with visions of the different ways I plan on seeing the life drain from his body.

The only thing that keeps me from doing so is the shackles that are laced with mountain ash, which causes me not to conjure my abilities. He had made sure to let the mountain ash touch my skin and burn my wrists every time I moved. When I sleep I awake to the violent sting of my shifting arms and when I am awake I barely feel the heavy limbs because I don't move them in fear of the burning. Now that the Tree of Light has been chopped down, I don't feel it. I don't feel the burn of the ash against my scarred wrists.

Pulling my hands free, I see the reddened and destroyed tissue and skin on my wrists in the shape of the shackles. I will bare these scars forever, but now that I am no longer bound to mortal life I can feel it. Feel the power running up and down my veins in a sporadic dance.

I have a power that only comes from a direct blood line of individuals and open my palms and let the room be illuminated by the sparkling blue electricity that dances along my palms. I have the power of lighting also called Storm magic. Other Fae like me have different forms of Storm abilities, but none of them have the lightning that I can create.

Now I get to finally do what I have dreamed of for so long. I walk up the stone stairs in the corner of the room and find the door to be locked which isn't very shocking.

I think of his room. The warm colored blankets and the creaky floorboards. I think of his grey hair and bulbous body. The spice filled scent of him fills my nose as I picture the repulsive man. In a flash of bright, blinding light, cold air fills my lungs and I am standing in his room.

The window is open letting in the humid summer air. A curtain billows and his bed is damp from sweat and the moist, soup-like air.

My lightning fills the room with blue light and I smile as the crackling wakes him from sleep. I begin to whisper, "Rywell, if I wasn't so blood thirsty I would take my time killing you. I have dreamed of this day since you stole me from my home all those years ago and I know that Prometheus will never give you the gift of Nirvana. You will find yourself rotting in the darkened pits of the underworld, which is where you belong you disgusting, torturous bastard."

"How did you get out?" he groans through a heavy sleepy voice.

"Is that really what you wanted to ask me?" I cock my head in an animalistic way and he starts screaming. "I would've assumed you wanted to know how I am going to kill you. Well to answer the question you didn't ask; I am going to turn you to a pile of ashes." I am a woman of my word so I direct the bolts of lightning to his bed and he begins to thrash and squirm wildly on the bed. The springs squeak loudly and I laugh at his shouting. I can't help but think that this is all a daydream and I am going to flash back to reality in the cellar.

Once he is done flailing and his heart has stopped beating I head down the hall and into his Lady's room where I steal a gown of the darkest purple and I brush out the blood from my silvery white hair with water and a bathing tonic. Braiding my hair, I leave his house and walk down the street towards one of Duke Rywell's client's house. I plan on killing every single man who stole my innocence.

CHAPTER TWENTY-ONE
~*Ariadae*~

Once the Forsaken had left the colosseum is when we started to move. I lost the leather sack of leaves somewhere during the battle and I didn't care. I need to get to my father before my mother does.

I mounted Jax and left Jeremiah and Zube behind at the colosseum to run back home. The night sky has passed and the sky is now becoming a warm gold. In about an hour, clouds will be visible and surrounded by blue light.

My pounding heart beats a hundred times a minute and I get frightened for my father. He was trapped inside his own body for so long; he has most likely woken up confused and disoriented. How could he be able to handle an entire army of Forsaken after that? He can't, so I plan on heading straight for the kingdom and bringing him to the Keep where it is safe and I will explain everything.

"Jax," I whisper in his ear. The white and black fur tickles my cheek. His heavy breaths are more audible now than his thunderous bounding steps. "I know you are running very fast but we need to get there quicker. Please."

He listens and all of the sudden we are going faster than before. My short hair slaps against my face and each wisp of hair feels like a bee sting. The sound of the wind is screaming and the brush breaking beneath Jax's feet sounds like thunder crackling.

In what feels like minutes we are approaching the foliage that I used to enter Elkwood. For a second I think once we break through my dad will be waiting for me, but I know he won't. He will not be anywhere near the edge of Elkwood.

Leaping from the brush we dart into the dirt and pass sentinels who are moving dead bodies and corpses swinging from the gallows. The streets make little rivers of blood flow down into the slums. We pass crying women and pale lifeless children. My mother has gotten here first. My pounding heart punches against my chest violently and I shake off the burn behind my eyes. So many people have lost their family and friends. How can we ever expect to bounce back from this?

She did all of this because I killed her sentinels and many soldiers on that bridge with the mountain ash. I ruined her social status by telling her people of the glamour, and I wore a titanium antler crown to her Summer Solstice. I am more stupid than I thought. I somehow thought I could do all of those things without her fighting back? I started this war, but it was going to happen at some point. I just kicked it into gear.

Jax stops in front of the courtyard before the castle and I ignore the corpses that hang at odd angles on the spikes atop the wall. Dodging dripping blood Jax shifts and sprints next to me into the castle and straight into the throne room. The blue aisle leads straight to the dais and a black feather sits on the velvet carpet. My mother was in here.

"Ariadae," his warm voice says and I look up from the black feather to the man of green eyes and hair just as fiery as my own. His eyes seemed to have sunken in and look hollow and tired but he is still the man I grew up with and loved. He is no longer that monster that had taken my father almost two months ago. "Where have you been?"

"Father," the words escape my lips before I erupt into tears and sprint for him. I hug him with every ounce of muscle I have and he wraps his hands around my back, squeezing tight. My body shakes in happiness and my beating heart calms. I am so glad she didn't hurt him.

When I pull away he looks confused. "I went into Elkwood and found the Tree of Light. I saved you." His face warms and I look at his eyes again. The smile doesn't reach his ears and his eyes aren't warm like they usually were. That's when I notice the cobalt crown of thorns still atop his head.

"ARIADAE," Jax screams before my father presses his sword straight through my naval. The steel grinds against my bones and the blood falls in a heavy waterfall that trickles down my legs.

My father holds my shoulder keeping me up and he pulls the blade from my stomach and I shudder in pain. I feel the cavity and air flowing through one side of my body and out the other.

"You arrogant child," My father hisses, His teeth black from the demon inside him. "The curse wasn't created by Elkwood or bound to the Tree of Light. The curse was from your mother and has been in this crown." Once the word crown passes his lips Jax takes my father's sword and swipes it through his neck making his head roll. Our bodies collapse in unison.

I feel my body getting cold as all the blood leeches from my veins. The marble beneath my back is hot from the growing pool of my blood. All I hear is a constant ringing which doesn't leave. Jax fumbles around me and tears fall from his eyes as his lips move. He is saying something but I can't hear him.

I spent about two months in Elkwood and now there is no saving my father. Not only was the curse created by Evaflora, but he is also dead. His corpse lay meters from me, his gilded sword slick with my blood, beside Jax.

I still feel the reverberations of the steel grinding against my ribs and bones. The blade hit my lungs slicing a small cut into the left lung making it deflate instantly. Air comes in fast shuddering breaths. I am wasting them; my last breaths spent just trying to get air.

Jax keeps running about trying to stop the bleeding and help me breathe. He is trying to save me but he can't. Odi said I was going to die and now I know I am. Death will be upon me before I realize that I am dead. I thought when the Dreag held my beneath the surface of the water after Gaston died, that I was going to die but I didn't. Now I know death is here and it makes me sick. Somehow the mind has a way of saying, "you're going to die." My life hasn't flashed before my eyes. I just have to watch as my vision keeps blackening and Jax is crying.

Death is beckoning me, trying to guide me to him and for some reason I want nothing to do but join him, so I do. I release my last mortal breath and leave the world I have come to know so well.

Darkness. Ariadae is standing alone in a dark abyss that pulses with negative energy. She has died and left her mortal life forever and she doesn't know what will become of her friends. Now she focuses on her choice, eternal darkness or ethereal light and happiness. The oblivion is a very manipulating, dark, evil being that takes many into its grasp, and obviously Ariadae doesn't want to be there.

Odi said that her friends will come to haunt her, and they do. In a wave of black smoke they appear; Novid, Gaston, Seri, and all of the sentinels and warriors she killed throughout Elkwood. Their bodies are falling apart and limbs are missing along with patches of skin revealing the bone beneath.

"I said you were going to join us soon," Gaston growls grimacing. He told her a long time ago before Ariadae entered the Rune Yard that she was going to join him and Novid soon, but Odi told her that if she ran from them she would never worry about them again.

"I will never," Ariadae shouts. "I don't want to die. I want to be with my friends."

"I'd run if I were you," Seri groans. Ariadae listens and sprints toward the light. The hoard of walking corpses fast on her tail, wail and shout her name, but she blocks them out and focuses on what's before her, the light, happiness, gratitude. What her friends have become is something she will never be. Odi told her what to do, and she listened.

She isn't fast enough. Novid begins to reach for the youthful girl, her skin smooth, her lifestyle kind, and her heart unbroken. The monsters have become ravenous and want to consume every ounce of her skin, making her but a husk. The light is only meters away and then she falls. Novid and Gaston dive onto her, so Ariadae in a last effort fight, kicks, thrashes and screams.

~Jax~

Her eyes are closed and I felt her last breath. The tears in my eyes make my vision a wild painting up close. I've watched this girl grow up and become a beautiful woman, but now I hold her lifeless body in my lap.

We went into that forest to save her father, and we made it to the Tree of Light. We grabbed some leaves and…Wait! She had a sack of leaves from the tree that she dropped…which I suddenly remember I grabbed before we left!

I pull the pouch from my belt and I pour the leaves over her body. Many fall out onto her wound and nothing happens. Panic shakes my bones and I begin to rub the leaves into her gut and they tear apart and vanish entirely. About three extra leaves are left behind but I throw the pouch aside and pray. *Please, Prometheus be kind and give her a second chance at life.* She has so much more to do. She needs to get married and rule her kingdom creating a life for herself where she can grow old with a king and children. Take mercy on this child.

I look down to her and I notice the wound is gone. Her blood is still all over the floor and my hands, but I am holding her cold body which is no longer bleeding.

"Come on, Ariadae. Fight for it. Fight for life," I whisper.

Her foot connects with Novid's face and he screams in painful agony. Suddenly the darkness vanishes and glowing water begins to rise. In an instant she is beneath the surface surrounded by the floating corpses and bubbles. The water reminds her of the healing water of the Ravine of Wisps but it isn't blue, it's white.

She starts to swim up. The surface of water is always up, and although she is dead she is holding her breath. She kicks and squirms, heading towards the surface. The monsters her friends have become kick right beneath her feet, swimming after her.

Her lungs are burning and her heart pulsating, she screams making bubbles dance and waltz from her mouth. She doesn't want to die and she doesn't want to become the monsters her friends have transformed into. If only the surface could be right above her, and there be air to fill her lungs. Ariadae notices the bubbles popping meters above her. She is almost there. Kicking, screaming, swimming, pushing, crying, glowing, fighting; she does all of these and breaks the surface of death.

<◇><◇><◇>

~*Ariadae*~

I take my first immortal breath.

~The End~

Acknowledgments

I want to start by saying thank you to *you*. If it weren't for people like you who took the time to read my book I wouldn't have any reason to write. I want to share my imagination with you and just the time you take to read a piece of my work is truly amazing, so thank you.

Next I want to explain my dedication. Heather Falotico was my seventh grade English teacher who sparked what I call my great awakening. She showed me the magic of novels and the power words can truly have. She is the only reason I started reading and found my love for writing. In eighth grade year she was moved up from seventh grade to eighth with me, and I had her again. I started writing novels and when I told her that I began writing a book we instantly became best friends! We talked for hours and spent days in class, which should've been for teaching, on my book and I had said to her one day when I was in her room for lunch. "If I ever publish a book the first one is going out to you." She looked a bit puzzled and asked why, but my response was, "I promise." And if it weren't for Heather this novel wouldn't sound so official and good. She makes my thoughts clear on the page and enjoyable for readers.

I would also love to thank Danielle, James, and many of my other friends who spent hours with me on the phone talking and letting me read chapters to them. You guys are amazing and I can't imagine my life without you. You're my biggest supporters and I know you'll be here for the long run. All of my friends, I love you guys!

And lastly I would like to thank my parents and brother who also spent way too much time listening to me blabber and bounce ideas off of them. You guys are the people who made me comfortable in my skin and allow me to be myself. If it weren't for you I wouldn't be happy with the life I have and for just being wonderful, thank you. And I love you.

About The Author

Photo by Patty McKenna

Zachary James is a high school student who has turned his hatred into a passion. His first novel, *The Rise Of Titanium*, is the first of many in the future. His best friend is his cat named Kitty who gives him love and affection, his human friends and family are good supporters too. If you want to stay up to date on any of the bookish details from Zachary James follow him on the provided social media below.

Twitter: *@_ZacharyJames_*
Facebook: *@Zachary James*
Instagram: @ZacharyJamesOfficial
Website: https://zacharyjamesnovels.wixsite.com/novels

The trilogy continues in...

THE REIGN OF QUEENS

~A Kingdom Of Diamond Antlers Novel~

Zachary James

CPSIA information can be obtained
at www.ICGtesting.com
Printed in the USA
FFHW022057210219
50614124-55997FF